THE LEGACY OF
ROSE VALLEY

LORESTALKER - Book 6

J.P. BARNETT

THE LEGACY OF ROSE VALLEY
Lorestalker – 6
Copyright © 2023 by J.P. Barnett

FIRST EDITION SOFTCOVER
ISBN: 1622536517
ISBN-13: 978-1-62253-651-1

Editor: Mike Robinson
Cover Artist: Richard Tran
Interior Designer: Lane Diamond

EVOLVED PUBLISHING™
www.EvolvedPub.com
Evolved Publishing LLC
Butler, Wisconsin, USA

Printed in Book Antiqua font.

Praise for the "Lorestalker" Series

BOOKS BY J.P. BARNETT

The LORESTALKER Series

The Beast of Rose Valley
The Kraken of Cape Madre
The Witch of Gray's Point
The Haunt at Hogg Run
The Devil of Misty Lake
The Legacy of Rose Valley

Prologue

Brynn Kerrison stepped from her rented Mustang onto almost scalding pavement. Her long, smooth legs, stretching from a pair of cut-off shorts, caught the attention of nearby fisherman and sailors, too busy to stop working but not too busy to leer. She slipped off her t-shirt and tossed it into the passenger seat, revealing a bikini top that only heightened the attention. Even in thin flip-flops, she stood noticeably taller than most women.

Brynn took a deep breath, then wished she hadn't. The air reeked. Emaciated cats chewed on dead fish either thrown away or stolen by the felines or cawing gulls. Sailors worked, seemingly unbothered by the stench. With her dark glasses, they wouldn't be able to tell what she fixated on: the one boat she'd come to find.

She walked down the wooden planks, forcing herself to take in the details of each anchored boat. Large ones, small ones. New, old. Some of them had catchy, clever names etched on the hulls. If she'd come on vacation, she might have chosen one of the newer ones with a name that might've generated some likes on social media. But no, instead she made her way to the end, where a modest vessel bobbed in the water, looking neglected with its barely legible name scratched in cursive.

Aunt Margie.

She stopped and took in the lone man onboard, working away, moving things from here to there, whistling happily. When he noticed her, he stopped his toiling. A broad, toothy smile stretched his leathered skin. He was tall and lanky, his eyes hidden behind dark aviators. His clothes looked second-hand, maybe third. Brynn resisted the urge to count the number of rips and holes in his wardrobe.

"Well, hello there, young lady," he said. "What can I do you for?"

Brynn flashed a smile of her own.

"Newt Goodreaux?"

He paused and wiped his hands on what was left of his jeans.

"Yes'm. You found ol' Newt. Why you lookin' for me?"

No *How can I help you?* or *Nice to meet you*. This man clearly distrusted strangers.

"Some folks down at the bar," she began, gesturing behind her towards the bar. "They said you were the best fisherman in Cape Madre. Told me that if I wanted to really see the Cape, you knew every inch of it better than anyone."

"I s'pose that's true these days."

He took a few steps forward, then leaped from his boat to the boardwalk. His weathered frame looked suddenly and especially lithe.

"And you are?" he asked, offering a hand.

She took it, intentionally lighter and softer than she normally would. "Name's Brynn Kerrison. I was hoping to charter your vessel to take me out there."

Brynn motioned to open water with her head. She looked at Newt's face and tried to imagine what his eyes might look like under the shaded glass. Brown, she decided. And squinting, as if she meant to play a trick on him he hadn't quite figured out yet. A trick that he wouldn't figure out until it was too late.

"Anywhere in particular you have in mind?" he asked.

"The vortex."

"Ah." Newt clicked his tongue. "So, you're one of *those*? Listen, all that stuff that happened out here in Cape Madre was a tragedy. Ain't no room for making a spectacle of it."

Brynn glanced away down the dock towards the other boats. She needed to go to the vortex. And she needed to go on this boat, with this man. She knew that only he could get her access to what she needed.

"Ya know what?" she said. "Maybe this was a bad idea. I don't know if you can navigate the vortex, anyway. I heard it's dangerous out there. And these other boats... they seem more seaworthy."

Newt let out a sharp guffaw. "*Aunt Margie* is every bit as seaworthy as any of these. And she has the best captain."

Now she had his pride at stake.

"Three hundred," Brynn said. "Cash. Up front."

He practically stumbled backward. Brynn took the opportunity to slide three, crisp hundred-dollar bills from the tiny front pocket of her cut-offs. His head followed her hand down, lingered a bit, then came back up with a smile even broader than the one he'd flashed when she'd arrived. He snatched the money from her hand without her even offering, then pushed it into his jeans pocket.

He jumped nimbly back onto the deck of his ship.

"Well, come on now," he said. "We'll lose the light if we don't head out soon."

She showed her own physical prowess by vaulting herself onto the deck every bit as expertly as Newt, eliciting a smiling nod from him as he headed back to the cockpit.

"I'm obliged to tell ya that there are life jackets under the bench there," he yelled out. "Can ya swim?"

She nodded, which seemed good enough for him.

The engine rumbled to life. Newt left it idling as he came back out and released *Aunt Margie* from her cleats, quickly pulling and stowing the ropes aboard.

Brynn sat and watched him work, steeling herself for the next part of her journey. She wasn't the same girl who'd almost lost her mind at Gray's Point. She'd come a long way. Made powerful friends. Survived life-altering events. The new Brynn didn't fear what came next.

She delighted in it.

Aunt Margie glided out into the Cape, leaving the smell of rotting fish for the fresh barb of sea salt. Newt kicked up the speed and Brynn's chin-length hair flopped in the wind, invigorating her. A good captain indeed.

The ride proved quick and smooth. She could tell they'd reached the vortex by the subtle change in the color of the water. Newt slowed the boat, killed the engine, then stepped out of the cockpit, leaving *Aunt Margie* adrift.

"Here she is." Newt said with a wide smile. "The vortex."

"So, this is where it all happened, huh?" Brynn asked with false demureness. "Where the kraken lived."

"Yes'm. Was a sight to behold. A dark time." Newt took off his cap and held it solemnly across his chest.

"How often do the babies come up?"

Newt slapped his hat back on, the smile disappearing into a frown. "I don't know nothin' about any babies. The kraken was unique. Nothing else like her out here."

Brynn stood and leaned over the side of the ship, peering into the dark water below. She knew Newt was lying. Newt Goodreaux was many things, but tight-lipped wasn't one of them.

There wasn't a bar in town that didn't have some drunk willing to talk about all the times Newt had let slip how he'd seen the baby krakens out there. Oddly, though, the information had never made it much beyond that. No news reports to speak of. She had to dig for the information on her own, though digging made it sound hard. It hadn't been.

She stood up, smiled sweetly, and took a step towards him, fully aware of what her body could do to a man. Especially one such as Newt.

"Listen, I'm just really curious is all. I absolutely love sea life, and some folks in town, well... they said you might have seen something out here, is all." She took two steps closer and watched him stiffen as she got within inches of him. "Just a peek? I won't tell anyone. I promise."

His Adam's apple bobbed. He staggered back two steps back, as if staying near her would prove dangerous. Little did he know the truth of that instinct.

"I...."

He stumbled to find a response. Silenced himself. Brynn stared at him, never letting her gaze wander. He deflated, his posture relaxing.

"Fine," he said, moving to one of the benches towards the bow of the ship. "But not a soul. You hear me? Not a single soul."

She giggled. A girly, shrill laugh that would have never come out without intent. "Of course, sir. Thank you so much!"

Newt grunted the reply of a man who already regretted his decision. Then he opened the bench and brought out a large frozen fish. Brynn didn't know what kind. She didn't care.

"I feed 'em sometimes," he said.

Brynn nodded eagerly and watched as he reached over and slapped the fish onto the surface of the water.

Slap. Slap. Slap.

Then a pause. And again. Only twice this time.

Slap. Slap.

They stood in silence. Nothing happened.

Newt whispered, "Just give it a minute."

Brynn nodded, no longer paying attention to the water, but to the boat. She surveyed every tool she had access to. A net. She'd need that. An axe behind glass. For some sort of fire safety purpose, she assumed. She didn't intend on using it, but it could help in a pinch.

Another whisper: "Look, look. Here they come."

And come they did. The water bubbled around them as at least a dozen small octopus-like creatures breached the surface of the water. They weren't babies, no, but neither were they anywhere near approaching the size of the infamous kraken of the Cape. The largest of them was no longer than she was tall, even with tentacles outstretched. One day, though, if left alone long enough...

The one nearest the boat grabbed at the frozen fish with one of its tentacles, enveloping it as if in a morbid little hug.

Newt laughed. "That never gets old."

The time had come. Brynn stepped towards Newt, shoulder to shoulder, and bent down over the side of the boat to watch the small octopus devour the fish. Newt pointed at the others.

"They're gonna all want some now."

He stood to get more fish, but Brynn stopped him. "Please, let me."

Newt nodded and leaned back over to peer into the water. Brynn took a step towards the ice-filled bench, then juked behind Newt, brought her hands up and shoved hard against the small of his back. He splashed into the water below without so much as a scream.

"What're you doing?" he yelled from below. "Get me outta here!"

Brynn ignored him. She fetched the large pole net she'd seen earlier and returned to watch the little octopuses moving towards Newt as he trod water. They didn't seem to be very discerning about where they got their meals.

"Lady! For God's sake!" he pleaded. "They're gonna eat me."

Yep.

He punched at them, swatting a few away or dunking them under the water. He tried to swim to the back where a ladder could save him, but from below and above, the octopuses swarmed him, wrapping around his arms, his legs, his head. Realizing he wouldn't make it to the back, he tried to scramble up the side, screaming, begging, all his cries falling on deaf ears.

A straggling, smaller octopus surged toward him, intent on getting its piece of the meal, but Brynn intercepted it with the net, scooping it out quickly and slamming it down on the floor of the boat with a *squish*. It searched for an escape, writhing its gelatinous body. She knew from kraken research that this thing posed no parasitic harm to her, but it could still cut off circulation to one of her extremities.

She picked it back up, dumped it into the icebox and slammed the bench shut. She knew octopuses could be crafty things, so she piled anything she could find atop the lid to weigh it down. She'd gotten the specimen she needed, and, secondarily, had taken care of the only witness. She glanced back over the side of the boat and saw nothing. The octopuses. Newt. All gone. Sunk into the depths. Hopefully never to be found, but certainly not before she'd be long gone.

Mission accomplished.

Brynn fired up the motor and pointed *Aunt Margie* back towards the docks. Within half an hour, she pulled the boat alongside the same dock from which it had departed. She hastily tied it to the cleats on the boardwalk, then hurried to her car to fetch the ice chest she'd brought with her.

The fishing boats were mostly gone. This time, no one paid her any attention.

Within minutes, she transferred her dying octopus to the ice chest and had it loaded into the car. She climbed into the driver's seat, and only then took a deep breath, surprised that her pulse wasn't racing.

She smiled. The new, improved Brynn.

She started the car, put it in gear, and sped back to Rose Valley.

Chapter 1 – Miriam

Hunched over a laptop, Miriam sat amid towers of boxes, having forged a workable maze offering access to the most important parts of her tiny, one-bedroom apartment.

She'd been here two months. Plenty of time to unpack. Yet she hadn't. Instead, the long days faded into sleepless nights. She only left to drop the trash in the bin, which she'd minimized down to once a week by producing little waste. Occasionally, she'd hear from Macy, but always about the upcoming wedding, and always short, curt, directed. Instead of hunting cryptids as the two had done together all through college, Macy now pursued a new mission filled with tulle and silk, flowers and cake.

Miriam knew it made sense. The logical next step. Macy, her best friend. Tanner, her cousin-almost-brother. They'd dated for almost the entire four — wait, no, five — years of college. Marriage made sense for them in that this-is-what-society-prescribes kind of way. For her part, Miriam did her best to be supportive. Planning weddings didn't fit very neatly into her wheelhouse, and despite being the maid of honor, she'd been given very little to do. Macy was nothing if not a good friend. She knew Miriam would be more of a hindrance than a help in most areas related to wedding planning, not to mention hate every second of it. Miriam appreciated it, while at the same time wanting more of a connection with her long-time roommate and only real friend.

Miriam stood from her chair and navigated through the maze to the fridge, where she fetched a Mountain Dew. Not much else filled its shelves. She ordered most of her food straight to the door, a surprisingly cheap option in a small town. The few groceries she did need came once a week in a giant cardboard box.

With no real direction and nowhere else to turn, Miriam had blindly followed Macy back to Rose Valley. Now, she rotted alone in an apartment, with no friends to check on her. Her dad lived in town, and though the relationship between them certainly had achieved formal cordiality, he hadn't gone out of his way to reach out to her.

She understood. She didn't exactly go out of her way to contact him either. For five years, Miriam had never been alone — hell, for twenty-four years, she'd never been alone. First, her parents, then her father, Tanner and Cornelius, then Macy. She considered herself an introvert who valued alone time more than most, so she didn't quite know how to handle this newfound feeling of being abandoned.

She downed half the Mountain Dew before mentally checking her hunger and deciding she could soldier on a few more hours. She made her way back to the folding table that served as a desk. She refreshed her screen, which showed the website for Skylar Black's team. In the site's rotating photos, she saw a picture of Gabe and tried not to focus on it.

They were still dating when she'd moved to Rose Valley. Gabe had looked forward to her moving with the anticipation of a young boy getting his first bike. The relationship had always been distant, strained, but his optimism, mixed with Miriam's resistance to change, kept them coupled far longer than prudent. She'd broken up with him not even a week after getting to town. Even though it had isolated her even further, she felt at peace with the choice. She didn't feel for him the way he did for her.

Macy said Miriam had gotten the *ick*, whatever that meant. Gabe's personality bordered on overwhelming, and, after spending time with him, she often found herself more exhausted than exhilarated. And no matter how hard she tried to feel otherwise, she just couldn't shake the feeling that she didn't find him physically attractive, despite all worldly evidence to the contrary.

If Miriam could feel romance at all, she hadn't found it with Gabe. Maybe she would never find it with anyone.

Her friends—if they could be called that—now consisted of cryptid enthusiasts scattered across a number of websites, some as general as Reddit and some as specific as her father's own forum community.

She clicked on a forum post about the Fresno Nightcrawler. The very idea of it was, of course, completely absurd. Miriam no more believed it a cryptid than she believed Oscar the Grouch lived in the trash bin in the back of the apartment complex. Still, she liked to keep up on what people called cryptids these days.

She could have tried harder to find work, but since Macy and Tanner would be out of pocket for at least a few months more, Miriam hesitated. She didn't want to go it alone, and though she could ask for Gabe or her father to consult on any cases she might pick up, she hesitated at that as well. Good or bad, psychologically sound or not, Miriam contentedly spent her days online, eating when necessary, going outside when unavoidable, and largely disappearing not only from the world around her, but also from herself.

Her desk vibrated. She barely noticed it at first, but then realized her phone rang nearby, its sound muted as always. She couldn't have chosen her ringtone out of a line-up. She looked at the caller, and felt a tiny flip in her chest. Someone she hadn't talked to in quite some time. Someone she respected. Someone she didn't expect to ever hear from again. Not really.

Tommy Wallace. Detective from Cape Madre. Her partner in bringing down the kraken, the only real cryptozoological accomplishment under her belt, despite pretty consistent work and one giant lake monster she never admitted to finding.

She answered. "Hello?"

She drew her knees up against her chest, resting her heels on the edge of her chair.

"Miriam Brooks?"

"Yep. That's me. What's up, detective?"

"Come on," the voice insisted. "Tommy, please."

"Tommy. Right. Long time."

"Yeah, sorry. I always mean to reach out, but you know how it is. Tourists, robberies, fights. Thankfully, no murders since, well... you know."

"That's good to hear."

"Yeah..."

He trailed off. Miriam let the silence hang. She didn't mind silence.

"Listen," he finally said. "I don't wanna worry you or anything. It's probably nothing. But, given your history and what we went through together..."

Miriam's brain raced through possibilities. Another kraken? She started working through logistics, right down to the minutia of whether her Sentra had gas. Macy and Tanner wouldn't be able to go with her, and she'd been avoiding any solo work, but she'd have Tommy. She could work with Tommy again.

All of this went through her mind in milliseconds.

"You remember Newt Goodreaux, right?" Tommy asked.

"Of course."

She didn't know him well, but she'd sat in on an interrogation of him — *the* interrogation that broke the case wide open. The slime ball was complicit as an accessory to attempted murder, and whatever the official law books called aiding and abetting a giant octopus that could control the human mind. That one probably didn't have a name, but Miriam wondered if maybe they'd entered an age where such a word needed to be drawn up.

"He's been missing for a while. Hasn't gone out on his routes. Boat's been abandoned, just sittin' on the docks. As you can imagine, I keep a close eye on him."

"Naturally."

"Anyway, it's probably nothing. He probably just went on a bender or something. Maybe went back east to visit his family in Baton Rouge. I dunno. It's just the first time he's left since the kraken, and I worry...."

Miriam didn't follow where Tommy was leading.

"I mean, he might blame you for getting Bark locked up. And we don't fully understand what it is that thing did to his brain. And you killed it. And well... maybe he harbors some resentment."

Ah. He worried that Newt might come for her. Cute. Miriam felt no threat from Newt Goodreaux.

"You're telling me to watch my back?" she asked.

He laughed mirthlessly. "Yeah. Something like that. Just in case, ya know."

"Thanks for the heads up," she replied. "I'll keep an eye out."

An easy promise to make. Miriam always kept an eye out. For everything. For anything. Her past exploits hadn't chased her down yet, but she supposed it would happen eventually, even if not with Newt. She felt perfectly defensible in her current life, anyway. Hard to threaten someone who never left their apartment.

"All right," Tommy said, his voice sounding a little lighter. "Thanks."

"Of course."

Miriam started wrapping up the conversation in her head, planning out all the niceties one needed for the end of a conversation with someone who'd saved your life but who you still felt cold and distant toward for psychological reasons too complex and terrifying to figure out.

But Tommy wasn't done with the conversation. Because he was normal. And normal people asked questions and shared information.

"I've been following the news a little," he said. "Seems like you're making a name for yourself."

"Kinda," she said. "Not sure it's a good name."

"No such thing as bad publicity, right?"

"Right." She quickly backtracked and planned a new path through the conversation. "How's Stacy?"

Tommy laughed again, this time more joyfully. "Oh, she's great. She moved into my place a few months back. We're getting adjusted to one another."

"That's great, Tommy. Congratulations."

Wait, was this something to congratulate? She couldn't be sure.

"Yeah, uh, thanks. Anyway. You've probably got some monster to hunt or something."

"Um, yeah..." she said, glancing at the forum post she'd been reading about the Fresno Nightcrawler. "Right. Cryptids never sleep."

She didn't know why she lied. Perhaps she worried that Tommy would think less of her.

He laughed. "They probably do. Doesn't everything?"

A soft smile crossed her lips. "Well, yeah, I didn't mean...."

"I know what you meant, Miriam," Tommy said. "Listen, if you need anything, let me know. I'm always happy to help out. And if you hear from Newt—"

"If I see him, you'll be the first to know."

"Great," Tommy said, pausing long enough that Miriam wondered if the conversation would carry on even further. Then: "Well, thanks again. Good talkin' to you after all these years."

Miriam nodded to no one. "You too. Later."

The call ended with Tommy's goodbye before Miriam could hang up. She relaxed in her chair and thought about Newt Goodreaux. Would he come for her? Would he even be able to find her? Though not particularly worried, her mind jumped at the chance to build a new plan of action—a new flow chart in anticipation of her past catching up with her.

Pushing that to the periphery, Miriam hit *Reply* and composed her scathing online rebuke of the so-called evidence proving the existence of a floating pair of pants—the preposterous Fresno Nightcrawler.

Chapter 2 – Macy

Macy paced back and forth. In front of her were two poster boards duct-taped to the wall, meticulously depicting a hand-drawn calendar spanning two months. Six of the eight weeks were swallowed by red cross marks.

Two weeks left. So much left to do. So little time. Why did she think she could plan a wedding in only two months?

Sure, she'd done some recon earlier, scoped out some places, done a modicum of research, but they were getting married in Rose Valley. Not like she was replete with options. Her photographer worked for the Rose Valley Reporter. Her venue—a ranch that had converted its horse barn into a dance hall—presented the only option in town capable of holding the number of people she wanted to invite. The cake would come from the only baker in town. The dresses from the only tailor, who had presented her with a laughable selection of options, but who had worked with her to get other considerations in stock. She did have a whole two florists to choose from, though. Yay for choice.

"You're never going to make it," Olivia said, reclining on the bed playing with a phone inches from her face. The seven-year-old girl that Macy had protected in Hogg Run now threatened to become a teenager. The snark had come early.

"Don't say that."

Macy collapsed onto the bed and put a pillow over her face. The warmth of her own breath helped to calm her nerves. A little.

She reminded herself that she had help at her fingertips. Her mom. Her stepmother, Kat. Her dad and Olivia, sometimes. Tanner tried to help but generally got in the way.

And Miriam. She hated all of this wedding stuff, so just her agreeing to be the maid of honor had been something of a miracle.

Olivia tugged the pillow off Macy's face.

"Okay, fine. Maybe you'll make it."

Macy smiled. Olivia played the part of a prepubescent plague most of the time, but their bond from Hogg Run ran deep.

"What is this?" Macy said. "Did you... no, I must be imagining it." She sat up, grabbed Olivia's hands and looked at her palms. "Did you actually put your phone down?"

Olivia responded by scrunching her nose and pulling her hands away. Macy laughed.

"I'll make it." She rose from the bed and inspected her calendar. "I have no choice."

As Olivia once again reached for her phone, Macy heard the front door open and the weighty sound of her dad's boots on the foyer tiles. She'd enjoyed living with him again these past few months, and still got that childish jolt of excitement when he got home from work.

"Probably a copycat," Cam said, his booming voice traveling down the hallway. "That thing is dead and cremated. No way we've got another."

Silence, until Macy heard Cam put down his keys and kick off his boots. She crept down the hallway to listen to the conversation.

"I'm not saying you can't do an investigation," he said. "Just keep it quiet. We don't need everything blowing up again."

More silence, then Cam falling into his chair with a *pop*, and the mechanisms kicking in and reclining. Macy tried to put it together with what little information she had. Something important and, most likely, related in some way to the beast. She had vivid memories of her hometown being turned upside down by that science experiment's murderous rampage, even as her mom and dad had kept her relatively distant from the whole ordeal.

Not Miriam, though. Miriam had been in the thick of the action. Pulled the trigger that ended the whole affair. She'd want to know if the beast—or anything related—had returned.

"All right, Dub," Cam said. "Keep me posted. You're doing good work." A beat, then: "Bye."

Overwhelmed by curiosity, Macy wasted no time leaving her hiding place in the hallway.

Cam smiled, his bushy mustache twitching, his eyes sparkling—a weird thing to see from a barrel-chested, sheriff-turned-mayor who could intimidate a T-Rex, but to her he'd always just been a big teddy bear.

"Hey, Mace," he said. "How's it going with the wedding planning?"

She took a seat on the couch next to him. He turned the TV on and horrific images of some murder flashed onto the screen. He muted it. The television never strayed from the murder shows in his house. He may have given up law enforcement as a profession, but never as a hobby.

"Good," she answered with a sigh. "Lots left to do."

He nodded, his eyes on the television. "Don't get too bent out of shape over it. The important bit is that you're married at the end of it. The day is just a day, but the marriage is forever."

She bit back a retort. He and her mom had gotten divorced right before Macy had entered high school.

He'd remarried Kat just a few years prior. Her mom had married Jake, Cam's high school rival. He hardly seemed qualified to talk about 'forever'. But, still, she appreciated the sentiment, and with Tanner she really did plan on it lasting, even as all the general cynicism in the air worried her. People hardly got married at all in her generation, it seemed, especially so young.

Not for the first time, Macy wondered if she and Tanner were rushing into things. But she pushed the thought away and re-vectored the conversation.

"Everything ok with Dub?" she asked.

"Huh?" He finally looked in her direction. "Oh. Yeah. Nothing to worry about."

Not what she wanted. He always tried to protect her, but monsters were her profession now. Surely, he knew she'd want the details.

She considered trying to subtly pull it out of him but decided on bluntness. "I heard you mention the beast. Something happen there?"

He laughed. "Nosy one, aren't ya?"

"Just curious," she said with a shy smile. Almost subconsciously, she knew how to get what she wanted out of her dad.

He looked back towards the television. "One of those mutilations again. Out at Watermelon Ranch."

Her mind whirled her back to the beginning of the whole ordeal. A sheep torn in half. It had seemed inconsequential at the time but presaged the deadliest period in Rose Valley history.

"Probably just a copycat," he said. "Some sick kids who think it's funny to get everyone riled up."

"Yeah, probably," she said quietly. Miriam would definitely want to know about this.

Macy stood from the couch, eliciting no response from her father who unmuted the TV. Surely, he'd seen all these by now. How many murders could possibly be documented?

She made her way back to her bedroom. Olivia had disappeared. Macy sat on the edge of the bed, grabbed her phone from the nightstand and pulled up her texts. Miriam hated phone calls. She wouldn't even answer most of the time. Instead, she'd reply with a text almost immediately after the ringing started.

Macy typed in a message with what she'd learned about the mutilation. It would be enough information for Miriam to get started. As capable a Sheriff as Dub might have been, Miriam would break the case wide open way faster.

As Macy's manicured thumb hovered over the send button, though, she hesitated.

If Miriam caught on to this, she'd pursue it like a bloodhound, at all costs. That usually proved a good thing, but the cost right now meant a maid of honor who would have even less interest in Macy's upcoming nuptials. Worse, Miriam almost always dragged Macy into whatever trail she followed.

Macy didn't have time for that. She knew the two of them had made a life of hunting down potential monsters. She knew they were qualified. She knew it might even lead to paid work.

But sometimes it was okay to be selfish, right?

She couldn't think of a better reason than her own wedding. Like her dad said, the mutilation was most likely a copycat. Some sadistic human, not a monstrous urban legend. They could sit this one out.

Macy deleted her message, put her phone back down on the nightstand, and turned her attention back to her wedding calendar.

Chapter 3 – Dub

Heavy was the head that wore the crown, and no one disliked the crown more than Dub Higgins. Unlike his predecessor, he had little interest in being famous. He didn't need to be a hero. He preferred peace and quiet. He preferred his guns collecting dust, and his phone lines full of pranks and fender benders. He'd had this, too, ever since taking over the role of Rose Valley's town sheriff. All the craziness had ended with Sheriff — now Mayor — Donner. Dub felt perfectly fine with that.

As he stepped out of his squad car onto flatland prairie, he flexed his bum hand, the tendons only barely stretching. It hurt and felt good at the same time, but today, he felt a deeper ache from his past. The beast had crushed that hand and made it nearly unusable. He didn't lose much sleep over it. He'd adapted quickly to one-handed life, and learned to do what he could with the damaged hand. But his hand was just a physical representation of deeper trauma. Not to himself, but to the entire town of Rose Valley.

A couple of police cruisers dotted the driveway and fields surrounding the house of Steve Witmer and his partner. Deputies busied themselves cordoning off the horse barn with yellow tape. Dub got within a few steps before the stench burned his nostrils. The buzzing of the flies came in a wave of sound, almost magnified after their confinement in those walls.

Dub peeked inside, long enough for breakfast to take a somersault in his stomach. He choked it back down.

He turned his attention to the barn door. Not hung on its hinges as it should have been. Mangled and resting a good twenty-five yards away. Not something he'd bet on a human being able to pull off.

His newest yet most capable deputy, Rodriguez, emerged from the barn and ducked under a line of tape. He slid a blue bandana from his face down to his neck. Dub clocked all the signs of nausea. Slightly dilated pupils. Pale skin. First time he'd seen the rookie this shaken. After taking over as Sheriff, Dub had vowed to bring on officers from outside of Rose Valley, and Rodriguez had been the first and only fruit of the effort. So far, he'd been an outstanding officer, outshining the other three.

"What've we got in there?" Dub asked him.

"A blood bath," Rodriguez said. "Every horse in there has been slaughtered. It'll take hours—maybe weeks—for forensics to piece it all together. I can't even tell how many horses were in the barn to begin with."

"Four."

Dub turned to find the source of the voice and spotted Steve standing a few feet away. He walked over and offered a hand, which Steve shook firmly. The two had known each other for just about their entire lives. Learned how to read and write together, played sports together. Dub still felt bad for the way he'd acted towards the man all those years ago, when he'd found out about…well, different time, Dub told himself. He only responded the way he'd been taught. What mattered was how he treated Steve now.

"How's Cory?" Dub asked.

"Shaken," Steve responded. "He's worried it's back."

Dub turned a glance towards Rodriguez, who took the hint and headed back to the barn. He took a deep breath of fresh air before stepping back inside.

"Let's back up," Dub suggested. "Start from the beginning."

"Sure," Steve replied. "Wanna go inside where it's cooler?"

Dub smiled. "Wouldn't mind that at all."

The two walked together in silence across the field, watched their feet across a cattleguard, and made their way up the concrete steps that had fallen away from the house a bit, leaving a gap. Once inside, Steve motioned to the kitchen table where Dub took a seat.

"Anything to drink?"

Dub removed his cowboy hat and sat it gently on the table before replying, "No, sir. I'm good. Thank you, though."

Steve sat.

"Cory around?" Dub asked. "It'd be good to get his statement, too."

"Nah. He headed back to Pecan Pass this morning to be with his folks. Said he felt safer there."

"Understandable."

Dub didn't figure Pecan Pass any safer than Rose Valley. Only a few miles separated the tiny communities. He remembered how quick the beast could be. How much ground it could cross in a matter of seconds. Distance wouldn't keep Cory safe. But if this thing was some kind of Beast 2.0, the evidence did point to Watermelon Ranch being a favorite attack point. After all, during that first saga, Jake Rollins had — unknowingly — drew it there. Jake lived an hour up the road now. So what could have pulled the beast to here this time?

Beast. It sounded unbelievable. Could be nothing of the sort. Turning his focus back to the room, he met Steve's gaze.

"So, tell me what happened."

Steve took a sip of water. "Woke up about, I dunno, three or so. Horses were making a ruckus. Cory didn't want me to check it out, but I didn't listen. Grabbed a shotgun. Thought maybe a coyote or something had gotten into the barn. It happens."

"Sure."

"When I opened the door, I knew it was more than that. Growls and screeches. The horses making inhumane noises. I almost turned back." Steve drifted off for a second, his eyes fixed on the window facing the barn. "As I got closer, I heard thuds. Sounds, like someone was swingin' them horses up against the barn wall like a baseball bat."

The sun shot through the window like a bullet, Steve's chintzy air conditioning barely able to keep up with the noonday heat, but still Dub shivered.

"I fired the gun there without taking another step," Steve continued. "It all stopped for a split second, then continued. Cory was at the door, waving me back."

"You didn't go back."

"'Course not. This is my lifeblood, Dub, you know that. I can't lose all my horses."

"But you did."

"I did."

"Did you see it?"

"You mean—was it the beast?"

Dub barely had to nod before Steve took a deep breath, looked around the room and back to Dub.

"I didn't see it," he said. "When I got close, some part of a dead horse flew out at me. Dodged it somehow. Fired into the darkness. Everything went quiet."

"Nothing running away?"

"Woods are out the other direction." Steve paused. "But was it the beast?"

The two men sat in silence. Dub knew the answer. Couldn't explain it any other way. Didn't suppose Steve could either. It didn't make sense, but Rose Valley's curse hadn't been lifted with the death of the first, apparently. Somehow, it made sense in a cruel sort of way.

"I don't know what else it could be, man," Steve said. "I don't know if it's the same one. Different one. But it ripped those horses to shreds. We've only seen something like that one time before."

"Maybe a prank," Dub said. "Some sadistic kids or something."

Steve laughed mirthlessly. "You know a kid that sadistic? A horse can put up a fight if it has to. They woulda had to come at them with a chainsaw or something. I woulda heard that."

"Yeah". Dub wanted to cling to the possibility, but his heart knew he couldn't. "What now?"

"You tell me, Sheriff," Steve said. "You're the boss."

In this moment, Dub wanted nothing less. He hesitated to take the same actions of his predecessor, worried about sending the town into a frenzy. The manhunt had left more than a few dead. The townspeople shouldn't have to worry about this thing. He needed to take care of it before it became more widespread. Before it attacked somewhere public.

In the distance, an engine rumbled nearby, stopped. A car door slammed. Dub looked to Steve. "Expecting company?"

Steve shook his head.

The screen door creaked open. Dub expected a knock, but the door opened instead, revealing the familiar silhouette of a man who hadn't been to Rose Valley in years.

"It's back," the shadow said, shutting the door and coming into focus.

Jake Rollins. The beast whisperer himself. Dub noticed how Jake had used the word *it* instead of *he*. Towards the end, with the last beast, Jake and Shandi both had insisted on humanizing the thing. Dub didn't think he'd ever be able to do that.

"How'd you get in here?" Dub asked, not even bothering to put any real threat into his voice. His deputies weren't accustomed to having to keep a crime scene.

"Just walked in."

Sounded about right.

Dub hadn't seen Jake in years, but he sized him up quickly. The clothes fit a little better. His face looked older, but more rested. The scruffy beard he'd worn before had disappeared. He looked alert. And worried.

Jake hadn't come just because Steve and Cory had a bad night.

"You're sure of it?" Dub asked.

"Positive."

Dub sighed. He couldn't pretend otherwise now. Jake turned his attention to Steve.

"You both ok?"

Steve stood and embraced his friend. "Yeah. We're fine."

"You saw it?" Dub asked.

Jake nodded.

"Like before?"

Another nod.

"Dammit."

"Yeah."

"We cremated that sonuvabitch."

Jake took a seat at the table. Steve went back to his original perch.

"I don't think it's Billy. It felt... different."

That explained the reversion to *it*.

"But you can control it?"

Dub asked the question rhetorically. The horse barn was such a shitshow that he'd noped out of the whole situation and assigned it to others. The only reason the beast would have turned away from Steve and Cory was if it'd been directed somewhere new. And only one person could direct these things.

"I...." Jake shrugged. "Maybe."

"Guess you're still a super soldier, then."

Jake laughed, but it carried no humor. "Yeah."

Dub's mind meandered through the options. His mind never raced, really. Everything came slowly to him, stewing and steeping. He didn't believe in acting quickly. He believed in acting deliberately, carefully.

"Probably should get Arrowhead involved. They created these bastards in the first place."

"Think we can trust' em?"

"Hell no," Dub responded. "But maybe they'll know if there were other... spears? That's what Deirdre called 'em right?"

"Mmhmm."

"How is this possible?" Steve asked.

"I don't know," Jake said with a shake of his head.

Time to act.

"Listen," Dub said. "I'm not going to stand on regulations and ceremony here. I'm not gonna try to pretend to be an expert. You can control this thing, or something close to it. We're gonna need that. As far as I'm concerned, you're a damn deputy now."

"Not sure I want the honor," Jake said.

"Tough," Dub replied. "Deirdre signed you up when she saved your life."

"We're going to need more than just an ability to draw it in," Steve suggested.

"More than the police, too," Jake said.

Dub propped his chin with his good hand. His predecessor had waited too long to bring in help, his delay inviting levels of death and carnage that Rose Valley never should have endured.

"She's back in town, right?" Dub asked.

"Yeah," Jake replied. "Moved here a couple months ago."

"Haven't seen a hint of her," Steve said.

"She killed the bastard the first time," Dub said. "She's the closest thing we've got to a beast killer. Think she'll help?"

Jake nodded. "You won't be able to keep her away."

"All right, let's meet back at HQ," Dub said. "You wanna get her, or shall I?"

Jake smiled, genuine admiration crossing his face. "I'll get Miriam there. You put the coffee on."

Dub stood, slapped on his cowboy hat, and bid the two men goodbye. He wouldn't be home for dinner, but he sure as hell hoped Jake and Miriam could repeat the impossible and put a stop to this thing before it got out of control—again.

Chapter 4 – Miriam

The Rose Valley Sheriff's Department wasn't much to look at, but the small building's rock facade did give it an air of sophistication. Such a tiny building with so many functions. It even housed a couple of holding cells, once destroyed by the beast then rebuilt in the interim. Miriam hadn't been there on that horrifying night, but could see the aftermath: subtle cracks on the concrete floor, scuffs along the painted cinder-block walls. Would the new beast wreak the same havoc?

Dub led her and Jake to an interrogation room. One of two. They had no conference rooms, really, but the larger of the two interrogation rooms had plenty of room for the three to stretch their legs or sit around a table if they wanted.

Miriam chose to stand. She glanced at the camera in the corner. Instead of feeling watched, she felt comforted. There would be a record of this plan. If it all went sideways and the beast ripped them to shreds, someone would be able to piece together what they'd meant to do, and maybe that would help the next set of people to bring it down.

After the dobhar-chú in Washington, Miriam had begun viewing her work as more preservationist than hunter, a change brought on by Kim's persuasive view of the subject. But the beast couldn't be granted such mercy. Not after what had happened the first time.

"We know a lot more than we did last time," Dub said. "So, this should be pretty easy. We'll set a trap out at the old Hargrove place. Use Jake to draw it in. Shoot it. Cremate it. Move on."

Could it be that simple? Miriam didn't think so.

"Hang on, now," Jake said. "That worked last time because Billy had a history with the old schoolhouse on that property. This beast isn't Billy."

"Are we sure?" Dub asked.

Miriam interjected. "They turned him into ash. Of course we're sure."

"Did you watch it burn?" Dub asked.

Miriam hadn't. Jake's subtle head shake confirmed he hadn't, either. Mayor Donner, sheriff at the time, had just handed the body off to Arrowhead Research and trusted them when they said they'd done so. In retrospect, trusting the very corporation that created the monster didn't exactly seem prudent. Then again, they were keen on cleaning up their mess. A mess that they never intended to create. The beast was a sin of their fathers, not that of Arrowhead's current leadership. A sin that would have stayed in the past had it not been for one demented scientist.

"We can talk to Arrowhead," Dub said. "But they're not going to be able to prove a thing. Just receipts, logbooks, that sort of thing."

"Even if they didn't cremate it," Miriam replied. "I shot it. More than once. Point blank in the head. That thing was dead."

A heavy silent pause, either because of the conversation or because interrogation rooms seemed built to produce that very effect.

Jake shuffled in his seat, stroked his chin as he had back when he had the beard. "I died, too. Yet here I am.

The stuff they pumped into us, though different, was meant for war. It was meant to keep us alive."

Dub stood up, threw his hat on the table and paced. The hardware on his belt rattled, echoing off the walls. Miriam didn't like the sound. She preferred quiet to think.

"That's not how Deirdre described it," Dub said. "She was sittin' in this very room when she explained it to us. The seeker got the healing juice, not the spear. Jake might be able to survive death, but that doesn't mean the beast could."

Miriam had never met Deirdre. The scientist almost didn't even seem real, just part of the ghost story leading up to Miriam murdering a man-beast. Deirdre had been the foremost expert on the hundred-year technology, but the beast had nearly separated her head from her body, so they couldn't exactly ask her opinion on the matter.

"Ok," Miriam said, working to slow the adrenaline coursing through her veins. "Let's say it's not the same guy. Different beast. Which is more plausible? That Arrowhead resurrected Billy Hargrove, or that they had other test subjects they told us didn't exist?"

"Well, if it ain't Billy, then how're we gonna predict its next move?" Dub asked.

"With me," Jake said, with no small amount of irritation and resignation. "It went to Steve's last night because I fell asleep thinking about how I'd be hanging out with him soon."

Miriam nodded. "So, we pick a new place. Get Jake to lead it there. Shoot it."

"Somewhere safer than the Hargrove place," Dub added. "A place we can control."

"And a big place," Jake said. "We can keep our distance. With plenty of light so we can hit our targets."

Dub flexed his hand, lifting it enough for Miriam to notice the gesture. He looked down and grimaced.

"The football stadium," Dub said. "We're in the off-season. There's light. Big space."

"You don't think it's too public?" Jake asked.

"Ain't much around here that isn't," Dub answered. "Not with the requirements we're talkin'. We'll cordon it off. Keep people far away."

"I dunno," Jake said. "I don't feel comfortable bringing it into town. If I lose control, or my mind wanders..."

Miriam considered the options. Certainly, it might be safer to lure it out into the woods or maybe even Steve's ranch. Not as much light. The woods would be problematic because of all the trees blocking their sight-lines. Steve's Ranch could work, though. It was mostly fields.

Not even any horses grazing, Miriam thought morbidly.

"What about Steve's?" Miriam suggested.

"No light out there," Dub said, sinking back down into one of the chairs. His weight caused the chair to creak, and the floor to vibrate subtly.

"We'll get some flood lights," she said.

"From who? We ain't got anything like that here."

"We buy them."

"With whose budget?"

Miriam paced. She stopped at the mirror, knowing it opened on the other side to a dim room where people could watch. They needed a setup like that. With the beast safely on the other side, where it would feel alone and safe. But that would just add more cost to an operation that already had no money to spare.

Yet she did know someone with both equipment and money. And he lived nearby, along with her ex-boyfriend. Hostile territory, but not as hostile as it had once been. For the most part, she and her father were on speaking terms, occasionally even warm ones. Gabe, on the other hand...

"We ask my dad," Miriam said, shoving no small amount of pride deep into her stomach. "If he doesn't have what we need, he can get it."

Dub nodded. "Good, good. I should've thought of that. Skylar's a friend of the community. He'll help."

Miriam suspected he would, but she'd made it her mission to distance herself from his shackles. Their new relationship was predicated on the fact that she didn't need him. Indebting herself to him seemed like a recipe for disaster, or, at the very least, a way of dredging up barely-dealt-with family trauma. Even the thought of having to think about all that made her stomach churn more violently than any encounter with the beast.

Every instinct told her to insist that Dub or Jake handle it. Dub, especially, had every credential needed to justify a visit to the museum. But Miriam knew her dad well, and if he found out she was involved but avoiding him, he'd only come on stronger. Her hand would be forced either way, and lives were at stake here. Logic dictated she go to him, and Miriam tried always listening to the logic, not the emotion.

"Okay," she said. "I'll go out there. Secure the equipment."

"Perfect," Dub said.

Jake remained quiet, his eyes fixed on Miriam. She ignored him but could sense the concern.

Over the years, Miriam had become almost an adopted daughter to Jake and Shandi. She'd spent holidays with the family and crashed on the couch multiple times on trips with Macy. They knew all about

Miriam's strained family relations, as well as her fumbling attempt at her first serious relationship. They'd dragged every inch of it out of her over time, even though she tried hard not to talk about stuff like that.

"It'll be fine," Miriam said, primarily for Jake's benefit. "I'm sure he'll be happy to help."

"Want me to go with you?" Jake offered.

Miriam considered it but decided that, even with Jake as a father-figure, it would prove more awkward than helpful.

"No, thanks," she said. "Tanner should be here from Dobie soon. I'll get him to go with me."

Jake nodded distractedly, his attention seemingly elsewhere. Tanner would be the better choice. Somehow, the weird upbringing Miriam and he had shared didn't make Tanner's skin crawl in the same way. Even during the dark times, Tanner always kept her dad apprised of their status. Tanner could keep the peace with her father, but that peace had already been steady for some time.

She worried much more about Gabe. Over the last few years, Tanner and Gabe had managed to bond in a way that Miriam hadn't seen since the death of her brother, Cornelius. On the one hand, of course she liked that Tanner was able to move on and forge new relationships, but on the other it left her in quite the uncomfortable position of breaking the heart of Tanner's new best friend.

God, relationships sucked. All of them.

Miriam preferred to consider herself a robot, driven by facts and routine, programming and efficiency. And for the longest time, that description fit her perfectly. But the tightly-wound cogs had started to loosen as Miriam began realizing she *did* have emotions—she just didn't know how to recognize them, name them, or deal with them. She still struggled. More often than not, Macy named Miriam's emotions for her. But at least she now understood that the uncomfortable knot in her stomach couldn't be attributed to her diet.

"It's settled then," Dub said, picking up his hat. "Let us know how it goes."

Miriam nodded, attempted to give Jake one last look of comfort, then steeled herself for a visit to the Skylar Brooks Center for Cryptozoological Research.

Chapter 5 – Jillian

Jillian gulped down her cup of coffee, not registering the scalding temperature or the bitter flavor, neither of which would have been worth savoring anyway. She clicked at the keyboard, slung her mouse around. It's all she did at work anymore.

She'd been working for Arrowhead Research her entire adult life. Her innate intellectual curiosity tugged at her, begging her to find something to better engage her mind, but after her impoverished childhood, she couldn't abandon the intense feelings of security and comfort having a well-paying job afforded her, even when other firms had come calling.

As a child, she'd been isolated from the rest of the world. Her parents were preppers, complete with the bunker and the guns. They hardly let her leave. Her mother had managed to educate her enough, but truthfully, without Arrowhead stepping in with what could only be described as charity, she'd never have amounted to anything. She would have died in that bunker with both her parents. But she wanted nothing more than escape, so she ran away, lived on the street—till she met a woman who would change the trajectory of her life.

Now that woman was also dead, leaving Jillian to find meaning in a life increasingly unfair and cruel. Arrowhead constantly constrained budgets and cut programs, the work to which she'd dedicated her entire career even as she'd not received so much as a token thank-you plaque or mug. She supposed she could thank Deirdre for that, but no matter the role the woman had played in bringing a mutant soldier to bear on the tiny town of Rose Valley, Jillian could never find the true fault of her mentor, not emotionally anyway. From Deirdre, Jillian had only known acceptance.

As she mindlessly clicked through files, looking busy, her phone vibrated. She picked it up. The front desk was calling.

"Hello?"

"Hi Dr. Vance." Jillian didn't recognize the woman on the other line. She barely talked to the front desk staff. "The sheriff is here to see you."

Jillian's heart seized. She noticed the flutter and took a deep breath. "I'll meet him in the lobby."

"I'll let him know."

The receptionist hung up without any exit pleasantries. Jillian stood and straightened her blouse, then slipped on her simple black loafers. She didn't have a mirror, but ran her fingers through her brunette hair, hoping to smooth down any fly-aways or tangles.

Her trek down the hallway to the lobby felt interminably long. She impulsively counted each soft clack of her shoes. She glanced haphazardly at her coworkers as she passed by their offices, but her mind raced forward, practicing responses that she'd already planned.

By the time she hit the button that opened the door to the lobby, Jillian presented nothing but smiles and business. The Sheriff stood, leaving his hat on the small couch and offering a hand for her to shake. She did so daintily. He would surely read into their every interaction, and though she wanted him to think her capable, she did not want him to think her strong.

"Hi, Sheriff," she said. "What can I do for you?"

She'd only met Dub Higgins once or twice, years ago during the aftermath of the beast. With Deirdre gone, it fell to Jillian to pick up the pieces. She'd dealt with the inquiries and investigations. The recantations and false promises. Her handling of the incident got her Deirdre's job. Not that it mattered. Arrowhead dismantled the department shortly after and stuck Jillian with rote research instead of thrilling scientific discovery.

"We've had an..." He took a beat to search for a word. Jillian guessed he'd settle on 'incident,' which he did. "...incident down at Watermelon Ranch."

"Oh?" she purposefully raised an eyebrow. After she'd escaped the bunker, she realized she possessed very few social skills. She'd practiced facial expressions in front of a mirror.

"Yeah." He bent down and picked up his hat. "Is there somewhere private we could talk?"

"Of course," Jillian replied. She turned and trusted him to follow, badged through the door, waited for it to open, then led him down the very long hallway she'd just come down. He stayed behind her, and she fought the urge to look back, focusing on the sounds of his boots and using the time to race through all the questions he might ask, and all the answers she might give.

When they arrived, she motioned to the door of her office. "Please. Have a seat."

"Much obliged," he replied, sitting down and setting his hat on her desk.

She pushed back the desire to swat his sweaty hat to the floor and instead took a seat across from him, the desk providing her both a barrier and a sense of ownership. This room belonged to her, as would the conversation.

"So, what happened?" she asked.

"We had an attack out there. Something killed all of Steve Witmer's horses."

Jillian almost shrugged, but corrected into mock horror. "All of them?"

"Yes, ma'am. Every last one. Torn to shreds."

"What could possibly do that?"

"Well." Dub shifted in his seat, his considerable weight causing it to creak. "Only time we've seen something like this is the beast. Given you took over after Deirdre's passing, I thought you might know something about it."

Deidre's "passing?" What tame phraseology. Her neck had been snapped by a war monster from World War II.

"As you know," Jillian replied. "We destroyed all research pertaining to the Seeker program."

"Right." Dub took a moment to look into her eyes. She met his gaze and tried to look weak instead of exasperated. "And Billy — he was the only Spear?"

"I mean, yeah. And we didn't even know about him. We thought he'd be long dead. It's not like we have some method of cryogenically freezing these things."

They did, though. They'd perfected the technology decades ago, and run the first tests even further back still. That knowledge was still classified, and Jillian didn't intend to jeopardize her clearances for a bumpkin playing Sheriff.

"Billy surviving the elements for that long in a cave," she went on. "The odds of that are infinitesimally low, Sheriff. And we have no record of any of the others escaping. Their bodies were destroyed long ago."

Jillian had gotten good at lies, but on that she didn't have to. Arrowhead, in fact, did not have in its possession any serum, seekers, or spears. They had, as promised, destroyed their experiments.

When the Sheriff rubbed his chin in thought, she offered, "Would it help to see the lab? It's been reclaimed. Full of drug-riddled monkeys and obese mice now. But you can see it if you want."

He didn't take long to consider it. "No. That's all right. I trust you, Dr. Vance. Why wouldn't I?"

On television, cops always had an edge to them. They always implied wrongdoing in hopes of making their suspects slip up and spill the beans. Not so with Sheriff Higgins. His words came only with the naiveté and charm of a man doing his best to survive in a world that had outpaced him and his old-fashioned values. He really did trust her, she thought.

"Well, if there are no further questions, Sheriff." She stood briskly and swept open the door. "I have a lot of work to do."

He stood slowly, hat in hand. He stopped at the door and gave Jillian a sweet, simple smile before offering her his hand. She took it and he held on a beat too long, looking in her eyes.

Trying to size her up? What would he find? She'd played her cards right. Told him all the half-truths that made for believable lies.

"Thank you for your time, Dr. Vance." He dropped her hand and stepped out into the hallway. "I can see myself out. You be careful, now, y'hear?"

A common saying in the south, but somehow, laced with just a tad bit of menace. *No.* Jillian pushed the thought away. She refused to succumb to paranoia. That had been the downfall of Deirdre. Well, that and hubris.

She watched him scurry down the hallway, made sure he exited through the gated doors, then returned to her desk, replaying the entire visit in her mind. No, she'd given up nothing. Told no outright lies. Arrowhead really had rid itself of the entire Seeker program after the infamous beast came to light. Sweeping everything under the rug, the company had refocused on other opportunities not as risky.

Power, Jillian had learned, was not held in the product, but the idea itself. Much like the atomic bomb, once an idea sprang into being, it could not be quashed. No matter how complex. How seemingly impossible. Nothing begged re-invention more than an impossible height known to be reachable by those with the willingness to climb for it.

No. Arrowhead didn't have a serum. They had no spears. The only seeker lived in another town programming computers. But she didn't need any of that. She had the only thing she truly needed.

Knowledge.

Chapter 6 – Miriam

The museum looked about the same as she remembered: meticulously upkept, a large, mostly empty parking lot and the exterior of a hiking cabin. Her father had dolled up the interior, though, with marble floors and all the modern amenities and technologies. She wondered if he still kept a prominent display of her accomplishments.

Miriam pulled into one of the parking spots next to the wheelchair-accessible ramp. Movement caught the corner of her eye, from just behind the main building. She saw metal fencing, thick underbrush, and a thick wall of non-native trees. What had they been up to out here?

Intrigued about what lay beneath the brush, Miriam itched to see it. She needed Tanner before her confrontation, though, so she checked her messages for his response to her request for help. He'd responded while she'd driven over: *Sorry, can't. Meeting Macy for wedding stuff.*

Miriam sighed. *Et tu, Brute?*

She understood the importance of the nuptials — she really did — but it had left her abandoned and alone, feelings she'd nearly forgotten with Macy's near-constant companionship over the last four years.

She fought off waves of panic. She couldn't remember the last time she'd had a meal, but now became acutely aware of being famished. She'd never been one to worry about her weight, and didn't own a scale, but she often forgot to eat these days. Not that she'd ever been a consistent eater.

Miriam stepped out of the car and headed toward the fence. If she had to do this alone, she'd take a moment to observe whatever new thing Skylar had collected. The fence towered above her, at least eight feet high. The dense weave of metal honeycomb gave the impression that the thing kept inside might be dangerous. She looped her fingers through it, held on, and peered through the leaves, desperate to catch the movement she'd seen before.

Her mind ran through the possible inhabitants. What sort of animal would Skylar deem important enough to cage up behind the museum? Surely not a cryptid. She would have heard of that by now. No doubt he'd chosen something meaningful, though. Something that would make a point, or at least encourage people to visit more often.

There!

She saw a shimmer of white through the foliage. Briefly. Like a mirage. Her eyes focused, making out the shape of it. The creature was mostly brown, but she could see the white, even as it somehow blended with the forest behind it. Her heart danced in her chest. She knew it wouldn't be anything groundbreaking, but still, it triggered that same emotional response she got when hunting a new cryptid. Perhaps Skylar had put this animal here for exactly that invigorating reason.

Eyes. Big, brown. A long snout, like a horse, or — more precisely — a giraffe. Big ears that flicked away at flies buzzing nearby, and weird, striped legs ending in black hooves.

An okapi.

In Rose Valley.

Miriam couldn't fight the smile that tugged at her lips. As a kid, her dad *always* brought up the okapi. Officially "discovered" in 1901, it provided the very best poster child for the study of cryptozoology. Of course, the African people had known of its existence for years, but to European explorers, this giraffe/zebra/horse amalgamation sounded downright folkloric. Even then, they only had bones to work with. A live one didn't show up in a European zoo until 1919, and then, eventually, in the US in 1937. An animal as big as a horse, so recently thought to be a myth, now standing in Rose Valley as if it were born here.

She delighted as it stretched its prehensile tongue around a branch and broke it off, chewing and chewing. She'd only seen an okapi in person one other time in her life. Even in zoos, this marvel of biology tended to be pretty rare.

"So, you've met Bessie," a voice came from behind.

Not her father. Worse.

She turned, the smile melting. "Hi, Gabe."

Her voice sounded weird to her own ears. Breathy and raspy, as if her body couldn't muster the oxygen to get his name out.

"Hey, Mimi."

She winced, not the least bit successful in hiding her response to that nickname. It reminded her of the mother she barely knew, of course, but now it meant even more than that. As a relic of a lost relationship. Of shared kisses and tender embraces. It all felt foreign and distant now. She bit her tongue at the thought of reprimanding his use of it, choosing to let it go in the name of peace.

Instead, she used the okapi for cover, motioning back to it. "When did he get this?"

"Just a few months ago," Gabe said, a hint of sadness in his voice. "He loves showing it off as an example of why cryptozoology is so vitally important, blah, blah, blah. It's a badass animal and all, but when you pay too much attention, you realize it's just a messed-up looking giraffe."

A hint of Gabe's humor, but without the bounce. Why so sad? Over her? Surely not. She could think of no viable reason why he should be sad over her.

"Anyway," he said, approaching the fence beside her. He gripped the links, focused on the okapi. Miriam did the same — it made it easier. "Have you been out to Watermelon Ranch?"

"Not yet, but I met with Dub and Jake," she said, her voice trailing off.

"The beast?"

"How'd you know?"

He chuckled. "It's Rose Valley. There are no secrets here. Funny how privacy works. Alone, you've got tons of it. In a big city? Endless supply. In a town of a couple thousand? None."

Miriam nodded with an almost imperceptible smile, unsure how to respond.

Silence stretched between them, leaving only birdsong and the okapi's subtle chewing. She knew she should say something, but preferred the silence. Wondered if maybe it said more than any words she could drum up.

"Need help?" he asked.

No judgment. No expectation. No indication that he meant to hold such a request over her.

She couldn't get out a "yes" so instead she said, "Dub and Jake... and me, I guess. We have a plan. To end this before it gets out of hand again."

"End it?" he asked. "Like you did before? With...."

She wondered if he'd almost used the word murder.

"...Euthanasia."

"I don't know," she replied. "I hope not."

Another bout of silence between them. Then, Gabe pushed away from the fence, changing tone and subject. "Wanna pet her?"

Any control of her emotions vanished, and a smile spread across her face.

Gabe laughed. "I don't think I've ever seen you smile like that."

She wiped it away, self-conscious. "I've loved these things since I was a kid. Never thought I'd be so close to one."

"Come on."

He walked away, gesturing for her to follow. She did, almost running into his back with uncontrolled speed. He stopped at a gate, fished in his pocket for a key and unfastened a padlock. She followed him inside. He ducked to scoop up a handful of hay and immediately offered it to her.

"Hay? Really?" She immediately sifted through information to determine whether the food would ultimately be bad for the okapi. Given other elements of its diet, it would probably be fine.

"Yeah," he said. "She likes it. You want her to like you, right?"

Miriam nodded as they stepped around a tree, and saw it in all its magnificent glory. Her heart sped up. She became a kid again. Not wanting to spook it, she fought the urge to rush to it, instead stepping softly and outstretching a hand full of hay. The creature stared at her, as still as a statue. She glanced back at Gabe. He stood a few feet back now, smile wide.

She froze once her hand got within a foot of the okapi's snout. It sniffed the air. Miriam's muscles tensed, the excitement only barely masking the part of her brain reminding her this animal could be dangerous. It outweighed her by at least a factor of three, and had sharp hooves and powerful legs. It could probably kill her half a dozen ways.

It shuffled its feet, stepped away, then bent its long neck towards her and nibbled at the hay in her hand. She let out her breath and slowly reached out with her other hand to stroke the fur. Objectively, it felt like a horse, or a cow, or any other kind of a dozen farm animals she'd touched over the years, but her hand tingled with electricity, as if she'd just laid hands on the Ark of the Covenant. She stroked it gently until it finished eating the hay and backed away to forage on the greener options nearby.

She watched the creature for another minute before turning back to Gabe. He stood silently with a smile, no quips or jokes. He'd always been good at that. Reading the room. Understanding when the situation called for silence, or maybe in this case, reverence.

"Thank you," she said. It came out in a whisper.

"Of course."

They left the cage. Gabe re-engaged the padlock. They stood outside, Miriam working up the courage to ask for what she needed. The guns. The lights. Everything. Anything.

"Listen," he said. "I know how you hate asking your father for things."

She did. She really did.

He continued, "He's not here right now anyway. So, give me the list. I'll work it out. Drop it off wherever you say."

No offer to participate. He'd finally learned that playing the protective man didn't have a place with her. Perhaps too late, but she appreciated the show of boundaries and respect.

She couldn't stop her face from broadcasting her relief. "Thank you. That would be amazing."

"No problem, Mimi," he said. "It's the least I can do."

The nickname didn't bother her this time—in that moment, she realized she didn't miss Gabe. Their relationship had never felt right for her, never authentic, never easy and natural like what she'd seen with Tanner and Macy. It would have never been possible, her and Gabe. Something in her core appreciated a lot about him, but never found him truly attractive.

No, she didn't miss him. But she did love him, in a way. Not romantically, but deeply. Gabe accepted her for who she was, and people like that in her life came in short supply.

She gave him one last smile and headed back towards her car, glancing back to say, "I'll text you the info."

"Sounds good," he said. "Oh, and Miriam—"

She turned around fully now, still inching backwards.

Gabe winked. "Kick that thing's ass."

Chapter 7 – Macy

Macy's heart fluttered when she heard the truck door slam. She dropped her laptop on the bed and rushed out to the living room in time to hear him knock on the door. Cam had insisted that Tanner didn't have to knock—he was practically family—but Tanner did anyway. Every time. Macy couldn't help but giggle as she opened the door.

He scooped her up, spun her around, then locked her in the most comforting of bear hugs. Her relationship with Tanner had always been close to perfect, but in the lead-up to the wedding, it felt downright blissful. She wanted it to last forever, even though part of her knew it probably wouldn't. Despite her hopes and dreams to the contrary, her parents' divorce still made her gun-shy about the whole "till death do you part" thing.

With their overly romantic greeting complete and the house empty, Macy grabbed his hand and pulled him back to her bedroom. They collapsed together on the bed and she rested her head on his chest. She loved the sound of his heart.

"How did it go?" she asked, in nearly a whisper.

Tanner sighed. "Good. Yeah. He was really receptive."

"Did he agree to the terms?"

Tanner ran his hand across Macy's back. She shivered at his touch.

"Yeah. He's got Gabe and Kent doing all the fieldwork. Since they lost Brynn, though, they don't have enough hands to handle it all. It'll take some re-arranging of responsibilities, but..."

Giddy with excitement, Macy leaned up and kissed him. "Good job!"

Tanner seemed less enthused. Macy worried that she'd pressured him into this decision, but also knew it was the right one. Not just for her, but for them both. And for the family they wanted to build.

"I'll hang back mostly, doing the research and all the logistics. Gabe's stoked at the prospect."

"No travel?"

"Well, I can't promise none, but Uncle Skylar agreed to keep it rare."

Macy tapped her fingers against his chest, enjoying the deep thrum that echoed into her ears. She relished the moment, letting their conversation fall into silence before moving on to more uncomfortable topics.

She sat up, cross-legged. "I know this is hard. I don't want you to feel pressured to make this choice. I know you love what you do."

"Yeah, but..." He leaned up and kissed her. He almost never initiated the kissing. "I love you more. Skylar had us running around the world our whole childhood. We were as much employees as kids. I can't do that to you. I can't do that to our kids. Mir can go out and become Skylar 2.0, but I want to be a completely different thing."

Macy's face twisted up in discomfort at the mention of Miriam. The elephant in the room. The one person they both loved, and that both had no choice but to disappoint.

"We need to tell her," Tanner said, falling back onto his pillow and staring at the ceiling. "She deserves to know so she can start planning."

Tanner was right, of course. Miriam's entire identity rested on her role as a cryptid hunter, and the tiny agency they'd built wouldn't work as a solo act. Without Macy, Miriam wouldn't be able to complete the simplest of tasks. Calling, interacting. All of it overwhelmed Miriam to the point of paralysis. But maybe Macy was underestimating Miriam's drive. Surely, she would adapt. Besides, these days most communication could be done via email or text, both of which made Miriam infinitely more comfortable than phone calls and video conferences.

"Yeah, I know," Macy replied, sinking back down to Tanner's chest. "But not now. I need her right now. I don't know how she's gonna react. After the wedding, ok?"

Tanner took a beat to respond. "Fine. But right after."

"It's not like we aren't going to help her transition," Macy said, as much to convince herself as him. "Once we're married, and we get back from the honeymoon, we'll make sure to set her up for success. We can teach her all the stuff we do, and help her find some new team members."

Tanner laughed. "Miriam's never going to accept someone else."

"She accepted me."

"True..." He trailed off and ran his hand up and down Macy's back, then a fingertip across the base of her neck. She enjoyed every second of it. She knew what he wanted. She wanted it too, but she couldn't let him change the subject just yet.

"We'll just have to find someone she likes. That gets her."

"Babe, I love Mir like a sister, but she doesn't like very many people." Tanner laughed again. "And honestly, I've lived with her my entire life, and I don't think I even *get* her."

Macy craned her neck to look up at him, but he didn't seem to notice. "Yes, you do."

"I don't know. Do you understand her?"

"Yeah," Macy replied. "She's got her quirks, but she's smart and driven and she's saved my life more than once. She cares about everyone. She just... doesn't know how to show it."

"Maybe."

They fell quiet again as Macy considered what kind of person might be a good fit for Miriam's lifestyle. Someone light-hearted. Personable. Someone to push Miriam outside of her comfort zone without making it seem like an intervention. They needed someone who would care for Miriam in all the little ways that Miriam hardly ever noticed, but who could also stand up to her when she got too pig-headed. Macy had been a natural fit for the role, but it seemed a miracle they'd ever found each other.

Then it struck her. She jumped up from the bed.

"I've got it!"

Tanner sat up. "Got what?"

"The solution."

"To us abandoning Mir?"

"Yes!"

"This I gotta hear."

Macy pounced on top of Tanner and pressed her lips against his. "It's gonna be perfect," she whispered.

Chapter 8 – Miriam

With gear secured and a rough plan formed, only the setup remained. As she put the Sentra in park, she observed the crates of equipment under the carport, half-covered by a windblown tarp. The barn would have been a better landing zone, but since it still overflowed with horse carcasses, Miriam could appreciate the carport as the next logical dropoff.

She stepped out of the car and pulled the tarp back further to examine the haul. She recognized Gabe's handwriting, its shaky scrawl listing each box's contents. The guns sat on top, with the lights and other things tucked below. She popped open the top of one and smiled at the waning sun gleaming off the gunmetal. One of the other boxes had the tranqs, but this one served as the backup plan: the one that would save them if nothing else worked.

Satisfied, Miriam replaced the tarp and made her way to Steve's doublewide, where she hopped up the steps and rapped on the door. Dub answered and ushered her inside. Jake sat at the kitchen table already, a yellow legal notepad in front of him with some illegible scratches. With the sun setting, the house felt abnormally dark, with only the pale-yellow light of a bulb hanging above the table.

Miriam took a seat.

Dub lowered himself across from her, and Jake gave Miriam a smile. She couldn't help but notice the dark circles under his eyes and the tinge of apprehension about him. None of them wanted to go through this again. Practice made perfect, though—a second round with the beast, Miriam felt, would tilt much more heavily in their favor.

"I saw the gear outside," Dub said.

Miriam nodded. "Yep. Looks like it's all there."

"Good."

"What about personnel?" Jake asked.

Dub leaned in. "I'll have a couple deputies. I'd never require this of them, though, so I'm bringing them in on a volunteer basis only. I expect at least two to show. For sure, Rodriguez. Cam'll be here as well. Always a cop first."

"I'll have Tanner," Miriam said. "And Macy as well."

Macy wouldn't like it, but she'd come.

Dub: "What about Skylar's team?"

Miriam hesitated. She explicitly hadn't invited them. Maybe she should have. But borrowing gear from them was as far as she felt comfortable treading.

"Negative. Just the weapons and gear."

Silence hung in the air for a split second, as if both Jake and Dub wanted to object. Neither did.

"Shandi's on her way," Jake said. "I couldn't keep her away if I tried... and I tried."

"What about Steve and Cory?" Dub asked.

"Steve wants to be here, trust me," Jake responded. "Cory's still spooked, though. Convinced Steve they should stay with Cory's parents out in Pecan Pass."

"Doesn't seem safe," Miriam said. "What if the beast just finds them there?"

"I've never been there. If the beast is following my thoughts, like before, then they should be relatively safe."

'Relatively' didn't seem good enough.

"Any way we can get him a weapon?" Miriam asked. "Some sort of protection — just in case."

"Yeah, we can do that," Jake responded. "I'll text Steve to meet me in town tomorrow morning."

Miriam nodded, satisfied. "Ok. So that's, what? Over ten people that'll be here on the property? That's a good amount. If we space them out appropriately, arm them well, we should be okay."

Dub and Jake both nodded, perhaps as much to convince themselves as to show understanding.

"What's the plan, though?" Jake said, continuing before waiting for a response. "Are we killing it?"

She didn't want to. She'd killed the first one and regretted it every day since. Tranquilizer darts had proven highly ineffective, though. The tech improved every year, and of course Skylar had the latest and best stuff, but Miriam worried that even the higher concentration solutions wouldn't manage to bring down the beast — assuming this one carried the same resilience as the first.

"I don't know," Miriam replied. "I'd rather not."

Dub frowned. "Look, I don't like killing anyone or anything, but we know how much of a threat this thing might be. I don't think we can afford to take the chance."

"Well," Jake said. "We can have a two-stage plan, like before."

"We barely made it out of that one."

"We had Steve using a weapon he'd never fired before." Jake looked at Miriam. "We don't have that problem this time."

No, hitting the thing wouldn't be a problem. Living with the consequences, however...

"Okay," she said. "I'll take point on the roof then, with the Gehringer." She looked at Dub. "Sheriff, you'll get the tracker. If you can get a good shot into its back or somewhere hard to reach, we might be able to track it if it gets away."

Dub nodded. Jake looked queasy.

In truth, Miriam didn't think the tracker would provide much use. The beast had enough intelligence to pull it out, maybe even attach it to some other moving object to throw them off the trail. But Skylar had the tech on hand; might as well use it.

Miriam continued, "Tonight, we'll set up all the lights and cameras and whatever else Gabe packed into those boxes. Tomorrow we'll gather everyone up just before dusk, give out the assignments, then let Jake do his magic."

"All right," Dub said, standing. "Let's do it."

Dub made his way outside. Miriam stood, but Jake stared at his notepad.

"You all right?" she asked.

He didn't answer at first, but then looked up. "Yeah. I'm..."

"We won't let it hurt you," she promised.

She wouldn't have believed her claim, but Jake seemed to. He gave a wan smile and pushed himself up from the table.

Miriam stepped outside. The ranch seemed eerily quiet. Even Dub shoving boxes around under the carport felt distant. Paranoia scratched at the periphery of her attention, and she tried to ignore the distinct feeling of being watched. The fields stretched in all directions, the closest woods at least two hundred yards away. Nothing could be watching that closely. She'd be able to see it.

She walked towards Dub and pitched in, unstacking the boxes so they could get to everything. They worked in silence. As she and Dub placed the boxes on the ground,

Jake popped the tops. Gabe had labeled everything with precision. Everything in its place. The boy couldn't always be counted on to pay attention to the details, but he seemed to have taken extra care this time.

Miriam stopped suddenly, her body stiffening before she registered the reason.

"Shh," she whispered. "You hear that?"

Dub shook his head, as did Jake. Miriam held up a finger, silently instructing them to remain quiet. At first, she heard nothing. A few crickets. Soft wind dancing through the brown, overgrown grass. Then—the creak of old wood. The squeak of a rusted hinge. She turned her head toward the barn and saw one half-hung door, waving back and forth.

She walked out from under the carport to feel the breeze against her face. So slight. No gusts. Not nearly enough strength to move a barn door, especially one hung on twisted hinges.

She glanced at Jake, causing the hair on her neck to stiffen. He stood straight as a board, his eyes wide, pupils dilated. What she'd detected with her ears, he had detected with some other intangible superpower granted him by Arrowhead's serum. Ever observant, Dub knew enough to reach for his sidearm.

Miriam looked for any variation of the darkening skyline, any indication that they were being watched. Stalked. Deep down, though, she already knew the answer.

A gunshot fired so close that Miriam's ears rang. She turned to find Dub, legs apart, shoulders square, smoke wafting from the barrel of his pistol.

The three closed ranks without a word. Miriam looked over the gear, searching for the box containing the Gehringer. It had been on top, but Dub had shuffled things around.

"What did you see?" she tried to whisper, the volume of her voice exceeding her intention.

Dub's eyes moved frantically. "It ducked behind the house."

"The beast?"

He only nodded and gave a barely audible *mmhmm*.

"Jake?" she asked. He didn't look at her, seemingly lost in his mind.

"There!" Dub shouted.

And so it came: around the house from the other direction, straight in front of Miriam, loping across the ground at a speed so rapid Miriam struggled to process it. A beast, like before. A man whose hair had grown untended, whose eyes had lost all humanity. Not as tall as the original beast, but every bit as formidable. She lunged for the Gehringer box just as the thing careened into her, knocking her back into Jake who did little to catch her, instead stumbling to the ground.

For her part, Miriam kept her footing enough to catch herself on one palm and get back to her feet. The gravel bit her skin, but she didn't feel the sting. She gave herself the space needed instead of the gun she wanted. Dub fired a wild round as they both retreated behind Miriam's car.

It wouldn't be safe enough, and she knew she couldn't stay. She peeked around to see Jake scrambling to his feet in what felt like slow motion as this beast slammed his fists into the boxes, kicking them across the yard, and scattering the contents. Dub's service pistol wouldn't be enough to keep this thing at bay, much less kill it. She had to get to the Gehringer, wherever the beast had flung it to.

"Take care of Jake!"

Without any verbalization of her intent, Miriam bound from behind the car, straight towards the beast, trying to give it as wide as berth as she could, counting on its fascination with the gear to keep her safe enough to pass. As she leaped over the cattleguard and registered the slowing of the beast's rampage, she knew her plan wouldn't work. She'd been spotted, identified, and classified as a threat.

Rightfully so.

She managed to dart out of the way of the wooden crate thrown her way. She saw the glint of the Gehringer in the grass just as the beast launched another crate, losing its height enough to hit the ground next to her, splintering apart and jabbing into her calf the jagged end of a two-by-four.

Miriam cried out and stumbled, pain surging up her leg. Her momentum kept her up for a few more steps, but she couldn't keep her balance, and started to fall for the ground. She reached for the Gehringer. Maybe — just maybe — she would be close enough to get the tips of her finger on the butt of the gun.

She struck the ground, and her fingers felt nothing but dirt and grass. She scrambled up to all fours, but immediately went down again as something grabbed her ankle. The beast held her with a loose enough grip that she could flip on her back and kick at his hand. He withdrew his from her ankle long enough for her to scuttle backwards, but he came again, this time bending over and swinging his ape-like arms towards her chest. His fists connected hard against her ribcage, stealing her breath.

She rolled. The beast pounded the ground once, but quickly corrected. Miriam tried to catch his swings, but the attempt only served to wrench her arms as the beast, by its own strength and momentum, pounded them against her own ribs. She steeled against the pain, realizing she wouldn't win a fistfight. She saw the glimmer of the gun just inches away now.

She took another blow to the chest, but managed to free her arms enough to reach. She felt it cool against her skin, jerked it towards her, then fully gripped it. She swung it around, but the distance between her and the beast had grown so slight that she had no room to properly point the barrel towards him. She fired into the air. Nothing happened. Just a *click*.

Of course, Gabe hadn't packed a loaded gun. He wasn't an idiot.

Miriam used the gun as a crossbar and managed to hold the beast at bay for his next barrage, but she knew he'd try to take the gun soon enough, and she wouldn't be able to win tug-of-war against this creature any better than she could win a fistfight.

Gunshots rang out from Dub's pistol, but if they were hitting their target, the beast made no indication that it mattered.

Then the beast stopped and grabbed its own head, stumbling back up to its feet and stepping back. Miriam fought through the pain in her chest, gasped for breath and scooted backwards until she could find her feet. She bolted for the carport, Gehringer in hand.

Jake stood next to the Sentra now, his eyes vacant and lost. He'd backed the beast away, but as he shook his head and Miriam heard the commotion behind her, she knew the effect had been temporary. Dub fired more rounds past her head. She didn't know whether he was a good shot, or she just got lucky, but she managed to close the distance without a bullet. The beast didn't have the same luck, each pop causing blood to spatter outward, but none of the wounds slowed the thing down.

Miriam searched through the scattered boxes and found her quarry quickly. A box of large bullets. She scooped it up and dumped a few in her hand.

"Hold him off!" she yelled at Dub. Dub kept firing. She knew he couldn't have many rounds left.

She loaded a round, flipped off the safety and put the butt of the gun up against her shoulder. These things worked better on tripods, the weight almost proving too much to bear. Her shoulder would have to do, no matter how much the kick might hurt.

The beast closed the distance, advancing quickly.

She fired.

"Run!" she yelled to Dub.

At short range, with so little time to aim, the bullet blew a hole in the beast's shoulder. It howled in pain. She reloaded and fired again. Each kick buffeted her shoulder, sending pain down her spine and exacerbating that in her chest.

The second bullet struck him in the neck. Blood poured out. More than spatter.

Its momentum didn't slow, however: one more step and he'd grab her. She reloaded again with the grace and speed of years of practice. She took no time to aim at all this time, instead working from memory, a grand trigonometry equation solved in mere milliseconds before she pulled the trigger one last time.

The beast's huge hand reached for her just as a bullet cut right through its forehead, leaving a gaping hole. It stumbled backward, a look of confusion briefly crossing its face before it collapsed in a heap.

Miriam breathed for what felt like the first time since the beast had appeared. She rapidly loaded another round, but, after several hasty beats of her pulse, realized she wouldn't need to fire it.

Chapter 9 – Dub

Growing up in the Higgins family, the old man didn't have much tolerance for education. While some parents might have aspired to enrich their children's minds, Old Man Higgins instead looked down on the aristocracy of the educated, encouraging his sons to pursue more blue-collar, salt-of-the-earth work. Lung cancer had taken the bastard years ago, but Dub wondered if his dad would approve of an elected position such as sheriff.

Or County Medical Examiner. The elected position of his younger brother, Jeb. Though he was a mortician by trade.

Blinking bloodshot eyes, Jeb met Dub at the door of the morgue. They grunted at each other with the familiarity of brothers before Jeb followed him inside to the exam room, recently decorated with the remains of a very dead, very bloody urban legend. Miriam stood next to it, clearly fighting the urge to grab a scalpel and get to work. Truth be told, this time Dub suspected her more qualified to perform an autopsy than Jeb.

The whole affair had spooked Jake enough that Dub had sent him back to the hotel.

Jeb sighed. He slipped on a white coat hanging by the door, then grabbed a pair of disposable latex gloves from a nearby box and snapped them on.

"What happened?"

"I shot it," Miriam replied coolly.

"Right. I can see that."

"It attacked us out at Watermelon Ranch," Dub said. "Miriam's heroics saved us from getting ripped to bits."

Jeb smirked and clapped Dub on the back as he crossed over to the exam table. "Glad you didn't get ripped to bits."

Dub supposed his brother being constantly surrounded by death made him capable of humor in its presence, but it hardly seemed the time for any kind of smiling.

"We need to know if he's been lobotomized," Miriam said.

Jeb stared at her like she'd grown a third eye. He looked down on the corpse of the beast. "That's gonna be a touch hard to discern, considering you put a bullet through his brain."

"Fair point."

"I'd settle for an ID," Dub said.

Jeb lowered his face to within inches of the beast's. Most of its remaining features were caked in blood and hidden by matted beard hair.

"Wasn't the last one from like World War II or something?"

Miriam: "Yeah, but doesn't mean this one is."

Jeb stood upright. "Well, I don't recognize him, and we'd probably recognize anyone from Rose Valley."

"Maybe not," Dub said. "He's been mutated or whatever. And under all that hair, he could be anyone."

"Sure, maybe. So, what's the plan here then?"

"First off, we need to keep it quiet," Dub replied. "Don't talk about this to Steph, or any of your drinking buddies."

"Okay. People are going to get word, though. I doubt you carried this in here yourself."

Dub clenched his jaw. If Miriam and he could have carried the body themselves, they certainly would have, but the creature weighed at least three hundred pounds, so they'd needed some help. He'd called in Rodriguez, who Dub felt could best keep a secret. If people heard about another beast on the loose, the situation would go from challenging to impossible to control. Rose Valley would become a media circus.

"We didn't," said Dub. "But I think we have a little bit of breathing room before word gets out."

"I say we clean him up," Miriam said. "See if we can get a look at his face. If he is a Rose Valley resident, or even an ancestor of one, you may recognize him."

"Good idea," Dub replied. "Also, fingerprint it. I can run the prints and see if anything comes back. We can try for DNA too, but that'll likely raise more eyebrows and tell the world about our kill sooner."

"What about an autopsy?" Jeb asked.

Dub started to respond in the affirmative, but Miriam interjected: "No. Not yet."

She shot a look towards the door and Dub took the meaning.

"Start cleanin' it up," Dub said to Jeb. "We'll be right back."

Miriam followed into the hallway. Dub moved down a few feet to give the door some clearance. He didn't figure Jeb cared one way or another what they talked about, though.

"What's up?" Dub asked. "Why wouldn't we want an autopsy?"

Miriam hesitated. "It's not that we shouldn't do one, it's just that..."

It took a few seconds for it to click into place, but Dub took her meaning. Jeb spent most days gussying up dead old ladies. Even when he did have to perform an autopsy for the county, they almost always ended up with benign conclusions. Heart failure. Cancer. Stuff like that. Jeb certainly didn't know the first thing about autopsying a science experiment.

"If not Jeb, then who? We need someone we can trust."

"I'm sure your brother's great, Sheriff, but we need someone we can trust, and who has the experience to do this right. There's no one more suited for this than Arrowhead."

Dub shook his head. "I know who they'd turn it over to, and there's no way in hell we can go that route. I don't trust Dr. Vance as far as I can throw her."

"You think she's involved?" Miriam asked.

"I wouldn't rule it out."

Since meeting with Dr. Vance, Dub hadn't made time to parse through his impression of her, much less impart the conversation to Miriam, but his reaction against turning this thing over to her was one of intuitive conviction—he just couldn't.

"That does change things," Miriam said.

"You know anyone?"

"There's Kent. Works with my dad. I haven't met him, but he's their go-to for doing field autopsies."

"Think he's up for this?"

"I don't know. He's barely out of school. I doubt he's ever autopsied a human."

Dub didn't like to think of this thing as human. That came with ramifications, the least of which meant having to arrest his civilian partner for murder.

Miriam continued, "And if we bring him in, we're bringing in the entire team. Once dad finds out about this, you won't be able to keep him quiet. Or out of the way."

"Good point. No offense, but this'll be a lot easier without Skylar on my back."

"None taken."

Dub didn't want to sweep this one under the rug. He didn't want the body to be consigned to an incinerator with not even half the necessary questions answered. The last beast died publicly, leaving no way to keep Arrowhead out of it, but this gave them the chance to hopefully close the books on not just this threat, but any other threat in this tangled lineage.

Miriam winced as she pulled out her phone and started scrolling through what looked like her contacts.

"You okay?"

"Yeah," Miriam answered. "Probably."

"Anything broken?"

Miriam ran a hand across her ribs and winced again. "Maybe."

"Let me run you over to the ER, get you checked out."

She ignored him, absorbed by her phone. Then her eyes went wide. "I think I know a guy. He doesn't have experience with this exactly, but he's worked on some weird stuff."

Dub decided to let her weasel out of the subject of her condition. He knew the type. If she wanted treatment, she'd seek it out.

"Think he'll help?" he said.

"I don't know. I'll make some calls and let you know."

"Okay, let's get back in there."

Miriam looked down at her Timex, then glanced towards the rising sun, now piercing the front lobby windows. They'd been up all night.

"Crap," Miriam said. "I gotta go. Just keep your brother from destroying anything useful, ok?"

Confused, Dub asked, "What could be more pressing than this?"

Miriam's shoulders fell as she sighed.

"A dress fitting."

Chapter 10 – Miriam

Miriam slammed the door and turned the deadbolt. Immediately she stripped off her shirt and tossed it in the trash. She'd learned enough over the years to have given up on cleaning blood out of her clothes. Easier to just get new ones. Every removal of a piece of clothing hurt, but she managed with only a barely audible groan. Once stripped, she hobbled to the bathroom where she took a good look at herself in the mirror.

A nasty bruise snaked up her shoulder from the kickback of the Gehringer. The use of a tripod was apparently more necessary than she realized. Whenever she twisted, or bent, pain shot through her chest. A broken rib or two, she'd wager. Not the first time she'd done that, and it certainly wouldn't be the last. Her leg stung, reminding her about the splintered two-by-four that almost took her out. Under caked blood, she verified a gash. That wasn't going to feel good in the shower.

She turned the knob to scalding and waited for it to heat up. With dawn barely behind her, she thought it too early to make her phone calls.

Stepping into the shower, she knew stinging pain and warm relief. She tried to make room for both feelings until the pain largely muted, and she could enjoy the water.

Back in Cape Madre — after she'd killed the kraken — she almost failed out of college because she'd hung back for weeks to study the carcass along with CDC. She'd made a few contacts there and considered calling in a favor with one of them, but bringing in the CDC would come with too much red-tape. She needed someone closer to home, more accustomed to small-town life.

She grabbed a rag and gingerly started scrubbing at the dried blood on her leg.

In the aftermath of the kraken, the one person by her side had been Jess Gearhart, the Jeb Higgins of Cape Madre, except far more capable. Not to mention experienced in taking apart a massive octopus with a brain-controlling parasite. Her sights were on Jess. He'd help.

In washing, she saw the gash was actually more a scratch. It stung like hell, but didn't require stitches. One less thing to worry about. Couldn't put a cast on broken ribs, either, so Miriam saw no reason to bother herself with an ER visit. It would all heal in time. Granted, rest would be better than a full day of dress fittings and cryptid investigations, but she never much cared for good sense when it came to such things. Miriam Brooks was not an idle woman.

Clean and slightly more alert, Miriam stepped out of the shower and slowly dried off. She threw her hair into a wet ponytail. She hated blow dryers. So loud.

On the way to the bedroom, she noticed the TV. She left it on, mostly on mute. She didn't know why. She guessed that it made her feel less alone.

The news was reporting about two inmates having escaped from a prison down south. She knew of it. Davies and Grimes had been locked up there, after their part in a few murders and other cultish activity back in Gray's Point. She watched for a few seconds, but didn't catch the names of the escapees before she heard the buzz of her phone.

She fetched it while glancing at her watch. She knew exactly who the text would be from.

Are you awake? it said. *Dress fitting today. Don't forget.*

Miriam tapped out *Yes, I know.* Truth be told, Macy's text showed a lot of restraint, considering the fitting took place in only thirty minutes. The nagging would have usually started earlier. Of course, Macy probably didn't know anything about Miriam's overnight antics... yet.

Though much more interested in the beast situation, Miriam really did want to be a good maid of honor. Kind of. More accurately, Miriam really wanted Macy to have a good maid of honor. Miriam wished it could be herself, but she knew she just didn't have the chops for it. Not a single ounce of the responsibility appealed to her.

She sighed. Her ribs regretted it.

Back in her bedroom, she managed to get dressed. She opted for an over-sized, long-sleeved T-shirt and jeans to minimize any looks of horror she might get from the bride-to-be. Macy probably gave explicit instructions about what to wear, but Miriam couldn't remember any of it. Other than her presence, what else could a dress fitting require?

She went to the kitchen and downed some ibuprofen and caffeine, slipped on a pair of comfortable shoes, and headed out the door. The drive was short. She parked on the curb and headed inside as fast as her broken ribs would allow.

She underestimated how long it had taken her to get dressed given her state, and immediately knew it when she walked into the store to a trifecta of disapproving stares from Macy, Shandi, and Olivia.

"You're late."

Chapter 11 – Macy

Macy collapsed onto the flower-patterned couch, hoping to stave off what she knew were overly dramatic emotions. She fought back tears: a rare occurrence. Facing imminent death at the hands — and tentacles — of giant monsters? No problem. Trying to wrangle her entire cadre of family and friends into something resembling a functional team? Too hard.

Miriam usually claimed the title of control freak, but Macy's inner Bridezilla arrived in spectacular fashion, threatening to usurp the title of the Rose Valley Beast.

Shandi sat beside Macy on the couch, resting a hand on her forearm.

"It's gonna be okay."

Something in Macy's brain tried to suppress a retort. Something in there really wanted her to reply with the sensible answer of *I know*, but instead: "No it's not! Olivia's dress is way too big. Tanner's tux isn't even here from Fort Worth yet. The florist hasn't called back. The caterer just asked for the dress code... at a wedding! Honestly, who doesn't know the dress code of a wedding?"

Shandi just rubbed Macy's forearm gently. A show of motherly love, surely, but instead it just felt patronizing. She knew Shandi was giggling inside. Macy would have done the same if not so intimately connected to the situation. She shot a glance at the dressing room door that hid Miriam from view. If

Miriam wouldn't clearly hear, her next rant would be about Miriam's lack of enthusiasm and participation.

"Maybe I'll grow into it," Olivia said from across the room. She was perched on a folding chair in the corner, and had buried herself in her phone.

"Very funny," Macy replied.

"No, seriously. Everyone says I'm growing up very quickly now." Olivia gave a goading grin that only a sibling could deploy with such perfection.

Macy stood and paced, barefoot on the short pile carpet. It burned her feet as she dragged them along, but she didn't care.

The shopkeeper offered, "Do you want to try on your dress again? It looked so beautiful on you. Maybe we could go through some veil options."

Macy shot the shopkeeper a look, but the lady seemed unfazed, Bridezillas being her particular brand of monster.

"What is *taking* so long?!" Macy yelled at no one in particular, though intentionally loud enough for Miriam to hear.

The door to the dressing room cracked ever-so-slightly and Miriam's voice came out meekly. "I might need a little help."

The shopkeeper hopped to it, heading towards the dressing room, but Macy stopped her. "No. Let me."

Macy noticed the shopkeeper look at Shandi in a silent negotiation of the best course, but ultimately slowed up and let Macy pass her by. Knowing Miriam's weird shyness about nudity, Macy slid the door open enough to get inside, then hastily closed it. She expected Miriam just needed help understanding the function of the dress—after all, Macy had never seen Miriam in one.

Yet Miriam stood there, a dress hanging loosely around her waist, dark purple bruises all along her chest, both above and below her bra-line. A deep red gash glared from her calf.

"What the hell did you *do*?" Macy said, feeling like a vessel might burst in her temple.

"Um." Miriam looked a little sheepish. She never looked sheepish. In the more rational part of her mind, Macy knew that meant Miriam really did care about this whole wedding thing. "Last night, I was um, working on that new beast thing."

"Did you fall off a ladder?"

"Um, no," Miriam replied. "The beast showed up."

The world stopped. The wedding seemed far away. Dresses seemed unimportant. For the first time in weeks, Bridezilla took a backseat.

"Oh my god," Macy said. "Are you ok? Who else was there? Was anyone hurt? Why haven't I already heard about this?"

"I'm fine," Miriam said. "Just a little banged up."

"What did the doctor say?"

"I didn't go to the doctor."

Macy sighed.

Miriam continued, "Jake and Dub were there. Both safe. Only the beast..."

She trailed off as Macy closed the distance between them. Miriam gingerly pulled up one side of the dress so Macy could help her get it over her shoulder, but instead of helping with the dress, Macy took Miriam into her arms and hugged her loosely, trying to be mindful of her injuries.

"You killed it, didn't you?"

She felt Miriam's head nod. Tears previously reserved for wedding mishaps now flowed down Macy's face. "I'm so sorry."

Miriam whispered. "I had to."

"I know." Macy stroked Miriam's hair. The memories of Hogg Run came flooding back. The night Macy watched a man tumble off a roof. A man she could have saved. A man she believed in her heart she had murdered, despite all evidence to the contrary.

After a few moments of silence, Miriam changed the subject. "I can't lift my arm high enough to get the dress on."

Macy sniffled and chuckled, pulling out of the hug. Miriam had stayed in the intimate moment longer than usual.

"Let me help," Macy said, taking hold of the dress. "It might hurt."

"That's okay," Miriam replied. "We need to know if it fits. For the big day, you know."

Macy tugged. Miriam grunted, but nodded. With effort, Macy got Miriam into the dress and pulled the back zipper up to her neck. They both looked in the mirror. Macy couldn't help but beam: Miriam looked beautiful. Well, she *would*, anyway, with a little bit of makeup and a brush.

"I look weird," Miriam said.

"You look great."

"Agree to disagree."

"At least it fits."

"Does it?" Miriam asked. "Feels a little tight."

"That's how it's supposed to look."

Miriam studied herself almost scientifically in the mirror. Macy laughed. "I'm serious."

"If you say so."

"Ready to get it off?"

"Yes please."

Macy laughed again, unzipped the dress, then helped Miriam shimmy it off — with no small amount of painful grunts along the way.

As Macy affixed the dress back to its hanger, she felt like a weight had been lifted. "At least now, we can just focus on the wedding."

Miriam worked slowly through getting her clothes back on. Her lack of immediate answer stirred Bridezilla back to life.

"Right?" Macy said.

Miriam hissed in pain as she leaned over to get her shoes oriented.

"We haven't told anyone yet."

"That's okay," Macy said. "Dub can handle all that media stuff."

"We're not going to. Not yet."

"What? Why not?"

"We can't trust Arrowhead. We need to know who this beast is and where it came from."

"That sounds suspiciously like you haven't closed the books on this one."

Miriam just looked at Macy.

"No," Macy said, shaking her head. "Let Dub handle it. Let my dad handle it. Hell, let *your* dad handle it."

"You know he can't keep his mouth shut."

"I'm getting married, Miriam." Macy was pouting, but didn't care. "To your cousin. It's only going to happen once."

"I know, I know. I'll be there."

"But I need you here — now — every day until then," she pleaded. "I have so much to do. I need help."

"So does Dub."

Wrong answer. Macy felt her face flush with anger. "Dub has deputies. I only have you."

"You've got your mom. Your sister. Tanner."

"But I want *your* help!" Macy yelled, loud enough everyone in the store could hear. She clamped her mouth shut.

Macy knew Miriam couldn't—wouldn't—give her what she wanted. As much as she loved the girl, Miriam was single-minded, stubborn, and only ever focused on the next mystery.

The tears came again.

"Listen, I have the schedule," Miriam said. "I'll be at every meeting you need me at. And I'll be at the wedding with that monstrosity on." She gestured to the dress.

"You promise?"

She nodded. "I promise. I'll even try to heal up some so I don't look like Frankenstein in a dress. No more fighting monsters for me until after the big day."

If only Macy could believe that. Miriam would fight whatever monster showed up, so hoping for no monsters was a better bet than hoping Miriam would stay away from them.

Macy didn't have anything else to say. She couldn't beg anymore. Miriam wouldn't be there for her in the way she needed. She had to accept that, no matter how she felt on the subject.

She wiped away the tears and opened the door.

"You're free to go."

Macy failed to hide the snark, but Miriam didn't seem to notice as she bounded out the door.

Chapter 12 – Dub

Dub woke up at half past noon. Maria had taken the kid to the park, giving him some rest after staying up all night, so the house felt uncomfortably empty. She didn't even know what he'd been doing, but as Sheriff, it wasn't the first time he'd been forced to keep her out of the loop. She worried a lot, but Rose Valley had no real violence to speak of — outside the government monsters that showed up every few years.

And for her sanity, Dub thought it better that she believe there'd only ever been one of those.

He checked his phone. There was a message from Jeb about the fingerprints. Dub would swing by and pick those up on the way to the station. A more definitive test might be needed if his search came up inconclusive, but for the first round he could run the prints through the database and see what shook out. He hesitated to run DNA because that would have to run up the chain, alerting more people to their kill and possibly bringing in Arrowhead. No. For now, he'd keep to investigating what he had control over.

He quickly dressed and headed over to the morgue. Jeb met him at the entrance with a brown envelope.

"Did you get him cleaned up?" Dub asked.

"Yeah. Wanna take a look?"

He didn't but knew he should.

"Yeah."

Dub followed Jeb inside, where the beast lay on a gurney, covered in a white sheet. Jeb pulled the shroud down to the shoulders. Cleaned up and shaved, the beast looked almost human again, which Dub found immensely uncomfortable.

He knew this guy. Not well. And the damage to the face made it impossible to know for certain, but Dub's gut did somersaults — he'd seen this guy before.

"Do you recognize him?" Dub asked.

Jeb shook his head. "Nope. I don't think so."

A Rose Valley native wouldn't be able to escape recognition by Jeb and Dub, so it couldn't be that. But still, it had to be someone Dub had seen or interacted with somehow. He'd bet his career on it.

Dub tapped Jeb on the shoulder with the manila envelope. "I'm gonna head to the station and run these prints. See if I can come up with an ID."

"Sounds good. Want me to start the autopsy?"

Dub hadn't found the heart to tell Jeb they didn't trust him with something this big. "Not just yet. Let's see if we can get an ID first."

"Are you sure? I'm curious to see what makes this thing tick."

"Trust me, Jeb. We all are. But gotta do things carefully. By the book. You get it."

"If you say so, Sheriff."

The use of the honorific stung a little, but Dub let it slide. He could handle a little tension with his brother if it meant solving the case that seemed destined to forever plague Rose Valley.

***

Nestled into his office at the station, Dub began the upload to see if he got any hits from AFIS. At one point in time, running fingerprints may have raised some eyebrows, but nowadays the computers did all the work. No one would notice this particular set of prints going through unless they did an audit. And he wasn't gonna audit himself.

Most times, the result came back pretty quick, but other times it took a few minutes. He didn't understand how computers worked and he didn't care to learn. In the meantime, he turned his attention to clerical matters. Emails, requests, documents to sign. Sheriff sounded like he lived a life of action, but it couldn't be further from the truth. Mostly, every day provided a new challenge to his overall mental health.

When the phone on his belt rang, he saw Miriam's name come up, and immediately answered.

"Hey, Ms. Brooks."

"Hi, Sheriff."

"What can I do for you?"

"Nothing. Just calling to let you know that I got in touch with my guy. Jess Gearhart. He'll be here by morning."

"Where's he coming from?"

"Cape Madre."

"What's this guy's resume look like?" Dub knew it wouldn't take much to have more experience than Jeb, but curiosity caused him to ask for qualifications.

"Coroner, like your brother. Except specifically trained for it." She paused. Dub waited. He liked waiting people out. Eventually, she continued, "Worked with him for a few weeks on the kraken carcass."

Ok. *Now* they had something to work with. The beast's taxonomy would have very little to do with a kraken, no doubt, but at least it meant Gearhart had worked with weird before. Dub would take that, given the situation.

"And you can trust him?"

"As much as I can trust anybody, yeah."

So not much.

"Ok," Dub replied. "I'll meet you at the morgue tomorrow morning, then. Say eight?"

"Sounds good. I'll be there."

She hung up without saying goodbye. Dub didn't mind the lack of pleasantries. He'd already clocked Miriam for that.

He sat his phone down on the desk and clicked back over to the tab running AFIS. He didn't realize how skeptical he really was about finding a match until he saw the program had reported one. He clicked on it, then sunk back into his chair.

It was a man he'd met only once or twice.

A man with a history of domestic abuse.

A man who'd been a suspect for the murder of his wife—a still unsolved murder.

And a man whose ex-stepdaughter lived right here in Rose Valley.

I'll be damned.

Dub jumped to his feet, rushed to his car and sped across town for a visit with Brynn Kerrison.

Chapter 13 – Miriam

Miriam hit the pillow hard, instantly regretting not getting in bed more carefully. She toyed with the pillows and blankets until she found a position that didn't add to the lingering pain.

Despite the noonday sun, she tried to sleep, but her mind didn't want her to. It wanted to plan, worry, deduce, speculate. It wanted her to get her lazy butt out of bed and over to Steve's ranch to see if she could track where the beast came from. Maybe find a cave or something similar, as she had with the first beast. But she knew she needed rest. More importantly, she knew that if she got herself into any more trouble, Macy would surely come unhinged.

Her mind swam like this for what seemed like forever. She drifted in and out of sleep before being jerked awake by a knock on the door. A playful, light knock. She ignored it and put a pillow over her head.

The knock came again. She remained quiet. They would go away eventually.

On the nightstand, her phone buzzed. She picked it up to read a message:

I know you're in there. Open up.

Miriam's stomach fluttered. She looked at the time and realized she'd been fighting sleep for hours, not minutes. She'd gotten more sleep than it felt like. She texted back *Coming* but went to the bathroom first. She smoothed her hair, wiped sleep out of her eyes and smiled at herself in the mirror. Did she look ok? She never knew.

She crossed the apartment, her eyes noticing every embarrassing part of it. Unpacked boxes. Half-drunk cans of Mountain Dew. A couch covered in unfolded — albeit clean — laundry. Nothing to be done about it now.

She opened the door and immediately fell into a painful hug from Kim Akana. Her trail-guide from her last big mission. The whisperer of Dobhar-chús. And someone Miriam thought about more often than she felt she should have. She knew, of course, that Kim would be coming in for the wedding, but hadn't anticipated seeing her today.

Kim smelled good. Flowery.

"Hey, you!" Kim said, finally releasing the hug.

"Um hi," Miriam stammered out. "What are you doing here? I thought you weren't in town 'til tomorrow."

"I took an early flight."

"Oh. Ok." Miriam thought she should say more, but didn't, instead shutting the door behind Kim and watching as she took in the filth of the apartment.

"Oh, Mir," she said. "Are you ok?"

Miriam brushed laundry into a nearby basket and offered up the couch to sit.

"Yeah," she replied. "I've just been busy."

If 'busy' meant surfing the internet.

Kim took a seat. Miriam sat beside her.

"All right," Kim said. "I can't keep a secret. I came early because Macy asked me to."

"Oh, right," Miriam said. "To help her with wedding stuff?"

"Umm..." Kim's Cheshire-cat grin beamed as she leaned over and tapped Miriam on the knee. "Something like that."

Oh god. Macy didn't...

"You're my babysitter?!" Miriam asked.

"I wouldn't call it that," Kim said. "Macy just said you could use some company."

Miriam growled. Out loud. Like an animal. How could Macy do this to her? How could she continue searching into the beast's origin if Kim reported every move back to Macy? Miriam didn't intend to miss the wedding. She didn't need a minder.

"Don't worry," Kim said. "I'm not gonna narc on you. Truth is..." She looked down at her hands. "I thought it'd be fun to spend some time together before I head back."

Miriam melted a little. Her anger for Macy didn't extend to Kim, even *if* the two had colluded to keep Miriam out of trouble. Truth be told, Miriam's biggest apprehension about the upcoming wedding didn't have anything to do with Tanner or Macy or wearing an uncomfortable dress.

At their last parting, Kim left Miriam questioning things. About herself. About her relationship with Gabe. And no matter how much Miriam tried to exorcise thoughts of Kim from her memory, she'd never fully managed it. And that irked her.

"Fine," Miriam said. "You better not."

Kim smiled. "I promise. I'll even help you figure out this beast thing, if you want."

Miriam felt warm inside. Finally, someone wanting to help instead of slowing her down.

Kim continued more solemnly, "But I have to make sure you get to the wedding on time, or Macy will kill me. That girl is scary sometimes."

"Don't I know it."

Calmer now, Miriam once again looked around the apartment, wishing she could clean it up with her mind. Kim seemed to notice Miriam's disdain for the situation.

"Need help unpacking?" Kim asked, the smallest hint of a tease in her voice.

"No."

Miriam stood, winced. Kim followed her up, reaching over and touching her on the shoulder. "Maybe we take the day off, hmm? Macy said you were pretty beat up."

"Yeah. Maybe." Somehow following Kim's advice seemed easier than following that of others.

"So, I guess I get the couch, then?" Kim asked, sizing up the raggedy hand-me-down couch that barely exceeded the length of a loveseat.

"What do you mean?" Miriam said, slow to catch on.

"For the week," Kim replied. "Macy said I could stay with you."

What?!

Miriam made a mental note to have a talk with Macy about her scheming. No one had ever asked or even implied that Kim would be staying at Miriam's place.

"Oh, did she?"

"Yeah. Why? Is that not the plan?"

Not the plan at all, but Miriam couldn't turn her away. Not Kim. So, she did something that Miriam very rarely did.

She lied.

"No, no. Of course, that was always the plan," Miriam said, imagining her tone more convincing than it probably was. "I just meant you don't have to sleep on the couch. You can have the bed. I'll sleep on the couch."

Kim frowned. "I don't like that idea at all. You need rest."

Miriam had no spare sheets. No pillows. Nothing at all one would need to sleep on the couch. This all seemed so much more complicated than it should have. She wanted Kim to stay. She really did, but she didn't know how to navigate all of this. She didn't know how to be a host to anyone. But she couldn't bear the thought of disappointing Kim, either.

And at once, Miriam's facade of cool, planned perfection fell. She didn't mean for it to, but she just couldn't keep it together. Lack of sleep, she supposed.

"Okay. Look. I don't have anything for sleeping on the couch. I'm sorry. I just... I've been busy and there's the whole thing with the beast, and Macy is just so... so..."

"Bridey?" Kim laughed.

"Yeah," Miriam replied with a sigh.

"Tell you what," Kim said. "You're tired. You need some sleep. Why don't you take a nap and I'll head to the store to get some sheets and stuff."

Miriam smirked. "You sure I'm not gonna run off? What would Macy say with you leaving me alone like that?"

Kim laughed and rolled her shiny black eyes. "You leave Macy to me. Come on."

Kim tucked her arm around Miriam's and walked with her to the bedroom. Miriam didn't need the help. She'd managed with her injuries all day. But strangely, she didn't hate the closeness. Kim had always been easy to be around compared to other people. She could be a troll. Mischievous. Straightforward and downright cavalier about uncomfortable topics. But she felt like... Tanner. That's what it was. That same feeling of home.

When they got to the bed, Miriam climbed in. Kim pulled the covers up to Miriam's chin then sat down on the edge.

"Comfy?" Kim asked.

THE LEGACY OF ROSE VALLEY

Miriam nodded, already feeling warm and sleepy. Kim stroked Miriam's hair. She froze, her mind immediately trying to remember the last time she'd combed it and washed it, but then she just gave in, closing her eyes and enjoying the sensation.

Miriam sleepily tried to talk about the beast, but she knew it didn't make sense. Kim confirmed reception of the message with quiet *mmhmms* and a few *shhs*.

Sleep came quickly, her mind wandering around and thinking about so many different things. Emotions came and went. The world swam by.

As she danced with consciousness, her last coherent thought was of Kim. She stayed. She stayed until Miriam fell fast asleep.

Chapter 14 – Dub

Brynn Kerrison sat behind the smallest desk that Dub had ever seen. She waved him in as she talked to someone on the phone. He barely managed to squeeze into the rickety office chair across from her, his knees hard against the back of her desk.

The offices for the Rose Valley Reporter hadn't changed in decades. The town grew. The paper grew. The building didn't. As such, one of their primary researchers apparently got housed in what Dub guessed was once a supply closet.

"All right, Dr. Vance," she said. "I gotta go. We'll talk later."

Brynn tapped the screen of her phone and put it face down on the desk. She paused for a beat before looking up and greeting Dub with a huge, white smile.

"What can I do for you, Sheriff?"

Dub remembered the girl from back when he'd investigated her mother's death. All evidence suggested that Brynn hated her mom, but she'd been distraught over the whole ordeal, so despondent she'd been damned near unreachable. It'd been suspicious at the time, and her now calm, confident exterior only heightened his suspicions in retrospect.

She'd changed a lot since he'd last really talked to her. She looked rested. Her hair meticulously kept. Perfectly applied smokey eye make-up. Clothes tailored to fit her more perfectly than most. But none of those changes were what bothered him. Her attitude seemed different. Defiant. Arrogant, like she knew more than anyone else in the room.

It reminded him of Deirdre Valentine.

"Was that Jillian Vance you were talking to?"

Brynn's eyes diverted briefly down to her phone. "Um, yes. I'm working on a story about Arrowhead. I was setting up a time for an interview."

Dub nodded. "Ah. Well, she's a bit shifty, that one. Hope you get what you need for the story."

As far as Dub knew, Brynn worked for the Reporter as a researcher, not a journalist. He noted the fact for future reference. Could be true. He didn't really know what researchers did. But he wouldn't have guessed interviews a part of her responsibilities.

He shifted to the task at hand.

"I know this may be a little delicate, Ms. Kerrison, but I'd like to ask you a few questions about your stepfather."

Her face remained impassive. Almost too impassive.

"That's fine," she replied. "The guy can rot in hell for all I care. Since *you* didn't nab him for mom's murder, he's probably beating some other woman somewhere."

Combative, right out of the gate. The accusation stung a little. Dub felt confident in their investigation, though. He didn't know who'd killed Anne Rickman, but no evidence suggested it had been her husband, Deke. Besides, Dub knew something Brynn didn't— Deke certainly wouldn't be beating anyone ever again.

"Right." He let the room fall silent, removed his notepad and pen, then looked her directly in the eye. She didn't break eye contact. "Does that mean you don't know where he went after the investigation?"

"Of course not," she answered. "How would I know? I hope I never see him again."

"He hasn't reached out to you?" he asked. "Tried to make contact?"

"Nope. Not a peep."

"I see."

She seemed annoyed. Rightfully so, perhaps, but her quick escalation to anger seemed odd. She'd been meeker when he'd talked to her after Anne's murder.

"Do you have any reason to believe he hung around Rose Valley?"

"Haven't seen him. Have you?"

Fair question. Rose Valley being so small, Deke wouldn't have gone unnoticed if he'd taken up residence. But Dub had seen him. Recently. In the morgue with a hole in his head.

Rather than lie, Dub redirected with another question. "Did you ever know Deke to work out?"

"What do you mean?"

"Like did he spend a lot of time in the gym?"

"Oh. No. Not that I remember. Worked on oil rigs, though, so, you know, pretty strong." She reached up to her cheek and brushed her fingertips against it, then lowered her hand back down to the table. Dub wondered if she even knew she'd done it.

He felt a pang of empathy in his chest. This girl—no matter how put together she seemed—had suffered years of Deke's abuse. Not in Rose Valley, but Dub had seen the domestic abuse reports, and they weren't pretty.

Dub leaned forward. "Listen, I know he's not a good man. I wish I could've brought him in for murder, trust me, I do. But we just didn't have the facts in our favor."

She looked away. Stared at the wall. "I know."

In profile, he could see the tears welling, ready to spill out, moving him to do something he knew he shouldn't.

"He's never going to hurt you again, Brynn... He's never going to hurt anyone again."

Her gaze snapped back to him, any hint of the pain and sorrow instantly gone.

She squinted as if she could peer into his brain. "Wha-What do you mean?"

"He's dead, Brynn."

"How?"

He couldn't tell her more. He couldn't risk an employee of the paper getting wind of a new beast. "I can't reveal the details at this point in the investigation, but he's gone. He can't hurt you."

"I know," she said, coolly now. "No one can hurt me now."

Dub didn't know what to make of the declaration. A mantra from therapy maybe?

"Right." He stood, having to push down on the arms of the chair to make sure it stayed in place, then shimmied back to the door. "Thank you for your time, Ms. Kerrison."

"Of course."

He turned to leave, then heard: "Sheriff."

He looked back at her. She now stood behind her desk, her height greater than his. They held eye contact for a couple of seconds, and he couldn't decipher the expression on her face. Not one of relief like he might have expected.

"Thanks."

He nodded and left, exchanging pleasantries with the staff on his way out to his squad car. On the surface, the interview hadn't told him anything new, but he'd gotten pieces. Pieces of a puzzle that still needed to be assembled. She might not have been a threat, or even involved, but something didn't sit right.

His brain couldn't find the root of his suspicions just yet, but it wouldn't stop until he could bring everything into focus.

Chapter 15 – Miriam

As they stepped out of the car, Miriam felt a rush of déjà vu. Alone. Outside. With Kim. Harrowing as the adventure in the Washington wilderness had been, Miriam missed those days. They wouldn't get lost in the wilds of Rose Valley, of course. To those from the Pacific Northwest, its trees were more like bushes.

Kim brought Miriam's thoughts to life with: "Why are the trees here so small?"

Miriam laughed.

"What?"

"Nothing. It's just..."

Miriam trailed off as her eyes surveyed the scene. It remained exactly as they'd left it the night before. By Dub's suggestion, Steve and Cory had stayed away. All the gear lay strewn about. Miriam couldn't resist glancing towards where she'd shot the beast. She could still see remnants of blood splattered across the grass. It turned her stomach.

Well rested from her nap, in a little less pain, and emboldened by a willing partner, Miriam intended to find something — anything — that would help her find the source of this new beast. She didn't even know where to start, really, but the scene of the crime made the most sense until Gearhart arrived to examine the corpse. She felt compelled to do something more than just wait. Waiting brought her nothing but anxiety.

As Miriam crossed the cattleguard, Kim hung back, taking in the scene.

"Mir... I'm so sorry. This must have been horrible."

Miriam walked the perimeter of the yard. "It wasn't great."

"At least you came out alive."

Miriam instinctively touched her bruised—maybe broken—ribs. "Yeah. At least there's that."

Kim smiled reassuringly and crossed the distance between them. "Ok. Where do we start?"

"Well." Miriam shifted her gaze to the end of the trailer and pointed. "It came from over there. Let's see if we can't figure out what direction it came from."

"Sounds good."

Kim took off towards the corner ahead of Miriam. Miriam hesitated, then followed. When she arrived, she looked at a ground mostly devoid of clues. Steve kept the grass well-manicured, which made it more difficult to discern where the dirt had been disturbed. Rose Valley didn't get much rain, leaving the ground dry and dusty. Not the best environment for molding the weight of something as big as the beast. Miriam didn't expect to find footprints.

She lifted her head to view the tree line in the distance. Not far. Something moving as quickly as the beast could cover the distance in a matter of seconds.

"Had to have come from the forest," Miriam said.

"Forest?" Kim asked with a laugh. "Do you mean grove?"

"Let's settle for 'woods,' all right?"

"Deal."

When Miriam didn't move, Kim led the way again. Miriam's stomach fluttered. Her hands felt clammy. Not because they might find the beast, but because of what happened last time she'd ventured into the woods of Rose Valley to find one. She'd lost a brother that day. Most days, Cornelius existed only on the periphery of her thoughts, but now, faced with this same set of oaks and cedars, she felt something she'd not truly felt in a long time — fear.

Kim seemed to sense it, returning to Miriam's position. Miriam didn't like to discuss Cornelius with anyone, and she hadn't spent nearly enough time with Kim for him to have come up. She considered telling the story, but right then couldn't find the courage. She didn't want Kim to view her as damaged. Compromised. Weak.

"You ok?"

Miriam nodded, then glanced back to the yard. "We should gear up, first. To be safe."

She headed back towards the yard, Kim close behind.

"I hate guns," Kim said.

"You seemed pretty fond of' em back when you were trying to keep Abby from killing the Dobhar-chú."

Miriam started picking through the crates, looking for something easy to carry. The Gehringer certainly wouldn't fit the bill, as much as she wished for the comfort of its stopping power.

"That was different," Kim said, hanging back. "I had something to protect."

Miriam found a pistol of the same model she'd lent Kim back in Washington. Kim took it reluctantly.

"Yeah, well, I'm not as cute as a Dobhar-chú, but carry this to protect *me*."

Kim beamed. "Not as cuddly maybe, but..."

Miriam pushed away the implication that Kim found her cute. Not because she detested the idea as much as she had a hard time believing it. Regardless, she knew she'd have time to overthink it later. Right now, she needed her head — and heart — in the game. She chose a pistol for herself, then fetched some already loaded clips to fill it with. She handed one to Kim, checked the safeties on both guns, then showed Kim how to attach the clip.

"The beast is dead," Kim said, dropping the gun to her side. "You killed it yourself."

"The second one, remember?" Miriam said. Unlike Kim, she confidently tucked the gun into the back of her jeans. "If there were two, maybe there're three."

"Or more."

"Exactly."

With that settled, Miriam led the way back to the woods. She looked to the sky, then to her watch. Sunset wouldn't come for another couple of hours. They could cover a lot of ground in that time. Maybe find something interesting.

Despite Kim's reluctance to use weaponry, Miriam still held confidence for her trail-guide-turned-friend-turned-possibly-more. When had that happened? When had Miriam started to think of Kim as more than a friend? She couldn't pinpoint it. Didn't try.

Only one thing mattered in the moment: Kim was an excellent tracker. A consummate outdoors woman. Miriam hated to admit it, but Kim's resumé offered more for a monster hunt than did Macy's. She implicitly trusted Kim to have her back no matter what. And in the woods of Rose Valley, one could never be too careful.

The lack of rain caused the trees to grow far apart from one another, providing plenty of room for the two girls to fan out. They did so without conversation, immediately falling back into the rhythm they'd established in the much denser forests of Washington State. Miriam studied the ground for any signs of disturbance, finding it as enigmatic as the dead grass in Steve's yard. She studied the branches next, not really noticing anything of interest. Most of them were taller than even the beast.

Then she stood back. Took in the bigger picture. Only then did she see something.

Cedar trees made their home among the smattering of oaks, mostly growing outward instead of up. She didn't notice any disturbed branches, but did see a path almost devoid of any branches—the only path something as large as the beast could hope to travel without running into and breaking something.

"What about that way?" Miriam asked Kim, mostly rhetorically.

Kim closed in beside her and regarded the path. "Looks like a game trail."

"Agreed," Miriam replied. "Let's check it out."

***

They walked for almost an hour. The banter flowed freely between them as the path wound and split. They occasionally had to double back to pick up a new one. Curious, Miriam opened the GPS on her phone to ascertain their position and direction. Without roads, the little blue dot didn't tell her much, but as they followed trails and what little clues they could find, she started to see an endpoint at the only landmark in the area big enough to warrant a label on the map.

"I think we're headed to Big Rock Clearing," she said, tipping the phone towards Kim.

Kim studied the map for a second. "Yeah? What's that?"

"A field of rocks. Big ones," Miriam said. "Like bigger than you've ever seen. You'll see."

They kept walking down the only path left to them.

"Anything special out there?"

"Other than the rock formation?" Miriam shook her head. "Not really. When we were hunting the first beast, we came across it. The locals already know of it, of course. Lots of teenagers go there to hang out. It's certainly a geologically fascinating location."

"Looking forward to seeing it," Kim said.

As the walk continued, Miriam wrestled with the memories of her first time in the woods of Rose Valley. As much as she hated discussing the pain of that day, she couldn't shake the feeling that she needed to tell Kim about Cornelius. The logical part of her brain told her that Kim should know for practical purposes, in case Miriam froze or something. But the softer part of her knew it was for more personal reasons.

"So, uh..." She started, pausing when her voice wavered. "I got something I wanna tell you."

Kim slowed, clearly intrigued. "Is it that you've missed me dearly?"

Miriam smiled and gently shook her head. "No. You already know that."

"Do I?" Kim squinted at her with a cock of the head.

"You should," Miriam said, eager to move along the conversation before she got too flustered to think straight. "But no. When I was here before. In Rose Valley. You know we hunted the beast and eventually killed it, right?"

"Of course."

Miriam started walking again, knowing her story would be easier to tell without the intimacy of eye contact. Kim followed suit, walking beside closer than before.

"We'd hunted for days, y'know. Looked into every corner of Rose Valley. Probably walked through this very spot over and over."

They came to another split in the trail. Miriam steered them toward Big Rock Clearing, having already decided it to be the destination of their travels.

"Anyway, one day we found a cave. Pretty small, but big enough that it looked like it could have housed something as big as the beast."

Her voice cracked even though she didn't want it to. Miriam sensed Kim's head turn to look at her, but chose to keep staring straight ahead, trying not to blink for fear of tears squeezing out. She flinched when Kim grabbed her hand, but then gripped back, appreciating the warmth of encouragement.

"That was it. The cave where it lived. We found its den. Stuff that it had collected. And we found a cheetah."

"A cheetah?" Kim seemed confused.

"Yeah. Escaped from the wildlife park. Tanner killed it. That's a whole 'nother thing both of us feel bad about. It was a mistake born of fear or over-training, but that's not the point."

Never a fan of any animal dying, Kim frowned. Miriam felt even worse for the mistake they'd made that day. The diversion from Cornelius' death, though, served to offer Miriam some resolve, so she used it to continue.

"After we left the cave, it—the beast, I mean— showed up. We didn't have the guns we needed to kill it, so we ran."

"Right. Of course."

"And, um..." Miriam's bottom lip trembled. She took in a sharp breath. If she could just get it out, then it would be over. "Cornclius didn't make it."

"Who?"

"My brother."

Kim stopped. Her hold on Miriam's hand forced Miriam to do the same. Without another word or further explanation, Kim wrapped her up. Miriam buried her head in Kim's chest. She'd never done this. Never cried for Cornelius in this way. After his death, she could only find hot, burning, all-consuming anger. She used it to avenge him, but it never really brought closure. She'd never made the time to mourn. Hell, she didn't even think she knew how.

For her part, Kim didn't say a word. She held Miriam until Miriam felt self-conscious about the whole thing and pulled away, quickly running her hand across her face to wipe away the tears and striking out back down the trail. Kim followed a step behind this time.

When the silence grew uncomfortable, Miriam said, "It's fine, though. I just thought you should know."

Kim caught up but kept walking, honoring Miriam's avoidance tactics. "It's not fine. But I'm glad you told me. You can tell me anything."

"Yeah." Miriam sniffled and found a small smile in the despair. "I know."

They walked quietly for a bit. Miriam pushed the feelings away. She felt better when she locked them into the recesses of her mind.

Before long, the trail opened into a clearing. *The* clearing.

"Wow," Kim said. "This is..."

"Amazing, right?"

"I don't know what I imagined, but this sure wasn't it."

Giant boulders littered the landscape in front of them. Most of the trees couldn't even reach the twenty-foot diameter of the biggest ones. Miriam couldn't count them all. She'd seen them before, but now stared in awe at how smooth and round they appeared. Nature never ceased to amaze her.

"This would be a weird place for the beast to live, wouldn't it?" Kim asked.

"Not necessarily." Miriam bounded forward and quickly scaled one of the rocks, using the pitted holes as foot and handholds. It didn't hurt as much as she would have expected. Maybe her ribs were only bruised, not broken. "The rocks have been here forever. Some of them have eroded with time. When we were here before, we found a lot of caves around here."

Miriam got to the top and offered a hand to Kim, who climbed up quickly behind her. They looked out over the landscape, now able to really take in the entirety of one of the world's biggest rock collections. They might not have found the beast's lair, but this sojourn sparked something in Miriam that reminded her how much she loved the hunt, not just because of the prospect of finding something unknown, but because of all the beauty in the known things that she so often took for granted.

"What's that?" Kim said.

Miriam turned to see Kim pointing into the distance. Miriam squinted, studying the red blotch on a distant rock.

"And there!"

Miriam followed Kim's finger to another shock of red against the white rock — which drew her eye to yet another. And another. Maybe a dozen of them, spread haphazardly across the domes of stone.

"Blood," Miriam said as her mind registered it all. "Carcasses."

"Animals? Deer?"

Few predators could be counted among the fauna of Rose Valley, and the ones it had were small and inconsequential. Most of them couldn't even scale these rocks. Whatever brought this carnage to Big Rock Clearing had been something more exotic than a bobcat.

Maybe this was all just the work of the beast she'd already killed.

Or maybe, the terror of Rose Valley was far from over.

Chapter 16 – Jillian

Though integral to the very fabric of Rose Valley, toward sundown not even Mikey's oft-bustling fast food joint could overcome the town's tendency towards quiet. As Jillian stepped into the diner, she noticed two old men playing chess off to her right, the sounds of cleaning from the kitchen, and a bored teenager leaning on the order counter. Mikey didn't let them have their phones on duty. Everyone knew that, because every teenage employee complained about it to anyone with ears.

She approached the kid and started ordering. He scrambled to find his notepad and a pen.

"Let me get a basket of fries and a Blue Ocean."

Mikey didn't serve alcohol, but he'd concocted a few drinks that sorta, kinda got their inspiration from cocktails. The Blue Ocean had coconut-flavored syrup, some blue liquid, and something from the soda fountain. Jillian never bothered wondering what. She liked the flavor. All of Mikey's drinks were crafted with the loving care of a soda jerk from the 1950s, transported to the modern day.

The kid rang up the order, read the total, and took Jillian's payment. She paid in cash and told him to keep the change.

She took the plastic numbered tent and slid into a booth in the back, as far away from both the counter and the chess players as she could get. The kid brought her Blue Ocean almost immediately after she sat down.

"Here ya go, Dr. Vance," he said. "Enjoy!"

She hated that everyone knew her in Rose Valley. She longed for somewhere she could disappear as a nameless face.

Taking a long sip from her drink, she pulled out her phone and flipped through social media, emails and the news. She didn't really absorb any of it. The fries came a few minutes later, piping hot, salty, and greasy, a mountain of them she knew she wouldn't finish.

"Thanks," she mumbled to the kid.

She crunched on a fry just as the bell on the door rang. Jillian turned to see the person she'd been waiting for. Brynn Kerrison's long legs closed the distance between them in a flash. She slid in across from Jillian and helped herself to a fry. She closed her eyes, as if savoring the treat.

"Mikey makes the best fries," Brynn said.

Jillian ate another one. "They're all right."

Brynn grabbed the ketchup bottle. "You mind?"

The ketchup came dripping out before Jillian managed to wave a dismissive hand. "Yeah, it's fine."

"So..." Brynn said, pausing for bites of potato. "He's dead."

"Who's dead?"

Brynn looked around, seemingly satisfied with how little attention they were being paid by the others in the restaurant. "Him. Dear old dad."

"Oh." Jillian's stomach dropped. Logically, it didn't matter that he'd died. For all intents and purposes, the experimentation had already killed him. But still, as long as he drew breath, she somehow justified what they'd done. She supposed, though, that they were long past the point of justification. No amount of mental gymnastics could ever free them from the quagmire they'd waded into. The only difference between Jillian and Brynn was that Brynn didn't seem to care.

J.P. BARNETT

"What happened?" Jillian asked meekly.

"Killed by that bitch, Miriam Brooks."

"Who's that?"

Brynn dusted her hands off, then rubbed them against her jeans. She reached for the Blue Ocean, pausing only briefly to raise an eyebrow at Jillian. When Jillian didn't protest, Brynn took a drink.

"Cryptid hunter chick. Skylar's daughter."

"Oh, that wacko out there with the museum?"

"The very same."

"How did she, you know..."

"Not sure. Didn't get to that level of detail when I coerced Dub into telling me about it."

Jillian ate another fry, even though her stomach warned against it.

"I'm..." Jillian paused to try to find the right words, unsure of exactly what Brynn wanted to hear. "Sorry for your loss."

Brynn laughed, loud enough she garnered sharp looks from the two men across the diner.

"Mind your business!" she shouted. The men went back to their game. If Brynn cared at all about her reputation in Rose Valley, she sure didn't show it. Jillian wondered what path through life had led Brynn to be so cavalier.

Brynn turned back to Jillian. "It's fine. Asshole had it coming. The problem is we're out one beast."

"*You're* out one beast."

Jillian didn't feel comfortable being included. Sure, she'd made the choice to assist, but assistance didn't mean ownership. In fact, she'd intentionally kept herself unaware of the endgame of this lunatic now seated across from her. Jillian got money and the chance to do something scientifically interesting. With the right application of her and Deirdre's work, she could cure disease and give humanity near immortality. Her work might change the world. She didn't need anything else.

"Right," Brynn admitted. "That brings us to the reason for the meeting."

Jillian shook her head. "No. I told you. Just once. Never again."

"Come on, don't be like that."

"Look what happened the first time," Jillian said, lowering her voice to a fervent whisper. "We can't do that to someone again."

She'd only agreed to the first one because of who they were experimenting on. Brynn had told Jillian the stories of her stepdad, how he'd beaten and abused them both for years, how that had gone too far and led to the murder of her mother. The man had escaped the law, too, so Jillian saw some poetic justice in using him for science. But even that had stretched her ability to justify her actions. She didn't think she could do it again.

Brynn popped another fry and chewed it slowly, never taking her hazel eyes off Jillian. "Listen, I get it. It's scary. But it's for a greater purpose."

"Yeah? And what's that?"

No answer. Just Brynn eating a few more fries and washing it down with the Blue Ocean that Jillian didn't intend to touch again.

"Don't you want to see how far we can push this thing?" Brynn asked. A not-so-subtle change in tactic, one with more hope of working on Jillian. "You've already made significant improvements on the previous attempts. Think what you could do with another go at it?"

Truthfully? A lot.

Jillian's mind never stopped coming up with ways she could improve the serum. She'd already removed the need to lobotomize the subject by utilizing the parasite salvaged from the kraken carcass that Brynn brought back from Cape Madre. She'd increased the muscle growth potential by ten percent. She thought she could do better. She knew she could.

Jillian sighed. "Who's the new subject?"

"Don't worry about it," Brynn said, leaning back into her booth. It seemed she'd finally sated herself on Jillian's fries.

"It's important," she said. "I'm not gonna hurt an innocent person."

"I can promise you this," Brynn said with a smile. "It'll be another criminal."

Brynn stood up. She shot a smile towards the kid at the counter, whose return grin was almost puppy-like. Jillian could imagine drool. Brynn didn't have a lot of friends in town, but she did seem to have a lot of fans. Mostly of the male variety.

"Let's meet up again," Brynn said, reaching into her jeans pocket and pulling out a wad of cash. She threw a five on the table. "We'll work out the details. I'll give you a call when I've got things in place."

Jillian didn't meet Brynn's gaze. She stared at the table, refusing to give a yes or a no.

"I'll be in touch."

The bell rang at Brynn's exit and Jillian inhaled sharply. She hated how Brynn just assumed cooperation.

Jillian shoveled the five into her pocket, gathered up the trash, and dumped it in the nearby bin. She shouldn't do this again. So many risks. So many moral questions. Sleeping had become hard enough already.

But when a message from Brynn flashed across her phone screen, Jillian already knew she'd answer.

Chapter 17 – Miriam

Miriam stumbled out of her car, regretting her entire night. After they'd discovered the massacre at Big Rock Clearing, the sunset urged them back home where Miriam paced the living room, talking ninety miles an hour. Kim watched on primly, occasionally poking fun at Miriam's exuberance. Once Kim couldn't take any more and fell asleep on the couch, Miriam took to the internet, uploading pictures of the carnage they'd found, and seeing if she could find any near-matches.

She found some. Of course, no one suggested the beast as the culprit. Most of them pointed at chupacabras, which Miriam could understand. When the first beast wreaked havoc on livestock throughout Rose Valley, chupacabras had also been the first suspect for those who knew it couldn't just be coyotes or bobcats. As much as she enjoyed the prospect of having chupacabras along for the ride, Miriam didn't really expect to find one. The question to her came down to exactly how many beasts roamed the woods.

With no sleep under her belt, she at least gave Kim the courtesy of getting some, choosing to leave her temporary roommate asleep on the couch instead of dragging her down to the county morgue.

The sun seemed far too bright as she crossed the pavement, as did the smile on Jess Gearhart's face as he waited for her approach, casually leaning against the brick wall of the morgue. She'd spent countless days buried in kraken guts with this guy, and not even that had quashed his good humor. Miriam couldn't imagine being that happy all the time. She found the very idea of it existentially exhausting.

"Miriam Brooks. The one and only!"

"Jess."

She offered a hand, which he shook professionally. Despite all they'd been through together, hugging would still be a bridge too far for two introverts who preferred picking apart dead things to interacting with the living.

Miriam glanced at her watch. "Have you seen the body yet?"

"Not yet," he said. "I was waiting for you."

"Let's do it."

They entered the morgue—only to immediately be met by Dub.

"Morning," said Dub. "You must be Dr. Gearhart."

"I am. Sheriff Higgins, I presume?"

"That's me."

The two men shook hands, wasting no time on other pleasantries before the threesome walked to the examination room, where Jeb had already prepared the beast's corpse for autopsy. Gearhart let out a low whistle when he saw the body.

"Damn," he said. "Was this guy a body builder or something?"

Already familiar with the beast's identity, Miriam had dug a little into his past. She'd found photos online of a leaner man. Not impossible that he would have put on such bulging muscles with hard work, but highly unlikely.

"No," Miriam said. "And I suspect he didn't have to go the gym at all for this."

"I guess we're about to find out," Gearhart said.

Before beginning the work, both Miriam and Gearhart dressed in white gowns, then donned masks, goggles, and gloves. By the time they were done, you could hardly tell one from the other. Gearhart grabbed a scalpel from a nearby table.

Jeb cleared his throat. "Looks like you've got this under control. I'm gonna..."

He didn't finish his sentence before leaving the room. Dub waved a hand. "Don't mind him. He's a little butthurt that we called in an actual professional."

Gearhart looked worriedly at the door. "I don't wanna step on any toes here."

"You're not. Not any that didn't need to be stepped on."

Miriam gave Gearhart a small nod to encourage him to continue, so he did, cutting with intense precision into the beast's chest cavity. He went through the motions of a normal autopsy. The blood and guts didn't bother Miriam in the least, but Dub started to look a little green.

"Why don't you step out and get us some donuts, Sheriff?" Miriam suggested. She quickly registered the look of disgust on Dub's face, so she amended with: "For after, I mean."

Dub smiled with relief. "Yeah, that's a good idea. Coffee, too?"

"Sure," Miriam replied, turning to Gearhart. "Anything specific?"

"Nope," he said, never losing focus on his task. "Whatever's good here in Rose Valley."

"Got it," Dub said.

He shuffled out the door. Only then did Gearhart pause. "Is it something I said?"

She couldn't see his smile behind the mask, but the crow's feet in his eyes gave it away as a rhetorical question.

Miriam didn't have much to offer. She'd autopsied plenty of animals, but a human seemed so much more complex. Every incision was fascinating as Gearhart pulled out organs, made notes, and generally grunted and squinted at everything he examined. Miriam didn't want to interrupt his concentration, so she stayed quiet, appreciating the exactness of the process.

After examining more organs than Miriam could name by sight, Gearhart finally spoke: "Nothing out of the ordinary, really. Lungs are a bit scarred. Guy probably smoked most of his life."

"Checks out," Miriam said. "Fits the profile I'd expect of this guy."

"Honestly, we'll probably know more after some lab work. The muscle growth seems extreme. I see some evidence that it happened rapidly, but it's hard to know how rapidly."

"How can you tell?"

Gearhart used the scalpel as a pointer, highlighting stretch marks along the biceps, thighs, and calves. "Muscle growth alone wouldn't cause this, so that makes me think it happened rapidly. Same as when someone gains weight, or whatever. Anything that stretches the skin can cause them."

"Makes sense."

Gearhart put the scalpel on the table and picked up a small rotary saw. "But, let's get to the good stuff. You mentioned that the previous beast had been lobotomized?"

Miriam nodded. "Yeah. Something about having to do that to make it more compliant."

"Ok," Gearhart replied. "Well, let's see if this beast is the same."

When the saw started, Miriam winched, and fought the urge to cover her ears. Gearhart worked quickly, though, opening the beast's head as if it'd come with a lid. Miriam didn't know much about what a lobotomy might look like. Other than the bullet hole, though, the brain looked pretty much exactly like she'd seen a million times before on a smaller scale, or on those forensics shows she sometimes watched.

"Definitely no lobotomy here."

"The old serum gave one person—the seeker, I think they called it—the ability to control the mind of the spear—this guy. Whoever made this surely wanted to control it, so how did they do it?"

Gearhart leaned in as if he didn't hear anything. He reached for the scalpel and gently scraped along the surface of the beast's brain. Then he moved to another portion and did it again.

"Hoooo-ly shit," he said, at a near-whisper.

"What?"

Gearhart put the scalpel down, looked at Miriam, then picked it back up and followed a similar pattern as before, poking and prodding at the brain. Though Miriam saw nothing out of the ordinary, she wouldn't really be able to spot 'ordinary' on a human brain anyway.

"It can't be."

"What?" Miriam said, more exasperated this time. "What is it?"

Gearhart set down the scalpel again and finally looked at her.

"I don't know how, but this thing's been infected."

"With what?"

"Diplomiriamus pseudopathaceum."

The blood drained from Miriam's face. She recognized the taxonomy, for no other reason than it was named after her. Named after her efforts in bringing its existence to light in Cape Madre, when she killed a kraken. When she stopped a small army of zombies being controlled by this parasite. The CDC had cured the people. The kraken was most certainly dead. And no one had seen this parasite since.

"That's impossible," she said.

"Maybe," Gearhart said. "But I studied it for months, Miriam. If this isn't the same parasite, then it's very similar."

It made no sense. Why here? Why now? Could it be coincidence alone that a repeat of a World War II super-soldier she'd killed had shown up in Rose Valley, infected with the parasite of a kraken she'd also killed? As a cryptozoologist, Miriam made a living on proving long odds, but not even she'd take a bet on this being a random accident of fate.

"I'll do more tests to make sure, of course."

"Right. Thanks."

Miriam's mind swam — until it hit on the shores of information from days earlier, the one she'd dismissed, about one of the zombie horde who'd been cured but who was now, conveniently, missing.

Newt Goodreaux.

There had to be a connection.

Chapter 18 – Macy

Breathe.

Everything would be fine. Macy just needed to make it through this barbecue, and then she could check on all the preparations and get some sleep before the big day.

They'd opted for a rehearsal barbecue instead of a dinner. Macy didn't want to stay up too late, and they didn't really intend to do any rehearsing. The logistics would be explained before the wedding, and she felt confident that everyone in the wedding party could walk and stand without practice. Even Olivia.

As she rolled mascara onto one of her eyelashes, she heard a gentle knock on the door of the bathroom. She paused and opened it to see Kim.

"Hey, Kim!" she said. "Come on in."

Kim stepped inside and Macy shut the door, turning back to the mirror to do her other eye. With only one set of eyelashes painted, she looked like a freak. Without mascara, one would be forgiven for believing she'd been born without eyelashes.

"Cute outfit," Kim said.

"Thanks," Macy replied, carefully not moving her face or head too much while she did. When she finished, she turned and smiled. "I'm the center of attention, right? Gotta look my best."

Macy turned to the full-length mirror on the wall and smoothed the bodice of her sundress. She really liked the way it hugged her body, and Tanner really liked the way it showed off her boobs. Yet she was beyond paranoid that she'd get a sunburn and look like a lobster at the altar. To avoid the possibility, she'd layered up on the highest SPF.

Studying herself, she decided on more lipstick. As she grabbed the tube off the counter, she said, "So how's it going with Mir?"

"Good. Just, you know, helping her do her thing."

"Is she still on about the beast?"

"Yeah," Kim said. "She's concerned there might be another."

Macy sighed. On the one hand, she admired Miriam's tenacity, but on the other, she needed a maid of honor with her head in the game.

"She's so damn stubborn."

Kim smiled. "Yeah, she is."

Macy detected a hint of admiration in her voice. She started to apply the lipstick.

"Do you want me...?"

Kim took a step forward and Macy handed her the tube, noticing for the first time that Kim had actually worn make-up. She'd never seen Kim in make-up before. It was subtle, nothing like the bright, garish colors that Macy generally went for. At least that meant Kim knew what she was doing.

As Kim carefully applied the lipstick, she said, "Don't worry. She knows this is important to you. She's already here, even."

Kim reached for a tissue and had Macy blot.

"Really? Like, early and everything?"

Kim nodded. "And showered and dressed."

Macy felt some of her anxiety melt away. Worrying about Miriam being in the right place at the right time had been causing her no small amount of stress.

"You're so good with her," Macy said.

Kim laughed. "She's not a child, Macy. I like her."

"I know," Macy said with a smirk. "That's why I called you in early. Also... she likes you, too. She just doesn't know her own mind sometimes."

"If you say so."

Macy looked in the mirror one last time and smiled.

"Shall we?" Kim asked.

"Let's do it."

Macy stepped into the hallway, following Kim out toward the backyard. Macy blinked a few times to adjust to the brightness of the sun, then took in the scene.

She spied Tanner across the yard, surrounded by her dad and Dub. She waved and mouthed *sorry* to him before heading towards their table. She didn't make it before being waylaid by a number of people offering compliments and well-wishes. This was just the rehearsal dinner, and it felt like too many people. Of course, it was meant to be just the wedding party, but then Cam had invited Dub and Dub invited Maria, and on and on it went until it got well out of control. The reception would be at least three times as many people.

Breathe.

Miriam sat alone at the table.

"Hi, Mir!" Macy said, as she took the seat beside her maid of honor.

"Hi." Miriam chomped on a piece of bread. "You look nice."

Macy smiled as she noticed that Miriam too wore make-up. Of course, Macy had demanded it for the wedding, but she didn't expect such high fashion for the rehearsal dinner, too. No doubt, Kim had done the honors, because Miriam didn't know a single thing about properly applying eyeliner. A window into Kim's preferences, perhaps.

"Thanks," Macy said. "You do, too. Thanks for coming. And early even."

"Of course."

Tanner broke away from the cops and showed up at the table as Kim sat across from Miriam. Olivia filed in from somewhere, tugging uncomfortably at her clothes before sitting down next to Miriam. Tanner leaned over and gave Macy a peck on the lips, careful not to mess up her make-up.

Just as Tanner sat down, people seemed to start taking the hint. Everyone shuffled around to their seats. Gabe showed up at the table and pulled the chair out next to Tanner. Tanner stood to greet him and Gabe took his hand, pulling him in for what Macy only knew how to describe as a bro-hug.

"Hey, *amigo*," Gabe said. "Got your new office all set up. Can't wait to get to work."

Macy felt her heart skip. Everything went into slow motion as Miriam cocked her head. Kim's face fell to a look of horror, and everything Macy had carefully curated for this day went to complete and utter shit.

"What does that mean?" Miriam asked.

Macy scrambled to find an explanation, only to have Tanner jump in first: "Nothing. Just an inside joke."

Miriam didn't seem convinced.

Kim tried to help with: "Did you learn anything cool from the autopsy?"

"A joke?" Miriam said, ignoring Kim. "How is that a joke? Explain it to me."

Even beneath the make-up, Miriam's face had turned red. Her brown eyes twinkled with something like embers.

Tanner looked helplessly at Macy, who looked at Miriam, then at Kim. Then towards her dad, who was just making his way up to the smoker to give a speech. He tapped a fork against a wine glass.

"Hey everyone," Cam said.

Macy hoped the formality of the toast would cause the conversation to die, but Miriam hiss-whispered, "Gabe. What did you mean?"

Gabe held up his hands and Macy knew they were cooked. Gabe couldn't lie to Miriam, not after the relationship they'd been through. Macy had worried that having a Maid of Honor and Best Man be exes would cause drama, but this wasn't what she'd expected.

Just as Gabe opened his mouth, Macy held up a hand. She saw no way out except to try to take control of the narrative.

She whispered frantically, "We were going to tell you after the wedding, Mir."

"Tell me what?"

"Tanner and I are going to be married."

"Yes, I know."

"And we want to start a family, you know?"

"Sure. And?"

Macy looked at Tanner, who offered a silent nod of encouragement. After this, there'd be no going back. Whether Tanner really wanted it or not, she'd be consigning him to be the guy in the chair while Gabe and Kent traveled the world looking for legends and fables. It's what he wanted, though. Right?

Macy tried to take Miriam's hands. Miriam would have none of it.

"We just think it would be better if we had a homebase. If we weren't traveling all the time."

Miriam looked at Tanner who grew stone-faced, then at Gabe, who completely turned away.

"Are you saying you're... what? Gonna quit?"

Macy's eyes watered up. "Yeah. That's the plan. Tanner got a job with your dad to work at the museum."

Miriam stood up, her chair toppling backwards into the grass. Kim stood with her.

"Miriam, wait! It's gonna be okay. I'm gonna work for you instead." Kim looked bashfully to the ground. "If you'll have me."

"What?" This time Miriam no longer whispered. Cam stopped mid-sentence. "You knew about this?!"

Kim nodded.

Macy stood up and tried to pull Miriam into a hug, but Miriam jerked away. Macy knew she had every right to be angry at having her day stolen, but she couldn't shake the feeling that she'd caused this. She'd kept Miriam in the dark. Treated her like a child who couldn't be trusted, instead of best friends. It was time to reap the punishment of her bad choices.

Miriam stormed off, slamming open the back door to the house. Macy rushed after her, with Kim hot on her heels. At the door, Kim caught up and pulled Macy back by the shoulder.

"Let me," she said. She reached up and carefully wiped away Macy's tears. "Don't ruin your make-up. This is your day. I'll talk her down. Don't worry. She'll be fine."

Macy sniffled and nodded. "Does she hate me now?"

Kim shook her head and wrapped Macy in a hug. "No, of course not. You know how she is. She doesn't like change. Especially spontaneous change. She'll come around."

Macy wriggled out of the hug, only to be horrified at every guest staring at her. Her own father scowled from the front. She couldn't tell if he was angry at being interrupted, or worried about her emotional state. Maybe a little bit of both.

Kim smiled and waved at the group.

"Sorry, everyone. Just, uh, a little, uh, wardrobe malfunction. We're handling it. Please..." Kim motioned to the crowd. "Continue. You're doing great, Mr. Donner!"

Macy couldn't help but smile a little when Cam took the compliment with pride. Kim disappeared into the house. Macy returned to her chair to a waiting, doting Tanner.

It would be fine. Kim would fix everything in time for the wedding. All Macy could do now was...

Breathe.

Chapter 19 – Miriam

Miriam set off into the woods hoping to get lost there forever. She could live off the land. Build a house in the middle of nowhere. Of course, she didn't bring any tools or supplies, so she knew she wouldn't really do that, but she needed to clear her head and could think of nothing better than disconnecting from everything. Kim, Macy, Tanner, and even Gabe had been blowing up her phone since she'd left the barbecue, but she ignored them all, left the phone in the car, and set out into the woods in dress pants and a blouse. A blouse! She never wore a blouse indoors, much less out in the Texas heat.

She wouldn't be gone long. Logic already dictated that she'd been rash and unfair, which heralded a return to sanity. Of course, Macy and Tanner deserved stability. Of course, they'd want a quieter life once they got married. Miriam didn't know why she'd never thought of the possibility. She liked the life they'd built, and yearned for further hunts in the future. She wanted it to last forever. But nothing lasted forever, and the woods were a bleak reminder of that as she thought, once again, of Cornelius.

Not really considering her trajectory, she headed towards Big Rock Clearing. Hardly a surprise. She'd left from Steve's ranch, after all, but her mind steered her almost without conscious thought.

And Kim!

Miriam couldn't believe Kim had known all along and never said a single thing. After all the time together. The personal conversations. Macy tended to treat Miriam like a child sometimes, which Miriam tacitly endured because sometimes it's what she needed, and it had become a feature of the relationship, but not Kim, who always treated her differently, always made her feel special. Having Kim involved hurt, leaving Miriam with no one to turn to.

So, she'd focus on the case. On the hunt. Solving the mystery. She couldn't talk it over with Dub—he was throwing back Buds in Cam's backyard. But she could return to the scene and look for clues. She wanted to believe it all went back to Brynn's dad. The one (or second) and only beast. She wanted to believe her paranoia came from trauma, not gut instinct. But somehow the kraken parasite got into Deke's brain, and that couldn't be coincidence.

Newt. Newt. Newt. How did Newt get involved? Did he have a grudge against her so strong that he'd intentionally infect people with the parasite? And even if he did figure that out, where did he get it? How did he use it to his advantage? Miriam conjured a mental map of Texas just to double-check that she hadn't gone crazy, and yep—Rose Valley sat nearly nine hours' drive from Cape Madre. Surely the range of the kraken couldn't extend that far, even if the cape held another. Of all the preposterous possibilities before her, that of another kraken in the vast Gulf waters so far seemed the easiest to believe.

She felt certain she could piece all this together if not for the overwhelming emotions coursing through her. She hated emotions so much. Well, not all of them. Not the way she felt when Kim...

Traitor.

She tugged at the neckline of her blouse. What the hell was this thing made of? Unlike her normal cotton t-shirts, her blouse had nearly soaked through with sweat already. She unbuttoned the top few buttons just as she came upon the clearing, having reached it sooner than she'd expected. Apparently, being lost in thought also caused her to lose time.

Looking around the clearing, her view mostly obscured by the giant boulders, Miriam didn't really know where to start. Without her phone, she couldn't take pictures. Without her kit, she couldn't take samples. She might as well have thrown darts at a dartboard for all the good this random excursion would do her. But, maybe distraction would prove the better outcome than discovery.

Having come the same direction as before, she spied the rock with the convenient hand holds and scrambled up, despite protests from her slippery dress shoes and some lingering pain from the beast's assault. From the top, she peered out across the rocks only to be struck with a sense of confusion. All the carcasses. All the blood. She couldn't see any of it. All of it had vanished.

She took a running leap from her boulder to one she judged close enough. She made it, tripping on the other side and landing on her knees. She heard the fabric of her khakis rip at the knee, and felt the sting of the burn of the rough rock on her skin. Flustered, she stood and kicked off her shoes. They tumbled down the round smooth surface of the stone until they hit the forest floor.

She flexed her toes. Yes. This would suit her needs better, even if she got a few blisters.

Looking down at her feet, she tried to remember if this stone had a carcass. She thought not, as she remembered all of them farther away from her initial location. Luckily, this one butted up against another boulder that she managed to skip onto with barely an extension of her leg. She reached the other side more comfortably this time, her toes easily gripping where her shoes had been unable.

She saw no sign of a carcass, so moved to the next boulder over. Finding nothing there, she moved on to the next, taking her longest leap yet with a semblance of grace. Again, no carcass. It hadn't rained, yet each looked as if it'd been cleared by something. Using her vantage point from nearer the center of the rock cluster, she looked again, closer, with a new theory brewing.

A theory quickly confirmed, too, when she noticed she could indeed pick out the rocks where the carcasses had been, not by blood but by the slightest difference in the color of the stone. Her starting boulder looked dingy gray, but some of the others were nearly white, revealing the chalky stone beneath the surface. Someone had cleaned up the carcasses carefully. Not with rain, but with something like a power washer.

To run a power washer this remotely into the woods would certainly require a generator, and getting a generator out this far would leave tracks.

Finally. A lead.

Excited, she sat down and lowered herself to the ground, enjoying the crunch of the dying grass against the bottoms of her feet. It reminded her of childhood, and made her question—not for the first time—why humans ever decided to bind their toughened feet with shoes in the first place. She felt certain that if she shunned her shoes more often, the ground would feel as comforting as shag carpet.

With a keen eye on the ground, Miriam wound her way between boulders. She ran her fingers along the inner wall as she worked her way through a shallow crevasse. She came to a junction and looked left and right before her eye caught a divot in the ground. Maybe nothing, but she headed towards it quickly until she got a good enough look to see not a divot, but an entire track.

Bingo.

She followed it like a bloodhound, snaking around boulders, generally losing all sense of direction except the one outlined by the wheel imprints. She stopped only when they stopped, not at the edge of the tree line like she'd expected but at the mouth of a cave. She peered inside and found the familiar inky blackness of something completely hidden from the sun.

Based on everything she knew about spelunking, the cave had to go down. As big as they were, it didn't make sense that the boulders could be connected in any cohesive system, not with the frequent gaps separating them. What she couldn't tell was whether it went down in a gentle slope or all at once with a big drop. If the latter, then her generator (and possibly its operator) would be lost to the cave. If the former, though, maybe they used the cave for storage.

So many questions, none of which got her directly closer to the creation of the beast. Maybe whatever service maintained these grounds came out to clean up the carnage, and maybe they really did store their stuff in here. Possible, but also unlikely. Surely, they'd build a structure for that.

If only she'd brought a flashlight, or her phone. Foolishly, she thought maybe if she stepped inside, she could see more. She brushed her toe against the mouth to ensure she wouldn't meet an immediate drop, then took a step inside. She felt tension on the balls of her foot. Then the tension broke. Something snapped. A *clang* reverberated through the cave.

Blinding pain shot up Miriam's right foot. She stumbled backward. The tug on her skin sent rockets of agony up into her calve, her thigh, everywhere. Glancing down as she lost her balance, she saw the tip of a nail ripping through the flesh at the top of her foot. She corrected enough to pull her foot off the nail in something resembling a straight line. Blood gushed out. Her head swam. From the heat, the shock, the pain... the loss of blood.

She fell hard on her ass, drew her foot up into her hand, and looked at the carnage. She couldn't make heads or tails from the injury with all the blood in the way. She took a deep breath, leaning back on her hands and staring up at the sky. Her mishap couldn't be classified an accident. She'd stepped on something that brought the nail up from the bedrock. She scooted over the mouth of the cave and peered inside, just barely seeing the tip of the nail glinting in the sun, straight up.

A booby trap.

Well, at least now she knew she'd stumbled on the right track, and she didn't for a second believe the beast set the trap.

First things first, she ripped at the seam of her sleeve and found that her blouse came apart easily. She used the fabric to wrap her foot, tying it tightly into a knot despite the pain it caused. That would stanch the bleeding, at least.

Miriam leaned heavy on her hands and pushed herself to her feet. The pain caused her to wobble, but by putting most of her weight on her left foot and tip-toeing with her right she managed to stay up. She'd want to come back, for sure, but for now she needed a clinic where she could get the wound cleaned and possibly even a Tetanus shot, though she'd had one fairly recently. She always kept up-to-date on her vaccines.

Hopefully the culprit hadn't also poisoned the nail, but if they had, Miriam wouldn't even make it back to the ranch. That worry hardly mattered.

Macy sure isn't gonna be happy to have a cripple hobbling down the aisle. All the annoyance and fury she'd felt before seemed distant and trivial now. She owed Macy an apology.

Her next thought sent her searching for her missing shoes, which she sorely regretted abandoning. She decided, though, that she wouldn't be able to wear one of them anyway, and opted to leave them lost among the boulders. Instead, she stumbled towards the trees, searching the ground for something she could use as a makeshift crutch. As small and sickly as the trees were, human-sized walking implements didn't often break off, but she did see something that might work. She shuffled towards it, only to be stopped when the crunch of the ground didn't match her slow steps.

Miriam turned. She saw a blur of blonde hair — then crumpled to the ground as the whole world went black.

Chapter 20 – Macy

Macy looked at her dress hanging on the roll-in rack and almost couldn't believe the day had arrived. She'd barely slept but felt wide awake. Today felt like a turning point in her life that she'd always remember. Always cherish. Though she valued independence and worked hard for her computer science degree, deep down, this day was the day she'd always wanted most. She didn't bother thinking about whether society conditioned her with that dream. It was hers now. Her dream finally realized. It felt like her life would be settled after today. She could move on to the next phase.

"Are you ready?"

Macy turned to see her mom at the door, thankfully carrying coffee and donuts. Macy took a cup of coffee, but spurned the donuts. She didn't want there to be any reason that her dress might not fit, even if it was silly to think a single donut could cause that.

"I am," Macy said with a smile. She felt calmer today than she had the previous, despite the calamity of Miriam's explosion. She just knew it would all work out. Miriam would show up when it mattered. She always had and always would.

Shandi pulled Macy into a half hug so as to not spill their coffees. "I'm proud of you, Macy."

"Thanks, mom."

"Now," Shandi said, putting her coffee cup down on a table next to the door. "Let's get to work."

Macy took as much of the coffee as she could in one gulp, then climbed into the folding director's chair in front of the vanity. The ranch they'd chosen as the venue had pulled out all the stops for the bride's room. This palatial point of preparation was one of the reasons Macy had decided, ultimately, to rent the place out for the wedding, instead of just using her dad's backyard.

She reached forward and unzipped the bag with her makeup. Not just the makeup she thought she'd need for the day, but all the makeup she could get her hands on. The stuff that belonged to her, to Kat, and even the shockingly small amount owned by Olivia. Shandi dropped another bag alongside her own stash. Nothing could be left to chance. Of course, she'd tested what make-up she wanted for the big day, but she wanted to be ready in case she changed her mind, or something didn't look quite right.

Shandi grabbed a brush and started by taming Macy's wild, red hair.

"Did you ever hear from Miriam?"

"Not yet," Macy said. "Kim promised she'd find her, though, and Miriam wouldn't abandon me. Not today."

"When are they are supposed to be here?"

Macy reached over to the table and tapped her phone. "Soon."

Since Tanner had so few friends in Rose Valley, the two had decided to go with just a maid of honor and a best man. At the time, the arrangement seemed perfect. Miriam on one side. Gabe on the other. Their break-up would make things awkward, but no more than the rift between Macy and Miriam that now existed. They'd chosen Olivia as the flower girl, despite her being too old for the job, but Miriam really wanted to include her somewhere.

Shandi and Macy went about making Macy look exactly how she'd imagined—until there was a knock on the door, and Kim let herself in.

"Kim!"

Kim looked tired. Worried. "Hi. Is um..." She looked around the room, dropping her shoulders. "Miriam here yet?"

"No..." Macy said slowly, getting up from her chair and crossing the distance to Kim. "She's not with you? You didn't find her?"

Kim shook her head. "She didn't go home. I called and messaged a hundred times, and looked all over town for her car, but didn't find it."

"Did you try Watermelon Ranch? She's probably just still on about that stupid, dead beast."

"First place I looked. Nothing."

"Oh," Macy said, trying to temper rising panic. "Well, she probably just went hiking or camping. She loves the outdoors. That's where she goes to clear her head. And cell phones don't work out in the woods here."

"Maybe," Kim said.

Kim was clearly concerned, but Macy couldn't bring herself to worry. Rather, she refused to let herself. This was her day, dammit. If Miriam wanted to go throw a hissy fit in the woods, so be it. Macy was getting married today, with or without a maid of honor.

"She can be such a baby sometimes," Macy said, coming off a little more harshly than she intended. "But I'm sure she'll show up. She probably just lost track of time."

Kim shared a look with Shandi that Macy willfully chose to ignore.

"Come on, Mom."

Macy climbed into her chair, then looked back over her shoulder. "Wanna stay and help me get ready, Kim?"

"Um, I'd love to. I really would, but I think maybe I should...."

Shandi jumped in. "That's a good idea. You go get Miriam and get her in the shower. We don't need her smelling up the altar."

Macy forced a giggle. "Yeah. That girl does not care when she stinks."

"Ok," Kim said. "I'll keep you updated."

"Thanks, Kim," Shandi said.

"Yeah," Macy said. "Thanks."

Macy turned to the mirror and smiled at herself. Everything would be fine. Every wedding had its mishaps. Miriam was hers. They'd all laugh down the road about how Miriam got her feelings hurt and went all emo on them right before the wedding.

Macy caught Shandi giving her one of those worried looks only a mother could muster.

"It's fine, Mom," Macy said. "She'll be here."

If ever a day needed the power of denial, this day was the one.

***

Macy woke up her phone and sighed. Thirty minutes. She had thirty minutes until she'd walk down that aisle, marry the man she loved more than anyone else, and start her life. Her new life. Without hunting cryptids. Without crazed murderers or mutant pigs. Without running. And, apparently, without Miriam.

"Where is she?" Macy asked. She'd already done so a dozen times. Shandi sat on the small loveseat without an answer, having already given up on trying to provide one. None of them worked. None of them assuaged Macy's frustration.

There was a rap at the door, and Shandi immediately moved to answer it. She pulled the door back to reveal a beleaguered Kim, beautifully outfitted in a slim-fitting blue dress that complemented the streaks of blue in her black hair. She also wore a frown.

"Nothing?" Shandi asked.

Kim shook her head. "I've looked everywhere. She's not answering her phone. I don't know what else to do."

"Are you talking about Miriam?"

The voice came from down the hall. Macy immediately recognized it. By the time she crossed to the doorway, the owner of the voice revealed themselves: Brynn Kerrison. Macy had seen her around town, but hadn't really interacted with her much since Gray's Point.

Brynn looked well, immaculately dressed for the wedding. The fact that she'd even shown up came as a surprise, and her being in the hallway seemed even stranger. Then again, right now, there were people everywhere.

"Yeah," Shandi responded. "What do you know?"

Brynn gave Macy a small half-smile of sympathy. "I saw her just this morning."

"Really?" Kim asked. "Where?"

"Out at Relics."

Relics Wildlife Reserve stood just outside town, a sprawling acreage with all manner of exotic animals, from giraffes to ostriches, cheetahs to wolves. It made some amount of sense that Miriam might go there. She loved animals, and, though she didn't talk about it much, Macy knew Miriam sometimes went to check on the cheetah she'd saved as a cub. After unfairly killing its mother, she'd always felt responsible for it.

"Did you talk to her?" Macy asked.

Brynn shook her head and frowned. "No. She looked like she wanted some space. Didn't want to intrude."

"Ok." Macy shook her arms as if to excise the nervous energy and started pacing the room. Shandi thanked Brynn, pulled Kim inside, and shut the door.

"Did you look for her out there?" Shandi asked of Kim.

Kim replied, "Only in the main parking lot. Is there somewhere else she might have been?"

"Yeah," Macy said. "They let her drive all the way back to the Cheetah pens."

That explained why Kim didn't find her.

"Let me get Dub to do a welfare check, ok?" Shandi said.

Macy nodded and watched as her mom rushed out the door. Kim sat on the couch and patted it to invite Macy to do the same. She didn't. If she sat, the energy would overflow and she'd surely explode. Instead, she paced. Kim watched her. The minutes ticked by, only the *whoosh* of Macy's dress filling the silence.

Finally, Shandi returned.

"Ok," she said. "Dub called out to Relics and got hold of one of the rangers. They verified that Miriam's car is there at the cheetah pens, just like you suspected. No sign of her, though."

"Can she hike anywhere from there?" Kim asked.

"Sure. They have tons of trails. Miriam would know them all."

Kim looked at her wrist, jumped up from the couch, and fished a phone out of the small clutch she carried. "It's Miriam."

Macy rushed over as Kim swiped up on the screen and opened the SMS app.

Tell Macy I just can't do it. I'm so sorry. Wish her luck for me.

Macy's heart sank as the tears burst out. Shandi wrapped her up.

"Why?" Macy sobbed into her mother's chest. "Why would she do this to me?"

"I don't know, baby," Shandi said. "It's not your fault."

Maybe it was a little bit her fault. Macy stayed buried against her mother, letting the tears flow. With them came some of the nervous energy she'd been burdened with. After a few minutes, she pulled away and sniffled, drying her tears, and saw Kim and Shandi looking at her expectantly.

"I need to talk to Tanner," Macy said. "He might not even wanna get married if Mir can't be here."

"Honey, it's bad luck for the groom to—"

"I don't care!" Macy screamed. "Get him!"

"I got it." Kim shuffled towards the door. "Be right back."

Macy collapsed on the couch. Shandi sat next to her.

"My makeup is ruined, isn't it?"

Shandi nodded. "A little, yeah. We can fix it, though."

Kim burst back into the room, with Tanner in tow. The second he crossed the threshold, Macy ran to him and wrapped herself around him. He looked amazing in his tuxedo, and smelled even better. Now that she had him with her, anything was possible again.

"Kim filled me in," he said.

Macy unpeeled herself and looked up at him. "What are we going to do?"

Tanner sighed. "I love Miriam. She's like a sister to me. But, you're everything."

Macy smiled, a rush of warmth covering the rage and sorrow.

"I don't want to put this off. I want to be married to you," he said. "Miriam can sort her own shit out. She'll come around, and we can work things out with her. What's important right now is you... and me."

He leaned over for a kiss. A kiss she'd received a million times over, yes, but one that felt more important than any that had come before. She closed her eyes, knowing that it would take away all the pain.

He stopped, though, when Shandi cleared her throat. Macy opened her eyes and looked at her mom in exasperation.

"Mom!"

"Save it for after," Shandi teased.

Tanner laughed and kissed Macy on the forehead instead. He winked. "See you out there."

"Ok," Macy replied, giving a small wave with only her fingers. "Bye."

He turned to leave, but then circled back. "You look amazing, by the way."

Macy shut the door behind him with a huge grin, internally conflicted but also at peace. She would marry Tanner today. Her relationship with Miriam would come after.

"Okay, lover girl," Shandi said. "Get over here and let me fix your makeup."

Chapter 21 – Miriam

The inky blackness seemed impossible. Miriam could see nothing. Not her hand in front of her face, and not any feature that would indicate where she'd been taken.

Drip.

Drip.

Drip.

Water. It echoed at a steady pace, but nothing she could reach felt wet. The air chilled her skin with a cool dampness. Certainly, she could feel the stone behind her, and reasonably assumed she had to be in a cave, deep underground, in the sort of cavern so cut off from the outside light that she'd go blind if she stayed here too long.

She'd awakened with a pounding headache, and tried to gather her bearings. It took her a few groggy minutes before she remembered that she did have a light on her, no matter how meager. She pushed the button on the side of her old-fashioned Timex watch and squinted into the green *Indiglo* light.

The wedding!

Macy would have already expected her, which brought hope, though only a small amount. Wherever Miriam had been taken, it wouldn't be easy to find, surely not on any map or down any known trail. Likely, she sat somewhere beneath the huge boulders of Big Rock Clearing.

Continually pushing the button, she held her wrist out toward her foot, where she found it artfully bandaged. She tried to flex her toes, focusing on each toe in sequence, trying to discern whether she could expect any long-term muscle damage. Thankfully, each responded to her command, though stiffly and with no small amount of blistering pain.

She got to her feet and limped around the perimeter, using the cave wall for balance. Solid rock met her fingertips with every slow step. But no cave could exist without a way out — she just hoped that way wouldn't be up. It didn't make sense that she'd have been bandaged up, then dropped down a hole, never to be retrieved. Clearly, her attacker wanted her alive, and having to repel down to get the prisoner seemed a poor design. So, Miriam continued limping about, certain she'd find an exit.

After traveling a good distance from her starting point, the texture of the wall changed into something smoother. Colder. Drier.

Metal.

Miriam scrambled for her watch, lit up the screen, and held it close to the wall. She found rivets, hinges, and the outline of a small portal that would serve large enough to push food through, when opened.

A prison, then. Deep under the woods of Rose Valley.

She beat on the door. No one came.

She screamed. No one answered.

She scuffled along the wall a little further. Finding nothing, she slid to the floor, managing to keep panic and hopelessness at bay. If she could gather what she knew to be true, then she'd have an advantage. And with advantage, she could form a plan. Someone would come for her eventually, friend or foe. Of that, she could be certain.

Carefully, she replayed the scuffle at the mouth of the cave. The trap. The nail. And then someone knocked her out, as the headache could attest. So who? She didn't have an image in her head, but she couldn't shake the feeling that it had been someone with blonde hair. Tall, so maybe a man.

Miriam sighed. All of it was far too fuzzy for her to make heads or tails of.

This all felt familiar, of course. She'd been trapped in a cave before, but this situation couldn't possibly be related. More likely, whomever decided to create new beasts did so here, at some underground laboratory to escape the gaze of Arrowhead Research, who surely watched the program like a hawk after everything had gone down with the original beast. Not for the first time, Miriam had simply stuck her nose somewhere it didn't belong, and this was her punishment.

Deep in thought, her ears stayed alert, listening for something... until they heard the scraping of metal.

Her captor drew near.

The door opened, scraping against stone, hinges squealing. She scrambled to her feet and drew her forearm up above her eyes to block out the blinding light coming from the other side. Pure, white, artificial light. Not from the sun above.

A silhouette stood in the doorway. Small, short, a thin waist and wide hips. Clearly, a woman. Not tall enough to be the person that had knocked Miriam out. The stranger's head seemed misshapen, too large for her prim body. The woman stood in the doorway without a word while Miriam stood transfixed, unable to see any detail and unwilling to trust her body enough to attempt an assault.

Another silhouette appeared behind the first, impossible to make out.

"Okay," said the new silhouette, a woman with a voice Miriam didn't recognize. "I've released them."

The first silhouette responded, "Wonderful. Let's see how much carnage our boys can create."

A chill ran down Miriam's spine. She absolutely knew that voice.

Chapter 22 – Macy

Macy stepped from the bride's room and looked down the hall to see her father standing at the end. Cam Donner. The sheriff-turned-mayor, who'd shepherded Rose Valley through arguably its direst and darkest moments, now smiled at her nervously, pride and even a little sadness coloring the edges of his usual bravado.

Macy returned his sheepish grin with her biggest smile. The tears about Miriam had all dried up. Now she focused on the future. This day. And part of this day meant she had a responsibility to herself, to Tanner, to all the people on the other side of that door to be graceful, beautiful and perfect. For just a few hours.

Cam offered her his arm as she drew close and she wrapped her fingers into the crook of his elbow.

"Nervous?" he asked.

Macy genuinely didn't feel nerves. She didn't mind being the center of attention, and the excitement of finally living this day overruled everything else.

"No." She tugged on his arm and giggled. "Why? Are you?"

The corners of his mustache turned up. "Only a little."

Macy faced toward the frosted glass leading outside. She could barely hear *Pachelbel's Canon*. That meant her turn would come soon enough. Gabe, having played no small part in the fiasco that was Miriam's cold feet, graciously agreed to sit in the crowd. Tanner and Macy would have no wedding party. They would only have Olivia to throw petals on the ground for Macy's trek down the aisle.

"I'm really proud of you," Cam said, not taking his eyes off the door. "Not just for this. For everything. School. Your... business." He seemed to have trouble searching for a way to describe her dalliances with cryptids.

"Thanks, Dad," she said, carefully and briefly laying her head on his shoulder.

The door opened. The wedding planner (if the ranch owner could be called that) waved them outside. Macy led the way, Cam following behind, where they relinked arms and stood facing the crowd. All eyes were on them.

No. All eyes were on *her*.

She smiled. Ok, fine. Now she felt a little nervous.

Everyone stood. She searched the crowd and spotted tons of people she knew, many of whom she loved dearly. Her mother was already crying, with Jake next to her rubbing her back. Gabe gave her a thumbs up and a goofy grin. Skylar sat next to him in his wheelchair. Brynn sat on the other side of Gabe.

Briefly, Macy wondered if the two of them might get back together now. She spotted Dub and Marie, Steve and Cory, Kim, Mikey. Way in the back, closest to where she stood, she even saw Wes. Her first boyfriend. It certainly seemed that the whole town had shown up.

Everyone, of course, except her very best friend in the world.

She took a deep breath as the *Wedding March* began, gently played from a piano off to the side. From the end of the aisle, Tanner locked eyes with her. He looked handsome, of course, but also ready. She playfully raised an eyebrow at him and he winked in return.

And then they were off, taking each measured step as slowly as possible, just like they'd been instructed. Everyone's gaze followed her, but Macy only had eyes for Tanner, gleefully anticipating getting nearer with each step. As slowly as the music played, time seemed to fast forward. Her father delivered her to the altar, shook hands with Tanner, and exchanged some words that Macy didn't hear. From the front row, Kim darted up to take the bouquet, which Macy only relinquished when she took a beat to register what was happening.

Cam wrapped Macy in a hug and kissed her on the cheek. His mustache tickled. She couldn't remember her dad ever having kissed her before, certainly not since she'd been an adult. Afterward, he went to the front row next to Kat and Olivia, then, when the pastor invited them to, they sat.

Macy looked into Tanner's eyes as he folded his hands over hers. Big, strong, warm hands. Her hands. His hands. They all felt the same now.

She never looked at the pastor as he began.

"I've never known a father to give away his daughter, so I will simply ask of you, Mayor Donner: do you give your blessing for this marriage?"

Macy had insisted on this part. She certainly wanted her father's approval, but didn't need his permission. She wasn't property.

Cam stood, nodded his head, and replied, "I do."

"Very well, then. Let us proceed."

A moment went by as the pastor shifted through the papers tucked into his scriptures. Macy focused on her soon-to-be husband.

The pastor began: "Good afternoon, family and friends, and welcome to this beautiful celebration of love as we gather to witness the union of Macy and Tanner.

"Today is a special day, not just for these two wonderful people, but for each and every one of us as we come together to share in their joy and support their love for one another."

Macy didn't hear much. She simply listened for her name or a direction that would tell her what she needed to do, just to be done with all of this. She wanted to be in the moment and remember it forever, but finding safe haven in Tanner's touch seemed more important than the words the pastor spoke.

"Marriage is a promise of love, a commitment to cherish and honor one another, through life's ups and downs, in sickness and in health. It's a bond that is meant to endure, a testament to the strength of love and the power of two hearts beating as one.

"Macy and Tanner," he continued. "As you stand here today, know that you are surrounded by love, by friends and family who are here to celebrate this joyous occasion with you."

Macy choked up. The most important friend wouldn't witness this. She didn't want to call off the wedding, but having Miriam absent felt like such a huge betrayal that Macy didn't know if their relationship would ever truly be able to recover. Their friendship would never be the same.

The tradeoff would unequivocally be worth it, but sadness still hovered over the moment. As if he sensed her sadness, Tanner squeezed her hands and drew her gaze back to his own.

Macy forced herself to take a deep breath, as much as her form-fitting wedding dress would allow. They would make it through this.

As she braced for the upcoming vows, she heard someone gasp in the crowd. Then murmuring. The pastor turned his back to them. Macy looked frantically across the field towards the woods, following the gaze of every person in attendance.

Macy clocked not one, but two giant men loping toward their location. Feral men, with huge muscles and insane amounts of shaggy, tangled hair.

Two beasts.

No, no, *no*.

Tanner tugged on her hand and she readily followed, her wedding dress tangling around her legs. Her heels stuck in the grass as they left the walkways that'd been laid for them. She never fell. Tanner's strength kept her on her feet, practically dragging her into the crowd. Running must have seemed cowardly, especially to Tanner, but he didn't have any weapons. In a perfectly organized universe, maybe, monster hunters would be armed while reciting their nuptials. Macy would remember that for next time.

Assuming next time came to fruition.

Once they got to the back of the crowd, Macy urged Tanner to stop.

"Hold on," she said. Reaching down, she quickly unstrapped her heels and kicked them off.

The crowds rushed around them, filtering through the small door into the barn-turned-wedding-venue.

"We have to make sure everyone gets inside!" Macy shouted.

Tanner nodded, only then letting go of her hand to usher people inside. Sweet that he had thought of saving her first, but the two of them had a responsibility to protect the guests, not just because it was their wedding, but because, on some level, Macy knew this wouldn't have happened if not for them.

She surged forward, back towards the altar, pushing people toward the door. At the back of the crowd, Macy met with Kim who, unsurprisingly, had already taken on the role of protector. Ahead of her, Macy saw splatters of blood and quickly gave up on trying to make out what was left of the officiant. Dub and Cam knelt behind two overturned chairs, both with arms outstretched, firing rounds into the beasts as they destroyed the altar.

Of course those two had brought guns. It was Texas, after all.

As valiant of a stand as the two men made, they didn't stand a chance. The beasts worked in almost perfect unison as they lunged forward, forcing Cam and Dub to retreat.

"What the hell are you doing, Macy?" Cam yelled. "Get in the barn!"

Macy didn't have a weapon. She couldn't compete. Fight. Even delay. They all needed to get into the barn. She turned to see most of the crowd gone. From around one side of the barn, Gabe rushed into the fray, a rifle on his shoulder. It would certainly have more stopping power than the handguns. He knelt and waved toward them.

"Move," he yelled. "Move!"

Macy rushed toward the door and slowed as Gabe got tackled. Not by a beast, but by —

"Tanner!"

Confused, Macy watched as Tanner wrestled the gun away from Gabe and hit him hard in the head with the butt. Gabe crumpled to the ground.

Ok. Weird way to get the gun, but Tanner's a better shot.

But Tanner didn't point the gun at the approaching beasts.

He pointed the gun at Dub Higgins — and fired.

Chapter 23 – Dub

Pain exploded like fire in Dub's shoulder. He stayed on his feet only barely, stumbling forward and landing against Cam's back. Cam held him up and dragged him along a few feet before ducking them both down behind the piano. Another rifle shot echoed, tearing through the wood of the piano and rending piano wires in a terrible cacophony.

"What the hell is that boy doing?" Cam yelled to no one in particular.

Dub didn't feel the need—or have the strength—to respond.

Cam peeked out over the top of the piano, only to quickly collapse back down as a bullet whizzed above. Instead of fighting, Cam changed tactics and turned to Dub.

"Are you ok?"

Dub looked down at the blood gushing from his shoulder. At least it was the shoulder of his bad hand.

"Been better."

Cam shuffled off his suit jacket, ripped his tie from his neck, and gently wrapped it around Dub's shoulder before pulling the two ends together hard. Dub hollered in pain as Cam tightened a knot, but that pain also brought some clarity. It hurt. Bad. But it didn't have to be life-threatening if they could just get out of this alive.

"Can you run?" Cam asked.

"Yeah. I think so."

"Ok." Cam shimmied to the edge of the piano and stuck his head out briefly. No shot came. "I'll cover you. You get into the barn."

"Where are the beasts?" Dub asked.

"I don't know."

The two monstrosities were nearby. Dub could hear the carnage of their destruction. Whether they settled for destroying chairs and altars or had moved to the barn, Dub couldn't be sure. Previous experience suggested that the beasts might avoid harming humans that didn't prove a threat, though the dead pastor attested otherwise. Clearly, these beasts played by a different rulebook.

"Shit!" Cam exclaimed.

Curious, Dub peeked around the other side of the piano to see Macy, hands up, slowly advancing toward Tanner. The muzzle of the gun pointed straight at her.

"Macy!" Cam yelled. "Get inside! Now!"

She didn't listen. Dub could make out her voice, but couldn't tell exactly what words she exchanged with Tanner. Whatever she said seemed to have kept him at bay long enough to stop the shooting.

"Cam," Dub said gently.

Cam didn't respond, instead yelling at Macy some more with no result.

Dub used his good hand to hit Cam on the shoulder. Dub dismissed the hate in his old friend's eyes. Dub would be mad, too, in this situation. Or perhaps, just scared to the point of anger.

Dub pointed to the side of the barn opposite Tanner and gave a series of hand signals they'd both used on the force. If they circled around the barn, they could come up behind Tanner. Of course, the beasts may hamper efforts, but a frontal assault wouldn't work.

Dub fully understood the danger that Macy put herself in with every slow step toward her groom, but he also intended to use that to their advantage.

Reluctantly, Cam nodded to Dub's plan and sprinted off toward the barn, keeping low enough that Macy's body blocked Tanner's view. Dub stayed behind the piano. Running wasn't in the cards for him. The pain seemed more manageable now, though. God, it seemed, really didn't want Dub to have two arms.

Dub's gun had a few rounds left in it. It's all he had on him, and even if he'd brought another clip, he didn't have faith that he'd be able to change it anyway. No one knew as well as Dub how poorly a handgun would fair against these abominable creatures. So, much as it scared him to even consider it, the best use of his position and skills came down to covering Cam—to shooting Tanner if necessary.

Dub prayed it wouldn't be necessary.

He listened to the echoing crash of the carnage. It sounded like the beasts had made their way to the front of the barn now. He could hear windshields shattering, car alarms blaring. They didn't seem interested in the people inside, but that checked out. The first beast tended to avoid people, operating off more an unbridled rage than anything resembling logic. Dub turned his attention toward Macy and Tanner.

Tanner's hand had fallen away from the trigger, but he kept the muzzle trained on Macy. He looked confused, regretful, embarrassed maybe. For the first time since he'd shot Dub, Tanner spoke. Unlike Macy, who's back faced Dub, Tanner faced directly toward the piano and his deeper voice carried further.

"Macy?" He phrased it as a question. Definitely confusion. "What happened? Where am I?"

Macy responded with something Dub couldn't make out, but he could discern the panic and confusion in her voice. Her pace quickened toward him just as Cam showed up behind him, gun drawn.

"Daddy, no!" Macy screamed, loud enough for anyone to hear.

Tanner turned, whirling the rifle as if it weighed no more than a feather. Cam reacted by sprinting forward, zigzagging to make himself a more difficult target. Tanner fired a shot, but missed. Cam closed the gap, seemingly unwilling to shoot his future son-in-law. Dub didn't blame him.

Right before Cam made it, his body slammed into the side of the barn as a blur of muscle took him off his feet. One of the beasts. The cracking of the splintering wood forced Dub out of his hiding space to protect his mentor, even as he worried that Cam might already be dead.

Unable to lift his bad arm, Dub aimed as best he could and fired at the beast. Macy used the confusion to get herself to Tanner, miraculously rip away the rifle and envelop him in a hug. Dub couldn't shake the idea that Tanner still couldn't be trusted, but he had bigger things to worry about.

Much bigger.

The beast bound toward Dub at a speed that he could never hope to outrun, so he didn't try. He simply fired until his clip protested its emptiness with a soft *click*.

Instead of tackling him, the beast swung with a wild punch. Only then did Dub notice something highly peculiar. This beast only had one arm. That didn't quite even the odds, but Dub still found strength in the irony of the situation. He hurled his gun toward the beast, which bought him enough time to scramble away while the beast swatted at the gun, knocking it away.

The beast advanced. Dub found strength he didn't know he had, not quite staying one step ahead, but managing to dodge each blow as it came. He couldn't do it forever. He needed backup. He needed another ally. No Gabe. No Cam. No Tanner. No Miriam. He'd exhausted the list of people who could hope to stand toe-to-toe with this thing. Dub did not want to be the last man standing, yet he focused on staying alive, not quite sure of his endgame.

But someone else found it for him as the blaring sounds of sirens filled the air. Dub heard tires come to a screeching halt, and Rodriguez yelling orders as car doors slammed open. A shot echoed and blood spurted out of the beast. Not enough of a wound to bring it down, but enough to draw its ire. The beast turned towards the cavalry, if two cop cars and four deputies could be called a cavalry. Each of Dub's four deputies fired at will, peppering the one-armed goliath with bullet holes, none hitting vital areas and none seeming to cause enough damage to bring the thing down.

Just when Dub thought the thing would advance on the cop cars, though, it turned back toward the woods. The other beast appeared behind Tanner and Macy.

Dub breathed, but his head swam, the potential end to the encounter robbing him of the adrenaline that had so far kept him upright. The second, two-armed beast pulled Macy up from the ground and tossed her toward Cam's unconscious—hopefully not dead—body, then jerked Tanner up by the bicep. When Tanner fought against it, the beast slammed a huge fist into the base of Tanner's skull. No more fighting from him. The beast picked Tanner up and tossed him over its shoulder, then followed the one-armed beast toward the tree line.

As Dub sank to the ground fighting his last seconds of consciousness, he saw Jake Rollins at the back door of the barn, standing as if entranced and pointing toward the trees.

Chapter 24 – Jillian

Jillian tried to calm the pure adrenaline flowing in her veins. Everything worked so much better than she could have ever imagined. Never had the seeker maintained such direct and focused control over the spears. Two at once, no less. In the vaunted history of the program, no one had even attempted such a feat. They'd never even released two beasts at once, because all data indicated doing so would cause a neural overload, rendering the seeker useless, possibly even a lifelong vegetable.

But this new seeker, empowered by Jillian's brilliant research and the potential of an evolutionarily developed parasite, surpassed all her expectations and dreams. The applications here could be infinite, especially if she figured out how to keep the seekers from turning into rage monsters devoid of soul or personality. Science happened one step at a time, though, and Jillian was more than ready to take on the next challenge. Her misgivings were buried under so much data and so much possibility that she'd lost touch with them entirely.

She'd only just snapped out of staring at the screens in disbelief when the metal door swung open. Brynn walked in, carrying a pair of heels.

"How'd it go?" she asked.

"You didn't see?"

"No." Brynn grabbed a chair, rolled it over, and plopped down next to Jillian. "It's not that I don't trust you, doc, but I didn't think staying was in the best interest of my health."

"Well, look."

Jillian pointed to the upper screens which showed cam video from the wedding venue. They conveniently had security cameras, but also commercial grade movie cameras as an upgrade package for anyone who wanted to commemorate the big day. The bride and groom hadn't opted for that exorbitantly expensive option, but since both types of camera had been wired into the network, Jillian had managed to find a way in. She wasn't a hacker or anything, but cowboys trying to make a buck off barren farmland didn't try very hard to secure their servers, either.

Brynn studied the images, pointing to one particular area. "Who's that?"

"The mayor."

"Dead?"

"I don't know. Maybe."

Having to admit that caused Jillian's guilt to bubble up, just a little.

"And that's Macy?" Brynn pointed at the woman in a white dress, now limping towards an ambulance that had just skidded to a stop in front of the barn.

"Obviously."

"Where's the groom?"

"Oh," Jillian responded. "You don't know. Of course, you wouldn't."

Another door opened, this one sliding open like a grocery store door or, more precisely, like one of the doors on *Star Trek*. In the doorway, she stood, draped in her cloak, revealing only a monstrous silhouette that didn't quite look human. Jillian knew the priestess under that garb was not at all imposing, in a physical sense. Still, Jillian shuddered at the sight of her.

"Tanner's on his way back here," the woman said, every word slow, methodical, foreign, dripping with poisoned honey, like she existed in another place and time.

"Here?" Brynn asked. "But why?"

Jillian bristled at the way Brynn talked to the priestess. Clearly the two of them had spent enough time together to be on very different terms.

"He proved useful. When he arrives, put him in the cell with Miriam."

"Useful?" Brynn asked. "What does that mean?"

The priestess disappeared back into her office. Lair might have been a better descriptor.

Brynn turned to Jillian for explanation.

"He shot the sheriff and protected the spears." Jillian reached over to a dial on the upper right part of her keyboard. "Here, look."

She scrubbed the video on one of the screens back to the point that Tanner had fought his best man for control of the rifle, aimed, and fired at Dub. Dub reeled back but didn't entirely fall, as Cam saved him and dragged him to safety.

"Is *he* dead?" Brynn asked.

"I don't think so. He was up and walking around. Looks like maybe he passed out right as the cops showed up. Well, the other cops."

"Ok," Brynn replied. "So Tanner. Why did he protect the beasts?"

"I don't know," Jill said with a sigh. "It's very bizarre behavior. Do you think maybe...." Jill cocked her head toward the door of the lair. "She conscripted him without us knowing?"

"Tanner Brooks?" Brynn laughed the sort of laugh only the truly confident used, devoid of any self-consciousness or reservation, not at all scared that she might insult Jillian's intelligence. In fact, she seemed to revel in it. "That boy is a puppy. He'd do anything for Macy or Miriam. If he's brainwashed at all, it's they who have him on a leash."

"Maybe he just missed."

Another boisterous laugh. "That guy doesn't miss. He's basically Hawkeye."

Given the chiseled jaw, rippling biceps, and general boy scout charisma, Jillian would have compared Tanner to another of *The Avengers*.

"Well, if he doesn't miss and he's not on our side, why would he do that?"

"I'm not sure." Brynn squinted her eyes in thought. "But I have a theory. I'll look into it and let you know."

Jillian suspected that Brynn kept things intentionally vague just to be irksome. Jillian wouldn't take the bait on this one.

"Fine," she said. "I'm going home, then. We're done for today, right?"

Brynn nodded. "Yeah, I guess. Mind if I look through this video?"

"Would you accept a no?"

Brynn smiled as if she'd been caught. "Probably not."

"That's what I figured."

Jillian sighed. Insufferable.

Jillian grabbed her purse and left, leaving Brynn and the priestess to plot their takeover of the world. She wondered if she'd ever get out of the literal rock she'd buried herself under in the name of scientific discovery.

Chapter 25 – Miriam

Miriam squinted against the light as the door opened again. She'd found sleep in the intervening hours, bringing with it the aches and pains of reclining on hard stone. She stretched, flexed her foot without as much protest as she expected, then stood just as the shadow in the doorway shoved someone inside and locked her into darkness again—this time with a stranger.

"Who's there?" she said, trying to sound stronger than she felt.

"Mi—Miriam?"

She recognized Tanner's voice, but still felt guarded. She'd seen what the witch could do with her mixed cocktails of drugs and hallucinations. It might be a trick. Yet none of her hallucinations in Gray's Point had ever spoken.

"Tanner," she said. "How'd you get here?"

"I don't know. I—" In his pause, Miriam detected fear. Possibly the threat of tears. Rare for Tanner. "I think I shot Dub Higgins."

"What? Why? Did he hurt someone?"

Miriam could fathom no other reason that Tanner might have chosen to harm the sheriff.

"No. Yes. I'm so confused."

She considered trying to find him in the darkness, but they'd never been a very physical family, and being able to hold him now would prove more awkward than helpful.

"Did she drug you? Like before?"

"She who?"

He didn't seem to know about their unwelcome visitor from the past.

"The priestess witch lady. From Gray's Point."

"She's here?"

"She is."

"I thought surely she was dead."

"She's not."

Tanner took a few beats before responding. "I don't think she drugged me. I haven't eaten or drank anything out of the ordinary."

"Was Dub, you know, Dub? When you shot him, I mean."

Back in Gray's Point, the drugs had caused them to see things that weren't there. Not only that, they'd misinterpreted the things that *were* there for other, more dangerous, things. Perhaps in this case Tanner perceived Dub as a threat. As something other than the sheriff of Rose Valley.

"No. I just..." Again, he interrupted himself, the fear in his voice escalating. "I had to protect them."

"Protect who?"

"The beasts."

All news to Miriam. "Beasts? What are you talking about? What happened?"

"The wedding. Beasts attacked. Two of them. They killed the preacher."

Family customs be damned, Miriam surged forward in the darkness until she came up against Tanner. She helped him to the ground, sitting beside him and rubbing his back. She looked at her watch, confirming the wedding would have happened hours ago.

"Is Macy okay?"

"Y-Yes. I could never...."

Miriam didn't respond. She didn't know what to say or how to say it. Everything had gone off the rails, and though some small part of her delighted in the fact that her suspicions about more potential beast activity had been well-founded, she wished that she'd been wrong. She wished she'd just been the paranoid cryptid hunter everyone was taking her for. But Miriam, for better or worse, so rarely found herself wrong on such matters.

She hated to interrogate Tanner under duress, but she needed information.

"Okay," she said. "So the beasts attacked. Killed the preacher. But why did you shoot Dub? Was he helping them? Is he in on this?"

"No. The opposite. He and Cam stood against the beasts and bought enough time to get everyone to safety. I shot Dub because... I had to."

"You had to? What does that mean?"

"I felt compelled to protect them."

Everything clicked into place. All that seemed blurry before suddenly came into focus.

"Like in Cape Madre? With the kraken?"

Tanner's response came out in a whisper. "Yes. Just like that."

"Okay. New question. Have you been in contact with anyone strange lately?"

He laughed a mirthless laugh. "Do you mean to ask whether I've been slapped around by a tentacle?"

"Right. Or something that could have transferred the parasite to you."

"No," he replied. "With the wedding, I haven't had time to do much."

"Wait. How did you get here?"

Miriam waited for him to form thoughts. It felt like forever. "One of the beasts hit me. Knocked me out. Must've carried me here."

"So she wanted you."

"I guess."

"But why you?"

"I don't know."

Miriam couldn't think sitting in the darkness. She needed some sort of sensory input to process her thoughts. She stood. Paced. Hobbled really. If the movement didn't trigger her need to feel something, the pain in her foot certainly did.

Truth be told, the witch's plans never really made much sense. World domination, *yada, yada, yada.* But she did act with purpose. And if she'd gone to all the trouble to recreate the beast and infect it with the kraken parasite, she meant to accomplish something. As far as Miriam knew, the woman didn't possess scientific skills, so she must have had help. From Arrowhead, no doubt. Or someone who worked there. But why Tanner? What part could he possibly play? And why him over Miriam, whom the witch seemed to have captured on chance alone.

Unless...

"The CDC never cured you," Miriam said, as resolute in her assertion as one could be about matters of almost supernatural origin. The witch didn't want Tanner specifically. He'd just been a happy accident.

"What?"

"They thought they killed the parasite after you were infected in Cape Madre, but they were wrong. It's still in there. It must have evaded detection somehow. It's not impossible to believe. It was new to them. Maybe it infects more than your brain. The kraken was dead, so they had no way to test that you were actually cured."

"Okay," Tanner said. "But those aren't krakens."

"Nope," Miriam replied. "But they have the parasite."

"What? How do you know that?"

"Right before the rehearsal dinner yesterday, I went to an autopsy of the first beast. Or second. Whatever. You know what I mean. Gearhart found the parasite inside its brain. The witch must be using it to control these new beasts. Her own personal army that will listen to her, no matter how batshit she gets."

"Woah."

Miriam heard Tanner shifting in the darkness.

"We have to get out of here," he said, the resolution in his voice back to the normal, strong Tanner that Miriam knew so well. "Macy might be in danger."

Miriam considered their predicament, trapped in the darkness behind a steel door that wouldn't budge, guarded by the witch, whatever cultists she'd brought to her side, and at least two artificially created monsters. Maybe the witch wanted to take over the world, or maybe—possibly, more likely—her motivations could be attributed to something much simpler. In Gray's Point, Miriam had managed to overturn the entire cult and end decades of surreptitious rule over a tiny community in West Texas.

The witch didn't want power.

She wanted revenge.

And right now, she held all the cards.

Considering the options, one thing seemed clear.

"Macy," said Miriam, "might be the only person who can save us."

Chapter 26 – Macy

Time did not afford Macy the luxury of crying, or mourning, or even worrying, really. Everything in her life had unraveled in a single day, and the job of picking up the pieces seemed to fall totally on her. She'd lost Tanner to a monster. Her best friend, MIA. And now the only person with the bandwidth to help was a trail guide from halfway across the country.

In truth, Kim kept everything together. She organized. Comforted. Kept things calm when they should have led to mass panic. Kim had been a godsend.

Since the wedding, Macy had spent hours navigating the winding halls of the Rose Valley Hospital, visiting one room after another and trying to keep up with all the injuries. Most were minor, caused by people trampling each other trying to escape the beasts. But some... some didn't have a definitive outcome, and those concerned Macy the most.

She came to one such hospital door and gently rapped on the frame. Her mother's voice penetrated through, only barely. "Come in."

Macy pushed the door open, met the red eyes of her mother, and handed her a cup of coffee from the nearby machine. Awful stuff, but Shandi wouldn't sleep as long as Jake did. If a coma could be called sleep.

Two beasts. Jake had commanded two beasts away from them, saving countless lives, but at a cost of some sort of overload. A neural meltdown. Hell, Macy didn't know what to call it. No one did. All she knew was that, after the beasts disappeared into the woods, Jake collapsed and never got up. Small-town life didn't attract top doctors in their fields, certainly not neurologists—Arrowhead research notwithstanding.

"Anything?" Macy asked.

Shandi shook her head.

Macy rubbed Shandi's back. "He'll be okay."

She didn't know if it was true, but she'd said "It'll be okay" so many times lately that the platitude barely held any meaning for her. Macy, an endless fountain of empathy, scared herself at the numbness she felt toward the carnage around her. She'd felt this way before, too. In Hogg Run. She hated it and hoped to never feel that way again.

It's exactly why she and Tanner had to get out of the game.

"Ok," Macy said. "Well, if you hear anything—or need anything—I've got my cell phone. I'm gonna go check on daddy."

She left one hospital room only to enter another just three doors down. She didn't knock at this one. The difference between being a daughter and a stepdaughter, she supposed.

Inside, she found Kat basically mimicking the state and position of Shandi. Olivia was around somewhere, popping in and out and not fully grasping the gravity of the situation, or, at least, unwilling to confront it. Macy didn't blame her. She'd have done the same at that age.

Without a word, Macy crossed to the opposite side of her father and looked down at his bruised face. The lacerations had been cleaned into blood red lines. She couldn't see evidence of the broken bones, but the doctor's brief of the situation made it clear that Cam faced a long road to recovery. Not many people walked away from being slammed into a wall with the force of a hurricane, but Cam would. Eventually.

"Hey, daddy," she said. He didn't respond, but his mustache twitched. "You're gonna be ok. Everything's under control out here. Don't you worry about that."

She knew that's what he would worry about if he could worry at all. As mayor, he had an elected duty to protect the citizens of Rose Valley, but it went much deeper than that. Protector was the only role Cam had ever fully embraced. He'd have a million questions when he woke, and ninety-nine percent of them would almost certainly be logistical queries as to how the aftermath of the attack was being managed. The answer, currently, would be "poorly." Macy intended to change that before Cam could ask about it, though.

She took his hand and squeezed, then gave a sympathetic nod to Kat before seeing herself back out into the hallway.

Next up on the rotation, Macy checked in across the hall. She knocked, but instead of someone ushering her inside with a word, the door opened wide and Gabe flashed her his infectious smile.

"Hey, *amiga*!"

Fully dressed with a bandage wrapped around his head, Gabe seemed nonplussed, as he often did. Tanner managed to give Gabe a mild concussion. Given the litany of injuries sustained by those who tried to stand up to the beasts, he'd gotten off pretty light. Of course, he also didn't accomplish much other than to turn Macy's fiancé against them. Macy shook the thought. Whatever happened with Tanner, Gabe couldn't be blamed. But what exactly did happen vexed her, filling up more of her thoughts than she could spare.

She'd seen too much to think Tanner had truly turned against her. He'd done that once in Cape Madre when possessed by a kraken. He'd seen shadow demons in Gray's Point. She couldn't fault him for any of that. No one could have stood against the techniques used on him in those instances. She didn't know what controlled him now, but she knew his heart.

No, she didn't blame him at all. But she desperately needed to save him.

She offered a thin smile. "Discharged already?"

"Yeah," he said. "I'm supposed to take it easy, but...."

"Gabe. You should listen to the doctor."

"Hell no, *chica*. They got my bro."

"Your bro gave you a concussion."

"Lucky hit. Won't happen again."

There existed no universe in which Macy would bet on Gabe in a fight against Tanner, but still, she admired Gabe's confidence. It was probably his best quality.

She sighed. "Fine. Kim's working some angles in the bereavement room."

"Sweet," Gabe replied. "I'll see you in there."

He rushed down the hall, leaving Macy with a surplus of hope. One more stop, then back to Kim to check in on efforts to find Tanner. And hopefully to find news of Miriam's return to civilization. She might have skipped the wedding, but Miriam would never abandon Tanner once she heard the news.

Farther down the hall, she knocked on yet another door. When she got no answer, she turned the handle, cracked the door, and peeked inside. No Marie. She opened up just enough to squeeze through, then quietly shut the door behind her. Dub lay on his bed, asleep, ample bandages wrapped around his shoulder. First his hand, now his shoulder. There seemed to be no end to what the beast would take from him, no matter its incarnation.

Macy whispered, "Dub? You awake?"

Dub had insisted on frequent updates of everyone, especially Cam and Jake, even if that meant waking him. Dub opened a groggy eye, seemed lost and confused for a few seconds, then focused.

"Macy," he said, shifting in the bed without so much as a groan. Good drugs must have been flowing through that IV. "Any news?"

"Not much. Jake's still in a coma. Dad's out of surgery, but hasn't woken up yet. They say he'll make a full recovery, though."

"That's good," Dub said. "God knows we need him."

"Yeah, well... we're not going to have him back for a while."

Dub nodded. "I guess it's on us, then."

As much as Dub acted like he was still in play, Macy couldn't count on anything more than counsel from him. She didn't know when he'd get discharged, and even then, he wouldn't be up for a manhunt.

He continued, "Any news on Tanner?"

"Not yet."

"Well, let me know."

"Of course. Need anything?"

Dub looked around the room. "Um, no. I don't think so. Marie should be back soon."

"Get some rest, okay?"

"I'll try."

She gave a small wave, and slipped back out into the hallway. Rounds completed, she headed back toward the front of the hospital, through the lobby, and toward the large conference room obscured by frosted glass. The white-noise generators, emanating from the speakers outside the room, made it impossible for Macy to hear what went on inside, so she wasn't prepared for the buzz of people talking when she opened the door.

Kim wrote quickly on a whiteboard, taking notes down from someone on the phone. Skylar's wheelchair sat in front of the conference table, which he'd covered in one giant map of Rose Valley. Gabe busied himself with a highlighter, marking things as Skylar pointed them out, occasionally arguing about the suggestion. Aside from Macy, Skylar was clearly the most motivated to find his nephew and ward. In the corner, Olivia texted on her phone. She noticed Macy first.

"Macy!" Olivia said, jumping up her chair. "So I talked to Benji and he said that Dirk told him that he saw the beasts out near Serendipity Ranch. And then Fiona says her brother was out dirt biking and saw them just a few minutes later, crossing the road over to Watermelon. Both said the beasts were carrying some guy. Has to be Tanner, right?"

Macy couldn't help but smile. Here she thought Olivia was just being an absent pre-teen when, really, she'd been digging up information all along. Gabe and Skylar seemed to be listening, shifting the focus from one part of the map to another.

"Thanks, Liv. That helps. Keep it up."

Olivia smiled with satisfaction and returned to her seat, her head already buried in her phone again. Meanwhile, Kim pulled a phone away from her ear and sat it on the table.

"How's everyone?" Kim asked.

"About the same," Macy responded. "You've got quite an operation going on here."

"It's not much, but it's a start."

"Got anything?"

Macy looked to the whiteboard, but Kim's chicken scratch proved difficult to read.

"Other than Olivia's sleuthing, a few things." Kim began pointing at the whiteboard as she spoke, as if the visual aid helped. "I talked to the wedding venue. They've got cameras. Like everywhere. They said they'd gather up the footage and get it to us. That may give us some clues about who these beasts are, and confirm what direction they were heading.

"I also talked to a deputy down at the police station. With Dub out of commission, they don't have a lot to offer but Officer..." Kim ran her finger down the list of writing, then tapped a word that looked like *rolodex*. "Rodriguez has already reached out to the Texas Rangers and the FBI. They'll send help, but he can't say how quickly or what kind yet."

Macy nodded. "Ok. And anything from Miriam?"

"Nothing. No texts since this morning, despite me sending oh...." She tapped her phone awake and swiped up the messages app. "About a billion from me. Mr. Brooks has tried, too. And Gabe sent one just a few minutes ago."

Macy could count just as many things to worry about as messages sent to Miriam, but as much as she needed to find Tanner, she also needed even more help to do it, and Miriam's disappearance was beginning to stretch the bounds of belief.

"Something's wrong."

"Yeah," Kim said with a nod. "This isn't like her at all. Think she got lost in the woods?"

Skylar let out an exaggerated *guffaw* from his wheelchair, but never looked up from the map. "Miriam does not get lost in the woods."

THE LEGACY OF ROSE VALLEY

"Ok," Kim replied. "Fair point."

Macy didn't want to voice her fear out loud, but she did anyway because she had no time for fear. "Do you think she ran into the beasts? Or another one?"

"Three beasts?" Gabe said. "Surely not."

"Well, we thought there could only be one, then there were two. Then from two to four. Maybe there're are eight now."

"They're not gremlins," Skylar said. "Whoever's creating these things still needs subjects. That's what's gonna limit them."

Kim nodded and started writing on the whiteboard again. "Yeah, yeah. That's true. I'll call Officer Rodriguez and see if he can check for missing persons reports in the surrounding area. They had to make these beasts from someone."

Of course, none of them knew who *they* were. Another mystery for another day.

When Kim finished writing, she turned back to Macy. "I don't know what Mir ran into out there, but I think we can all agree that something's keeping her from getting back to us. Which means..."

Trembling, Macy sighed, unready to accept that she'd have to spearhead this without Miriam's expertise.

"Which means," Kim said, "we're searching for two people."

Chapter 27 – Miriam

Miriam needed answers, and the first of them came when the door to their cell flipped open. She looked at Tanner, able to see him for the first time since he'd been thrown in the brig with her. The scuffle he'd had with beasts seemed to have left him no worse for the wear. At least he didn't have a hole in his foot.

The look he returned echoed her thoughts. *Trap.*

Since she could remember, her and Tanner had shared an almost supernatural bond. There'd been offhand jokes about telepathy, but it wasn't that. They'd both grown up in the shadow of a man who'd left no room for anyone but himself. Speaking often brought more harm than good, and many a hunt required silence anyway so as not to spook the prey. As such, they'd adapted well, learning to read body language and other cues.

Trap or not, neither of them intended to wait for someone to arrive at the door. Per usual, Miriam took the lead, while Tanner crept behind. She trusted no one more than Tanner to have her back, especially against a potential trap.

While she crept, she weighed the possibility of someone waiting behind the door to attack. If so, why open the door and then hide? Her captor had shown a penchant for theatrics back at Gray's Point, so perhaps this unexpected release was just more of the same.

As she climbed the stairs slowly, she took solace in the fact that the pain in her foot only felt like a distant sting. The bright white light of the room flooded her senses only for a few seconds before everything came into focus. No one pounced on them. Why did they want her and Tanner to see all this?

They stood at the precipice of a room full of nothing but tech: on her right stood a tower of humming computer servers. Next, a desk with a handful of monitors. Then a refrigerator with a glass front that might, in other circumstances, be used to hold sodas, but instead held vials of liquid. There, the cave turned a corner into a blank wall with nothing but a door in the middle. The door out, Miriam presumed.

On the other wall, she found two closed doors flanking a metal table covered with equipment: beakers, two powerful microscopes, and a messy stack of papers. An upper shelf contained even more stuff that looked like lab equipment. This underground network of caves appeared more than just a prison. The new beasts must have come from here, not Arrowhead. She still refused to believe they weren't somehow involved, as no one else could possibly have the technology or the knowledge for creating these creatures.

Her eyes wandered first back to the computer monitors, hoping to find some clue, no matter how minor, but on each one she found only a login screen. If push came to shove, she'd try to guess a username and password, but she didn't think that path would lead to success. Tanner moved to the fridge and peered inside. A shake of his head told her that he didn't know what exactly filled the vials, which meant Miriam wouldn't have any more luck trying to identify them. Safe to assume it related to the serum used to create the beasts.

Next, she moved to the lab bench, scanning her eyes over the equipment and landing on the stack of papers.

The front page looked like a cover sheet to an official report, most notably displaying in big block letters: *SEEKER SERUM v8.0.5*. For the first time, Miriam considered that maybe the witch didn't intend just to create beasts, but also the serum that allowed control of them. Possibly combined with the parasite from the kraken. She didn't know enough about the science to even guess at what the combination might yield, but mind control paired with mind control sounded potent.

As she reached to uncover more of the report, the door to her left slid open with a hiss. She jumped back, Tanner quickly closing ranks.

Bristling for a confrontation with the witch, Miriam instead saw someone else in the doorway. Tall. Blonde.

"Brynn?"

Brynn laughed, not without some menace. "Surprise!"

Miriam's head filled with questions. She had expected the witch to build a new cult, but she would have never placed Brynn among its ranks.

Gray's Point had left Brynn broken and deranged enough to leave Skylar's employ and pursue a quieter life as a research assistant for the town paper. Then her mother had died under mysterious circumstances, presumably at the hand of Brynn's stepfather, though he'd never been charged. Now his altered body waited in line for cremation.

Though curious as to why they'd been released, Miriam's flowchart instead led her to a conclusion that jumped many steps in the conversation, but even on the best of days she didn't have an interest in pleasantries, and certainly not when held captive.

"You did this," she said. "You turned your own dad—"

"Stepdad," Brynn said by way of interruption. "And he had it coming."

"Because he killed your mom?" Miriam asked.

Brynn's eerie smile turned into more of a smirk. She stood to the side and waved the two of them into the room she'd emerged from.

"That's in the past," she said.

Miriam glanced at Tanner. He nodded subtly. If Brynn saw it, she didn't let on. The two of them could certainly overpower Brynn should they attack, but they knew so very little about who else might be hidden in this bunker, or the protocol for getting out. They might need Brynn for that. Miriam returned Tanner's suggestion with not a shake of her head, but a dart of her eyes that clearly conveyed the message: they might choose to attack, but not yet.

Instead, she took a step toward Brynn, then into the next room. If the last had been built for research, this one felt like they'd stepped into a therapist's office. Peaceful music played from some hidden speaker. A cozy couch sat in the middle, facing a large, wing-backed chair sitting in front of another door. On either wall hung tapestries, depicting images like those found in tribal art. It only took Miriam a second to understand the meaning of both — transformation, shape-shifting. Skin-walking.

So the crazy witch still believed she could turn into animals. Some things never changed.

"I'll leave you to it," Brynn said. She disappeared back through the door, which immediately closed just as the one opposite opened.

And there she stood in the doorway, like a menacing gargoyle. Everything the witch did seemed calculated for dramatic effect, but it no longer held any fascination for Miriam. The coyote pelt, hanging loosely over her frame, seemed no more dangerous than a puppy.

"So we meet again," the nameless witch said, motioning to the couch. "Please, have a seat."

Having beaten the witch once before, Miriam felt curiosity stronger than fear. She sat. Tanner followed suit. Only then did the witch take the seat opposite, tossing back the hood of her cloak to reveal her face in full. She looked much the same as Miriam remembered. Raven black hair. Dark vacuous eyes. Her features sharp as knives with high cheekbones and a pointy chin. Not quite the witches you'd see on Halloween, but laughably close. Except...

One thing Miriam distinctly remembered from before was the witch's age. She'd worn a lot of makeup to try and cover it up. In the end, Miriam guessed the witch to be somewhere north of fifty. But the lady sitting in front of them, though undeniably the same woman, didn't look a day older than thirty. Hell, she might have looked younger than Miriam—certainly at the moment. She did wear some makeup, but it seemed light and fresh, applied more to evoke a certain aesthetic rather than to hide the signs of aging.

Miriam looked at Tanner, verifying that he'd clearly noticed the same thing.

"As you can see," the witch said. "I found someone else for the ritual."

The ritual. Back in Gray's point, this whack job had tried to get Miriam to kill her own father, claiming that doing so would bring the witch everlasting life or youth or some kind of nonsense. Miriam hadn't put stock in such a claim then, and didn't now. Surgery. Botox. Better make-up. Carefully planned lighting. Hallucinatory drugs. Miriam would accept any or all of those answers before she'd believe that some sort of blood magic gave this woman her youth.

"Right," Miriam said. "Obviously."

"You know," the witch continued, seemingly oblivious to Miriam's snark. "You're really a thorn in my side."

"I'd rather be a bullet in your head."

The witch feigned shock. "Such violence. But then, this is what I expect from you."

Exasperated, Miriam sighed. She remembered mostly everything about the witch from Gray's Point but she'd forgotten how incredibly slowly she talked, trying to lace every word with honey and threats.

"Just...what do you want?" Miriam asked.

"Thanks for asking. It's simple really. You took my town. Now I'm going to take yours."

Miriam actually laughed at the absurdity. Out loud. Miriam hardly ever laughed out loud at anything, but couldn't help it with the pure unadulterated idiocy of it all. She'd fought beasts and krakens, taken down cults, and competed with the best hunters in the world to find a giant otter in the Pacific Northwest. This woman's grandiose delusions of taking over a town felt downright silly.

"Yeah?" Miriam asked. "And how do you plan to do that? You've already kinda tipped your hand, lady. You've got two beasts out there roaming the city that everyone has seen. The cavalry is coming, I'm sure. Just a matter of time before they link back to you."

"We'll see."

"Good luck with that. So what do you want with us then?"

"Isn't it obvious?" the witch said. "I want you to live through it all. I want you to watch your friends and family die."

Fed up with the nonsense, Miriam gave Tanner a slight nod. They would attack—now. The two of them could easily overpower this tiny woman, no matter her age. They could bring her down before Brynn returned, who would also be no match for the two of them. But Tanner shot his eyes in the other direction, signaling a disagreement. Miriam widened her own eyes, protesting his protest. The look he gave her chilled her to the core. He looked scared. Of this woman? Impossible.

But then he looked at the witch and his expression changed. Miriam had only seen Tanner look at one other person that way—Macy.

The damn witch had taken the damn parasite-laced serum and turned herself into a damn kraken who Tanner now had no choice but to be infatuated with, and, obviously, would refuse to fight.

Probably, she thought with a sigh, if push came to shove, he would even attack her.

Chapter 28 – Macy

The guard at Relics Wildlife Reserve eagerly waved Macy through. They didn't want Miriam's car parked on their property, and since she had few other leads, Macy was more than happy to pick it up. She and Kim had driven over in Tanner's truck to check out the scene. For her part, Macy was currently in between cars, having given her old Sentra to Miriam. In this case, though, that worked out. Macy still had a set of keys.

As they neared the cheetah pens, Kim pointed into the distance where Miriam's car sat against the tree-line. It hadn't been mentioned that Miriam had parked so far away from the pens, which seemed significant somehow. Usually, she parked right next to them since she wanted to see the cheetahs. Macy steered the truck down the gravel path and parked alongside the Sentra.

Kim jumped out before the vehicle even came to a complete stop. She sprinted toward the pen, Macy close behind. Fanning out around the car, both girls peered through the windows. Nothing seemed out of the ordinary. Miriam kept the car clean and empty, save for a bag of gear in the backseat.

"What are we looking for?" Kim asked.

"I don't know," Macy replied. "Anything that gives us an idea of what she was up to, I guess."

In truth, Macy didn't expect to find much from the car. If Miriam ran into trouble, she more likely found it in the neighboring woods. Briefly, an image of the dead preacher popped into her head as she imagined the same happening to Miriam. She paused, feeling pale.

"She's ok," Kim said. "I know it."

Macy gave Kim a wan smile. If anyone could survive double beasts, Macy would certainly bet on Miriam.

Macy reached for the bag and unzipped it. She found a pistol, some rope, evidence bags, flashlight—the kind of things they always packed for a hunt. But Miriam hadn't taken this with her, so she clearly didn't expect one. Macy couldn't help but feel guilty. She knew she'd made the right choice, but the timing sucked and she could have delivered the news a little more gently.

Having found nothing of note in the car, Macy peered through the trees down a well-worn path leading into the depths of woods. They'd need to go there, but Macy wouldn't make the same mistake Miriam had. She wouldn't display the kind of bravado her father might have, either. Help would be coming, and Macy intended to leverage it. They'd come back here and search the woods in force, not alone.

Kim seemed to have other plans. Having found the bag herself, she checked the pistol for ammo. She grabbed the flashlight as well, though dusk wouldn't come for hours yet.

"Ready?" she asked.

Kim's confidence almost swayed Macy to agree.

"No. We wait. For the Rangers and the FBI."

"What if they don't get here in time?"

"They will."

Of course, Macy had no way of knowing that, but she wouldn't let foolishness force her hand. She didn't have the skillset that Miriam had, and as much of an outdoorswoman as Kim was, she also didn't have the experience to be fighting giant, bigfoot-like science experiments. They could get Gabe and have half a chance, maybe, but only half and Macy didn't like those odds, either.

"Let's take the car back to the station," Macy said. "Get Rodriguez to run prints or look for hairs or something. I dunno. All that stuff they do on Forensic Files."

The possibility of destroying some of the evidence did briefly cross her mind, but law enforcement in Rose Valley had already been stretched to its breaking point. She wouldn't take risks with lives, but she would take them with evidence, because deep down, she knew that cops wouldn't save them from this. When it came to the monsters, they always had to do it themselves. Without Tanner or Miriam, though, Macy questioned whether they had a chance at all.

When Kim didn't immediately relent, Macy tried again. "You take Tanner's truck. I'll take the car."

"But she could be in there," Kim said, motioning to the woods. "She could be hurt."

"And she could be dead," Macy said, shocking herself by saying it out loud. "And if we go in after her, we might just follow her. I can't risk that. Not when help might be coming."

"Might," Kim said. "Rodriguez doesn't consider Miriam a top priority. She left on her own."

Kim looked wistfully towards the trees again and Macy felt a swell of sympathy. As much as Macy wanted to keep them safe, Kim followed her heart, always quick to help a wounded animal. And in this case, it was even more than that. Macy could see the signs. The mutual admiration between Kim and Miriam had started at Misty Lake, and despite the time and distance, the bond hadn't lessened. If anything, it'd grown. Macy batted away unexpected feelings of jealousy to losing her best friend.

"Fine."

Macy held up her hand briefly until Kim caught her meaning, then tossed the keys to the truck. Kim caught them.

"See you at the station."

Macy climbed into her old Sentra, the seat hugging her just like she remembered, but when she reached for the steering wheel, alarm bells triggered in her head. Throughout college at Dobie Tech, Miriam and Macy had shared this car. With less than two inches of difference in their heights, Macy had never had to adjust the seat. She glanced in the rearview, which showed her the ceiling. Likewise, the side mirrors were completely misaligned.

Miriam hadn't been the last one to drive this car.

A clue. The first. Macy reached under, pulled up the seat, adjusted the mirrors, and took a deep breath. Maybe she could do this, after all.

***

Macy left the car in the hands of Officer Rodriguez. Kim had already briefed him on everything, so Macy didn't have much to say as he took the keys from her. She kept the knowledge of the seat to herself—for now. He promised a quick turnaround, but Macy didn't really expect he'd follow through. They seemed to be onboard with finding Tanner on account of him being kidnapped in front of the whole town, but they were less interested in Miriam. Macy suspected that finding Tanner may also turn up Miriam, though, so she took the help where she could.

Macy climbed into the truck next to Kim, eager to talk about her suspicions.

"Something's wrong," Macy said.

"No shit," Kim said, putting the truck in drive.

"No, I mean, Miriam wasn't the last person to drive that car."

"I wanna dig into that," Kim said. "But first, where are we going?"

"Well, if she didn't drive her car to Relics, then someone else did. And if Miriam didn't go to relics after the barbecue, then where did she go instead?"

"We've already checked her apartment. Didn't seem like she'd been there."

"Right. You know, Miriam. How would she have handled being overwhelmed?"

Kim thought for a second, then pulled the truck over, checked her mirrors, and swung a U-turn.

"She'd want to be alone, and distracted with something else."

"She'd go back to what she knows."

Kim nodded with excitement. "The hunt."

At the only light in town, Kim turned right and veered Tanner's truck toward Watermelon Ranch.

Chapter 29 – Dub

Sitting in a hospital bed, Dub felt helpless and hopeless. Marie brought around the baby from time to time, which lifted his spirits a little, but keeping a baby entertained in a hospital proved difficult and Dub understood that they also needed to spend some time away. As sheriff, he had no shortage of townsfolk looking in on him, but mostly he just wanted to get back to the job. He worried about Tanner, sure, and he knew that Miriam might also be in trouble, but he had more to protect than two cryptid hunters.

The town of Rose Valley had been changed forever when the first beast came along, and from the hospital, Dub knew he was only getting small snippets of the panic that had begun setting in. The town didn't even have Cam to keep tensions down.

He'd kept his most tenured officer on a tight leash—or as tight of one as he could via phone. Rodriguez had only joined the force a few years ago, but quickly rose through the ranks as a dependable and hardworking officer. He followed orders, had a good gut, and was generally liked by his coworkers. Dub, however, didn't think him ready for the pressure that would come with a case this big, and worried what that might mean for the efforts to find Tanner and Miriam, or the monumental task of bringing down these new monstrous threats to Rose Valley.

So, Dub intended to do what he could. That meant making a few phone calls, and—assuming he got discharged soon—making a few visits. Given his run-ins with the various beasts over the years, Dub didn't feel much help on that front, and he sure as hell wasn't eager to confront another, but his gut churned with suspicions. He could help put those to rest, at least. Lying in a hospital bed wasn't good for much, but it did give his mind the space to start putting together some puzzle pieces.

First on his list: Dr. Vance. She'd denied any involvement after the first beast attack, but with three in the last week, Arrowhead couldn't keep its head down any longer. Whether complicit or not in the creation of these particular beasts, Dub held them ultimately responsible. Had they not ever meddled with the very laws of nature, Rose Valley would still be the sleepy little town it yearned to be.

He swiped through the contacts on his cell phone until he got Dr. Vance's direct number. He dialed and waited.

He got a voicemail greeting but chose not to leave a message, instead backing out to the contacts and dialing Arrowhead's main number. This time, after two rings, someone picked up.

"Arrowhead Research, how may I help you?"

Dub cleared his throat. "Hi, yes. This is Sheriff Higgins down at Rose Valley PD. We had an incident recently that we think might be related to some of your research, and I was trying to get ahold of Dr. Vance."

"Oh, hi Sheriff," the voice said. He didn't recognize the young man on the other end, but surely would if he could see a face. "I can't speak to any of that, but let me redirect you to Dr. Vance's line."

"Wait— no," Dub said. "I've already tried that. She didn't answer."

With no immediate response, Dub worried that he'd already been transferred, but eventually, the man spoke again: "I see. Um. Let me patch you through to someone who might be able to help you."

This time, Dub received no chance to stop the transfer. It immediately started ringing through to a different line, quickly answered with: "Hello?"

Dub went through the same rehearsed explanation from before, confident that there'd been no time for the assistant to have relayed the message. The woman on the other end of this call sounded much older than the assistant. Dub suspected it might even be the CEO of Arrowhead, June Weathers, though he'd never met her. She commuted from Fort Worth every day, where she no doubt lived in some overly secure palatial property with eighteen bathrooms.

"Well, Sheriff, I can assure you that Arrowhead had nothing to do with your 'incident' and we will do everything we can to make sure you have the resources you need to stop this threat."

A practiced speech for an all-too-often occurrence. Dub hadn't mentioned the beasts, but he had no doubt that she knew exactly what he was talking about. Macy and Tanner's wedding overflowed with guests that worked for Arrowhead. The story would have made the rounds faster there than anywhere.

"I understand, Mrs. Weathers." He voiced the assumption of her identity to keep her off-balance. He paused to let her correct his assertion. She didn't. "It would help a lot if I could talk to someone with intimate knowledge of this... phenomenon. Could you get me in contact with Dr. Jillian Vance, perchance?"

He could hear papers shuffling on the other side of the phone, then whispers, a door shutting. He didn't know what any of it meant. Maybe nothing. Maybe everything. He waited her out, rather than try to rush the conversation. He had nowhere to be, anyway.

"Sheriff," she said. "I'm sorry. But that's not possible."

"Why is that, Mrs. Weathers?"

"Dr. Vance parted ways with Arrowhead Research yesterday."

"May I ask the nature of her departure from the company?"

Another pause. "I'm afraid I'm not at liberty to discuss the personal matters of former employees."

"No?" Dub responded. "That's a shame. I was really hoping to find something that could help me resolve this matter."

Talking about it so clinically made Dub feel dirty, but he had to play the game. If he spooked her with threats and plain talk, she'd hole up, and then he wouldn't get anything at all. Tough lesson he'd learned shortly after taking up the mantle of Sheriff.

"Again, Sheriff, I don't think Arrowhead can help you. We've cleaned house on this matter, as you well know."

"Uh huh," Dub said. "And did Dr. Vance have some trouble with this cleaning? Is that why you had to let her go?"

"Mr. Higgins," she replied, dropping his title as her voice took on the tone of a disappointed teacher. "You know that I can't reveal that information. I never said we let her go. Please don't put words in my mouth."

"Right, right. You didn't mention the nature of her departure," he said. "Let me ask you this then. Did your other previous employee, Deirdre Valentine, have any direct ties to Dr. Vance?"

The silence on the other end of the line spoke volumes. He could almost hear the woman bristling on the other end of the phone. He'd stepped too far. Been too direct. They both knew what he was accusing Dr. Vance of, but June Weathers had to toe the company line, keep to the story, and stay out of the limelight. Since the first beast, it was all that Arrowhead could do to shirk their involvement.

"I think this conversation is over, Sheriff. Best of luck to you and your investigation. I'm sure you will reach out if you need anything further."

Code for: don't call again unless you have a warrant.

"Well, Mrs. Weathers," Dub said, as diplomatically as possible. "I really appreciate your time. I'm sure we'll figure this out. One way or another."

Code for: I'll tear down your company if I have to.

"Have a good day, Sheriff."

"You too, Mrs. Weathers."

The other end went dead before Dub even had a chance to pull the phone away from his ear. He hadn't gotten any details, but he understood the form of it. Dr. Vance hadn't just quit. Not in a million years. Arrowhead most certainly had let her go, and Dub would have bet dollars to donuts that the beast attack on the wedding had given them the cause they needed, though they might have suspected her of meddling with the serum long before that.

Dub's gut seemed to be offering more than just a hunch. If he could find Jillian Vance, he could find the beasts. And Tanner. Possibly Miriam.

He flipped back over to his contacts, dialed up Rodriguez, and put him on the task of finding the good doctor with all due haste.

Chapter 30 – Macy

As Tanner's truck rumbled over the Watermelon Ranch's roughly hewn gravel path, Macy looked across the expanse of dying grass to see the old guesthouse. When she'd been in high school, the first beast attacked her house, forcing her and her mother to retreat here, where they stayed with Jake for a few days. Or, as Macy tended to think of that period: *how I met my stepdad.*

Now, the old shack looked abandoned, much like Macy felt at the moment. She knew they hadn't left her like this willingly, but everyone she counted on in difficult situations was either missing or incapacitated. Not the week she'd imagined just a few days earlier.

Kim parked the truck in front of the cattleguard leading into the yard of Steve's trailer.

"That's weird," she said.

"What?"

"Before. When Miriam and I came down here, there was tons of equipment here."

"Oh."

Macy looked around and saw none. Not even a scuff on the ground that might have indicated the presence of anything.

"Maybe Gabe came and got it?"

"Yeah," Kim said, handing the keys to Macy. "Probably."

They both got out of the truck — well, fell out really. Tanner had his truck jacked up all the way to heaven.

Not something he'd done before moving to Texas. Macy blamed Gabe's influence. Before becoming a cryptid hunter, Gabe had been a grease monkey.

"Where do we start?"

"Well," Kim said. "Before, we stopped here." She walked over the cattleguard and stopped just on the other side. "And picked up some weapons, because, you know — Miriam."

"Hard to fault her for her caution now."

"Fair point."

Macy crossed over to Kim and studied the ground. Closer, she could see more evidence of the gear that had once been here: depressions in the grass, scuff marks in the dirt. Somehow, that made her feel more confident that Gabe had just retrieved the gear. Skylar would certainly want it back, especially given the circumstances, and Macy wouldn't blame him. They'd need it. All of it.

"So then," Kim said, walking across the yard and pointing past the end of the trailer. "We went out there."

"Into the forest?"

Kim giggled. "Woods. Yep."

"What?"

"Nothing. It's just... you Texans really don't know how to classify your tree gatherings. Miriam tried to call it a forest, too."

Macy laughed, despite the anxiety knotted in her chest.

"Sorry, the woods. And we can't go in there without more firepower."

Kim sighed. "Come on, we need to do something. Rodriguez is dragging his feet. We don't know when the help is coming. Dub might not get out of the hospital for days. If we don't find her, who will?"

Of course, that made sense to someone who practically lived outdoors. Someone who hadn't been almost murdered by a mutant pig or its maniacal keeper. Someone who hadn't seen their whole town under the spell of the beast. Though, maybe Kim deserved a little credit. She had risked her life to save a family of giant otters from a hellbent trophy hunter.

Maybe Kim just had bravery where Macy had none.

Kim continued to prod. "We'll have each other's backs. And we can leave at the first sign of anything creepy. I'm up for a run."

She jogged teasingly in place, giving one of her classic Cheshire-cat smiles. Though Macy was about as straight as they came, she could see the appeal that Miriam found in Kim's playful personality, and the beautiful balance it would offer to Miriam's general seriousness.

"Fine," Macy said. "First sign of trouble, and we're out of there. Got it?"

Kim saluted. "Yes, sir."

"You still have Miriam's gun?"

"Right here," Kim said, producing the pistol from behind her back. "It's loaded and ready to go."

"It won't stop a beast."

"We won't fight a beast."

Hopefully they also wouldn't *find* a beast, because they wouldn't be able to outrun it. But Macy didn't want to voice that part out loud. It would only make it harder for her to push back the nerves and venture out into the trees. She psyched herself up by reminding herself not of the bad parts of Hogg Run, but of the good—how she'd persevered against all odds. At Misty Lake, she'd managed to live through two hunters who wanted her dead, and multiple nights alone in the vast wilderness living among giant monsters. Perhaps uncanny survival was a better superpower than bravery.

"Lead the way," Macy said, motioning out past the house.

Kim set out resolutely and Macy scuttled off behind, only pulling up alongside when the path became clear.

"You sure you can retrace your steps?" Macy asked.

Kim shot daggers at her. "Did you forget what I do for a living?"

"Right."

"So, in a bit. A long bit actually. It's a good hike. We'll get to Big Rock Clearing."

"I know that place," Macy said. "Kids in high school used to go out there to make out."

"Oh yeah?" Kim asked. "Did you...?"

"Oh no," Macy said with a laugh. "I was a total nerd in high school."

"Didn't you date the high school quarterback, though?"

"Well, yeah, but we never did anything," Macy replied. "I had to get out of Rose Valley and he wasn't the ticket. He's still here, in fact. Never left."

"Seems to happen a lot around here."

"Yeah, it does. But after leaving, this is the only place I could imagine coming back to. The only place I could put down roots."

Kim shook her head. "No thank you. The whole idea of roots sounds icky to me. I want to travel. See everything the world has to offer."

"I dunno," Macy said with a shrug. "I think I've already found the best of the world."

The conversation fell silent as Macy thought of Tanner and how much she needed him to make her world make sense. If something happened to him, if he didn't come back, if they didn't find him, it wouldn't be like all the other stuff she'd endured. Losing Tanner would be something she'd never come back from.

Kim started whistling, which helped pass the time as Macy tried to guess the tune. This became their distraction as the minutes slid by until they eventually arrived at the clearing. The looming boulders reminded her of everything that told her to stay away.

She'd never considered this place to be particularly ominous before. The boulders provided cover for illicit teenage activities, their remote location offering distance from watchful parents. Today, though, the rocks seemed gargantuan, the tree shadows foreboding. Macy didn't consider herself psychic or anything, but she knew in her bones that they'd find something significant here.

Kim sprinted ahead and quickly climbed one of the rocks. She knelt and offered a hand, which Macy made use of on account of having laughable upper body strength. From the top, Macy's heart felt a little lighter. She no longer had corners to fear, as she could clearly see the entire cluster of boulders. Not that a beast couldn't easily scale one of them, leap across like a goat and murder them in one fell swoop.

Kim made a running leap to the next rock over, landing with the grace of a gazelle. Macy did the same, but dropped with a thud, falling to her knees and staying up only by planting one of her hands against the stone.

"Good job," Kim said, laughing while also helping Macy to her feet. "So before, there were carcasses all over the tops. Now they're gone."

"Eaten by scavengers, maybe?"

"No. There'd be bones left behind. And it hasn't rained, so someone cleaned it up."

A shiver shot up Macy's spine at the image of some unknown, evil cabal cleaning up dead animal carcasses in the middle of the night.

"All right, let's get outta here."

"What?" Kim asked, clearly opposed.

"First sign of something creepy. You promised."

"But we haven't found anything," Kim said, just a hint of a whine in her voice.

"We found enough to come back with backup and bigger guns."

Kim looked at Macy, as if to judge the seriousness of the request. Then she pouted.

"We don't know that Miriam even came here, though."

When Macy didn't relent, Kim dropped her shoulders and scuttled back down to the ground. Macy sat down first, and then lowered herself, scooching her butt across the stone and surely destroying her jeans. Better than breaking an ankle, though.

Back below the boulder-line, Macy dusted off her butt and oriented herself to the way they came. Her eye caught something.

She turned back, looked again, and saw it among the dead leaves and drying grass. She crept over, some part of her worrying that she'd found nothing but bait for a trap.

When she got to it, she picked it up. A shoe. And another just a few feet away, which she also scooped up. She didn't immediately recognize them, so she showed them to Kim.

"These look familiar to you?"

Kim went white, her eyes wide. "Those are Miriam's."

Macy looked back down at her prize. Sure, they were roughly the right size for Miriam's feet, but dress shoes? Miriam never wore dress shoes. Hell, Macy didn't even know her friend *owned* any dress shoes.

"How do you know?"

"Miriam wanted to wear overalls to your rehearsal barbecue," Kim said. "And they were adorable on her, don't get me wrong."

Macy didn't immediately take the meaning.

Kim continued, "Who do you think got her dressed in grown up clothes for you?"

As Kim's explanation became clear, leaving no doubt as to the owner of the shoes, the silence of the forest suddenly echoed with something like a howl. It reverberated in Macy's very soul. She'd heard that sound before, years ago when the beast smashed into her house and forced her and her mother to flee. It could be nothing else.

She shoved the shoes into Kim's arms. "Time to go."

This time, Kim didn't protest.

Chapter 31 – Miriam

Food and bathroom breaks—that was it. They got no other interaction. They filled the time discussing how to get out, how to cure Tanner, whether Macy would find them or whether she'd even try. Of course, she'd try if she could, but being locked in an underground prison, the aftermath of the wedding could not be calculated—at least not after Tanner's knock to the head. For all Miriam knew, every single guest in attendance had been killed after. She doubted it, though. Whatever the witch's plan, it didn't seem to be mass murder.

She wanted the town, and a town served no purpose without pawns.

Safe to say that she would want Macy dead, though. It would hurt Miriam, and avenge some small part of the witch's losses in Gray's Point. So, Miriam tried to maintain hope that Macy had survived the wedding and that they would all get out of this alive. Fear of death never bothered Miriam much. Others dying frightened her, but her own death seemed inconsequential, especially if in service to some necessary outcome. And she could think of nothing more necessary than saving Macy, Tanner, Kim, and all of Rose Valley. Oh, and her father, of course.

The one thing the witch had gifted them so far was time. Time to think. Time to plan. Time to consider all options. And time to study their environment. Building a prison door into the natural cave entrance did not come easily. Though she could see little, Miriam found flaws. For one, it didn't sit flush against the floor or the walls. The cracks were tiny, and no light seeped through, which implied the other side had some sort of material to cover them. Though large and heavy, the door didn't provide the sort of protection of, say, a bank vault door. Thick and metal, yes. Indestructible, no.

As far as she could tell, the latching mechanism worked like any other door, which didn't provide much security at all. The real security came from a deadbolt. Miriam assumed a long one. Disabling that would be tricky, but she had some ideas.

"Should be about time for the next bathroom break," Miriam said.

"Good. I need to piss like a racehorse," Tanner replied.

Always a strange saying. Why specifically a racehorse? Did they pee more than an average horse?

"You know I can't see anything, right?" Miriam said. "Just go pee in the corner or something. It's a cave."

Tanner grunted as his clothes shuffled against the stone. Miriam presumed he was standing up.

"That's awkward. You're like my sister."

"Cousin. And it's just biology. Everybody pees."

"You know what I mean, Mir," Tanner said. "I know we're cousins. But I think of you like a sister. The sister I never had... and always had."

The comment made Miriam uncomfortable. The Brooks family did not share feelings. Miriam blamed Macy for this, out there making Tanner think he could just go sharing his deepest feelings on a whim.

"Thanks," Miriam murmured. She felt the same, but didn't quite know how to say it without dying of discomfort.

"No, I mean it," Tanner said. "It's important that you hear it. In case we don't... you know."

"Tanner Brooks, you shut your mouth," Miriam protested. "We're going to get out of here. And you're going to get married to Macy and have lots of cute annoying little babies and run for town council and coach the little league team and be a scout master. You'll probably be mayor one day. You *are* marrying into Rose Valley royalty, after all."

Tanner laughed. "And you'll be there for it all. Because you're like a sister to me."

Miriam growled. "Fine. I love you, too. Now shut up."

"Hey now, I didn't go that far."

Click.

The deadbolt slapped open, cutting them off. The door creaked back, bathing them in light and forcing Miriam to squint against the onslaught. Still, she could only make out a shadow.

"Who's first?" a voice came from the door. A new voice. So far, it had only been Brynn.

"You go," Miriam said to Tanner.

"Thanks, sis," he said, using the rare light to shoot her a teasing wink.

Seriously, who taught him this? He had once been so serious. Just like her. Maybe it was Gabe. Yes. Probably Gabe. That boy *never* took anything seriously. Unlike Kim, who could switch between the two when necessary, and always felt supportive-yet-playful. Miriam forcefully pushed away these thoughts too, frustrated at her wandering mind.

Tanner left with the new person, and Miriam sank back into the darkness. Brynn had watched her like a hawk. New girl might not. The intervening time waiting for Tanner to relieve himself like a horse gave Miriam an opportunity to plot new courses, new branches, new possibilities. No one had ever called Miriam charming, but she still considered that maybe she could win over this new person somehow. Brynn did not lack for reasons to hate Miriam, even before the descent into a cult. This change of the guard gave Miriam reason for hope.

After a few minutes, the door opened again. Miriam already stood just inside, ready for her turn. Tanner walked in, gave Miriam a silent look to indicate they might have a new opportunity, then stepped into the lab to finally see her new captor.

A woman stood there, not much taller than herself, with brown hair and light brown eyes, a slightly over-sized nose and thin lips. Faint freckles dusted her face, rare for someone with darker hair. She was of slight build, especially compared to Miriam, without an ounce of fat or muscle. If it came down to a brawl, there would be no contest. The woman looked tired. Maybe anxious. A little bit lethargic.

"You're new," Miriam said, as they crossed the main lab.

"Not really," the woman answered.

"Well, I've never seen you."

The woman sighed and opened the door to what Miriam had begun calling the operating room. Inside, medical devices hummed around a giant hospital gurney. She'd asked Brynn questions about the room, but never got any answers.

"Is this where you make them?"

The woman didn't answer, but did pause in a way Brynn never had. Maybe Miriam had hit a nerve.

"It must be fascinating," Miriam said, playing to a hunch about this woman's role in the cult. "To watch them transform, I mean. Does it happen, like, immediately, or does it take time?"

The woman fully stopped in front of the gurney. Miriam remained nearby, trying to make herself as little of a threat as possible.

"It takes time. It's..." The pause lasted a few seconds, while the woman searched for words. "Difficult for them. But, yes, fascinating."

"I'm Miriam, by the way."

"I know who you are."

"Oh, right. Well, um, what should I call you?"

The woman looked at her as if to judge her worth. Miriam met the gaze.

"Jillian."

"Nice to meet you, Jillian. So you're, what? A scientist?"

"Yeah. Or, at least, I'm supposed to be. A doctor, actually. Though, I'm not sure I can claim that at this point."

"Hippocratic oath and all that?"

"Yeah."

Jillian rested her hands on the gurney, staring at it as if it had taken everything from her. Miriam took the opportunity to wander around the room, testing how much of a leash Jillian intended to keep. Apparently a long one—there was no reaction to Miriam's movement.

"I wouldn't feel bad," Miriam said. She actually would have. "Science has to push the boundaries sometimes, right? If no one does it, then breakthroughs are never achieved."

It sounded pretty good, Miriam thought. Whether she sold it, though, was a different matter.

"That's what I used to think," Jillian said. "You know, Dr. Valentine never wanted all this, either. But there's just so much promise, and here, I was given an opportunity to test it on someone who wouldn't be missed. I mean, I know I'm not Batman or whatever, but it felt profound to test this stuff on a murderer."

While Jillian monologued, Miriam scanned the supplies along the wall, looking for something she could use. She finally decided on a roll of gauze, which she quickly pocketed, ready with the excuse of needing it for her foot. Jillian didn't seem to notice, though, so Miriam kept quiet. She replayed in her head everything Jillian mentioned, seeking the appropriate response.

"A murderer? You mean Deke?"

"You knew him?" Jillian asked, seemingly surprised.

"No, not personally. I know he wasn't a good dude, though."

"He killed Brynn's mother."

That hadn't been proved, but Jillian believing it did explain her willingness to experiment on him. It did not, however, explain why she'd inflicted this horror on two other people. Miriam wanted to press, but worried it would only come across as an accusation and ruin whatever level of comfort they'd achieved. She had a new tool, and information about the weakest link in the witch's cadre. That seemed enough for now.

Miriam pointed toward the bathroom door. "Um, I'm gonna...."

"Yeah, yeah. Of course."

Miriam didn't actually even need to use the bathroom, so she sat on the closed toilet and counted the seconds. She then unrolled some toilet paper, concerned that the sound of the roll would carry. She quietly opened the top, dropped in the paper and flushed, making sure to drop the top to sell that she'd just finished. She then washed her hands. Since she'd arrived, she'd never *not* felt dirty.

When she exited, Jillian hadn't moved, still leaning over the gurney in contemplation. When she didn't immediately respond to Miriam's entrance, Miriam cleared her throat.

"Oh sorry," Jillian said. "Let's go."

Miriam followed her new friend back to the cell, making an effort to stay a step behind. She took the gauze from her pocket and unrolled it until she had more of a squishy ball than a tight roll. Jillian pulled open the door. Miriam turned, obscuring the gauze behind her back.

"Hey," she said, stalling for time. "Don't beat yourself up. Good people do bad things, sometimes."

Jillian gave a drawn smile. Miriam leaned against the door frame, shoving as much gauze as she could into the deadbolt hole. Just when her delay started to seem fishy, she managed to get the last of it in.

"See you in a few hours," Jillian said.

"I'll be here."

Miriam disappeared back into the darkness, praying that Jillian wouldn't notice that the deadbolt wasn't going to turn as far as it normally did. A big risk. But one that seemed to pay off when Miriam heard a nice, muffled *click*.

Chapter 32 – Macy

Macy refused to make the mistakes of her father. He'd enlisted the help of the entire town to bring down the first beast, yet in the end, it'd only taken Miriam. A lot of inexperienced people had died that night. Macy couldn't ask the same of them again. She could only take those who understood the risk and had the necessary skillset. That may or may not have included her, but she didn't want to live a life without Tanner and Miriam. They'd saved her too many times to count. She needed to repay the favor. She owed it to them both.

She would lead an army, but it would be small and agile and prepared.

They'd moved their base of operations from the hospital to the Rose Valley Community Center, a large spacious one-room building. Hardly anyone ever used it except for the odd family reunion, but it gave Macy and her crew space to spread out. So far, she didn't have much. Herself, Kim, Gabe. Skylar to help with logistics, but he would be no use in a fight. Rodriguez promised himself, the other three Rose Valley police officers, four FBI agents, and two Texas Rangers. Dub would hang back, not yet ready to be of use in the field, but with his release from the hospital, at least he stood with them at the center, helping where he could.

Everyone except Dub's promised officers stood around Skylar's map as he tapped the circled Big Rock Clearing. All the reports pointed to that location, but

Kim and Macy's discovery there clinched the deal. There could be no doubt that, somewhere in that clearing, possibly underground, they would find at least Miriam, and likely Tanner and the beasts. Macy couldn't shake the feeling that there would be more to it, though. Someone controlled those monstrosities, and not knowing who bothered her. Jake controlled them accidentally, but the appearance of three beasts in such a short time, and the fact they very intentionally crashed her wedding, left no doubt in Macy's mind that these weren't accidents. Somewhere out there, an evil version of Jake had to be orchestrating this mayhem.

"Ok," Macy said. "So we attack there. We'll need those weapons back from y'all."

She directed the request to Gabe. "They're still at Watermelon Ranch. With all the chaos, I haven't had time to go pick them up."

Macy glanced at Kim, who shared the look of surprise.

"We were just out there," Macy said. "Place is picked clean."

"Hey, boss?" Gabe said, turning to Skylar. "You know anything about that?"

Skylar shook his head, a rare moment of silence from the blustery old man.

"How are we going to do this without the appropriate weapons?" Kim asked.

A good question, but Macy worried more about where they might find the missing weapons. If neither Gabe nor Skylar collected them, then someone else did. Someone very likely not on their side.

Dub shuffled in his seat, his weight causing the chair to creak. "I've got one rifle from that night," he said. "It's in evidence down at the station. The one Miriam used to kill Deke—the second beast."

"What about ammo?" Macy asked.

"We've got plenty of that," Gabe replied.

"Two beasts. One gun," Kim said. "Seems like long odds."

"Who's our best shot?" Macy asked.

The group looked at one another, waiting for someone to either volunteer a name or a skill. Macy caught Gabe's eye and could immediately tell that he was being quiet in order to seem humble. Of course, he'd want the job. He wanted Miriam safe as much as she wanted Tanner home.

"Obviously, it's Gabe, right?" Macy said, sending a broad smile across his face. All the guy wanted was a little recognition every now and then. Gabe loved Tanner like a brother, and Miriam as more, but Macy had seen the toll taken on Gabe's ego in trying to live up to those two legends.

"I could do it," Kim offered, half-heartedly.

The desire was there, but even Kim surely knew she didn't have the experience required to properly fire a rifle as potent as the one in question. Tension between Gabe and Kim over Miriam? Cute.

"Gabe's good," Skylar said. "Best we've got, given the circumstances."

Gabe looked wounded.

The dynamics of this group were nuanced and complicated, and Macy could see it all. Kim might get in Gabe's way to prove herself to Miriam. Skylar might lay on too much criticism and cause Gabe to buckle under the pressure. Dub's need to live up to Cam's legacy might lead him to make irrational decisions. Macy couldn't control any of that, but she counted on the one thing they all had in common: love. For Miriam. For Tanner. For Rose Valley.

She wasn't foolish enough to think that the power of heart could bring down two science experiments and whatever cabal backed them, but she did believe in their ability to put everything on the table, and to lead an all-out assault that would at least have a hope of success. In Hogg Run, she'd had to survive much of the night alone, but this time she'd have people with her every step of the way.

"Ok," Macy said. "So we'll get the rifle from evidence and get it to Gabe." Gabe and Dub both nodded. Macy turned to Gabe. "That means you'll be on the peripheral, hidden. When the beasts show themselves, you do your thing."

"Right between the eyes," Dub said. "Nothing else is gonna stop'em."

"Got it."

If Gabe doubted his ability to shoot that precisely, his face didn't show it. Macy chose to borrow some of his confidence.

"What about the rest of us?" Kim asked.

"I guess..." Macy thought for a second. "I guess we're bait. But we should be armed. We've still got smaller stuff, right? Pistols? Shotguns?"

"Sure," Dub said. "This is Rose Valley. We've got that stuff in spades."

"That won't protect you from the beasts," Skylar warned.

Macy shook her head. "No, but these things can't be working alone. We might run into something less resilient. Something we can kill with a standard gun."

No one responded, no doubt each pondering what that might mean. Killing the beasts seemed like mercy, but killing another human, even if they were responsible for creating the murder machines, would be difficult for anyone. Macy had killed a man in Hogg Run to save her own life, and that of her stepmother and stepsister, and not a day went by when she didn't wonder if she could have made a different choice. It stuck to her. She almost welcomed the memory, now. Remembering it seemed the least she could do, the best way to ensure she'd only kill again when absolutely necessary.

She turned to Dub next. "You've got the backup coming?"

"Rodriguez is on it. He's got it all set up."

"Good. We'll need it."

For all the years that had passed, and all the experience this group possessed, they found themselves in almost exactly the same position as the group that had gathered years ago to kill the first beast—a small band fighting against the odds, baiting a creature that had taken so much from them. It had only barely worked years before, and Macy worried she didn't have the same expertise. No Miriam. No Tanner. Not even her father to lead the charge.

But they couldn't wait. Every minute increased the odds that they'd never recover Tanner or Miriam. Macy couldn't stand by, as she had so many times before. Her friends wouldn't save her this time. It was time for her to repay the favor they'd bestowed on her in so many other instances. This ragtag group had to work with what they had... *for better or for worse.*

The thought caused a shiver to run up Macy's spine. She longed for the moment when she'd finally be able to make that marital promise to Tanner.

Chapter 33 – Miriam

Miriam didn't tell Tanner of her ploy, and he didn't seem to notice the difference in the sound of the deadbolt. As much as she wanted his help in attempting their escape, she couldn't trust him. She knew she could best (almost) any foe, but Tanner outsized her by a considerable amount and she couldn't hope to defeat him at the same time as Brynn or Jillian or the witch. Plus, she didn't want to hurt him. Multiple contusions would be a horrible wedding present.

Miriam waited. She intentionally refrained from conversation, listening carefully to his breathing. The boy could fall asleep anywhere. He'd already dozed on and off, and she just needed him to be asleep enough for her to get out and shut the door behind her. She'd come back for him, of course. After the witch had been neutralized. Until then, she had to treat him as hostile. Among those she might have to fight to gain her freedom, Tanner would provide the largest, most difficult obstacle. She saw both Jillian and the witch as trivial, so she focused mostly on Brynn.

And of course, she couldn't rule out the beasts. She didn't think they stayed in the lab. She'd seen most of it and hadn't seen anywhere the beasts could have been kept safely. Even with the influence of the serum, the creatures were largely feral. Though the witch's cocktail of serum-plus-kraken-parasite may have given her a slight edge over someone like Jake, it surely wouldn't be enough. Miriam expected, then, that the beasts were kept offsite. Maybe even allowed to roam free in the woods of Rose Valley.

That gave her time. Given the choice, she had to take out the witch first. Unconscious, she wouldn't be able to command the beasts back to the base.

A lot of *what ifs* for sure, but desperate times...

Once Miriam felt certain that Tanner wouldn't immediately react to her movement, Miriam crept toward the door and listened. When she heard nothing, she pushed on it gently, pleased to feel it move ever-so-slightly, more than it had before her intervention. She took a deep breath, flexed her hands, then balled them into fists.

She counted silently to herself.

One...

Two...

Three!

She rammed her shoulder into the door with all her weight. It rumbled, hung for a second, then gave in to her strength. As it swung open, she reached for the gauze, jerked as much of it out as she could, then slammed the door behind her and locked the deadbolt. Inside, she could barely hear Tanner's muffled screams as he'd realized what she'd done.

She spun, ready for a fight, but the room was empty. She searched for a weapon. There were a few cables on the shelves, random computer equipment, random lab equipment and papers. Nothing that Miriam would have considered a traditional weapon. Undeterred, she reached for the heaviest thing she saw — the microscope. She wrapped the power cord around her hand to ensure she wouldn't lose her grip, then tied it around itself. It would make a formidable — and possibly deadly — boxing glove.

She wrestled with a decision she hadn't made beforehand — to go for help and leave Tanner, or clear the base and make sure Tanner came with her. She looked at the two doors, one leading to the medical lab, the other the witch's lair, then to the exit which would lead through the cave. She'd been unconscious when she'd come that way, so she didn't know what to expect. Certainly, more traps, which might incapacitate her, end her right back up in the cell.

Miriam moved toward the witch's lair. The lab door slid open and she stopped. Brynn's face dropped in shock. Miriam acted quickly to take advantage, closing the distance between them and swinging the microscope hard at Brynn's head, but Brynn moved in time and swung a brutal fist to Miriam's ribcage. She stumbled backward. Brynn pressed the advantage, aiming another punch at Miriam's nose, but quick thinking forced Brynn to slam her first into a microscope instead as Miriam brought her weapon up just in time to serve as a shield

Brynn screeched in pain, flexing her fingers as she pulled her fist away. Miriam stepped forward and jammed the microscope into Brynn's belly, hoping to wind her. They dodged each other's swings, only occasionally landing a glancing blow. To Brynn's cheek. To Miriam's shoulder.

Miriam stayed close. Giving Brynn's longer reach any leverage would end poorly. Brynn awkwardly had to keep her elbows tight, which Miriam used to predict each punch. When Brynn threw, Miriam countered, focusing on the body now, bruising Brynn's ribs with the microscope. The microscope was heavy, though, and Miriam could feel her arm tiring.

Unable to easily disarm herself, Miriam switched tactics, stutter-stepping backward until she could turn safely and slide the computer chair at Brynn. Brynn caught it and slung it away toward the entrance.

"You won't get out of here," Brynn said.

"Watch me."

"Just give up," Brynn said.

"No!"

"Ok. Your choice."

Brynn sprinted forward, leading with her right fist. Miriam pulled her microscope up to block, but Brynn expertly pulled the punch and landed a left into Miriam's temple. The room swam for a second while Miriam tried to keep her balance, giving Brynn the opportunity to follow-up with a hard right. Miriam went down this time. Straight to the cold, stone floor, all attempts to catch herself foiled by the momentum of Brynn's punch. Brynn dropped down and straddled Miriam, landing another punch before Miriam gained enough awareness to start blocking with her forearms. When she did, Brynn moved the punches to Miriam's ribs. Miriam tried to punch back, couldn't reach Brynn's face, and settled for potshots to her hips instead.

Anger cut through Miriam at the thought of losing. She pulled back her microscope boxing glove and threw it at Brynn's stomach, just below the ribcage. The blow sent Brynn reeling, left her wobbly enough for Miriam to buck herself free. Brynn crawled back toward her but Miriam scrambled backward in time to avoid another assault. When Brynn surged again, Miriam brought the microscope up just in time at just the right length, clipping Brynn in the chin. Her teeth chattered as she flew backward and didn't get up.

Still panicked, Miriam shot to her feet on pure adrenaline, ignoring the pain across every inch of her body. She rushed to Brynn only to find her well and truly unconscious, possibly more from hitting her head on the stone than the uppercut with the microscope. Miriam doubled over and coughed and spat blood on the stone.

She looked at the exit, knowing it to be the only real option available to her now. She couldn't hope to win another fight in her current state. She untangled the microscope from her hand and let it tumble to the ground.

As she hobbled toward the door, she heard another open.

"Stop!"

Miriam stopped and turned. The witch stood in the doorway of her lair, her familiar cloak draping her frame, with its creepy, dead coyote eyes staring into Miriam's soul. No weapons. Smaller than Miriam in every way. The path out unblocked. Miriam shoved open the door and took a step into the cave beyond.

"If you leave," the witch yelled. "I'll turn him into one of them."

Miriam took a ragged breath. She couldn't leave Tanner, not even for the promise of help. Not now. She turned back toward the witch.

"Good girl," the witch said with honeyed menace. "Back to your cell."

Miriam walked slowly back into the room, toward the cell door, intending to convey defeat. The witch didn't move, standing in her doorway, possessed of all the confidence in the world that Miriam would obey. But Miriam didn't have the kraken parasite in her. She did not obey. Not the witch. Not anyone.

When Miriam drew up next to the witch, she lunged to the side and swung her fist at the woman's face, stunned when the blow didn't connect.

Had she misjudged? The witch seemed to have evaporated in front of her, but she knew that couldn't be the case. Brynn must have inflicted more damage than Miriam realized. Only a few steps away, deeper into her lair, the witch smiled at Miriam, looking no more hostile than a kitten. Miriam pushed forward and unleashed a flurry of blows, each one expertly dodged. The witch seemed to move with superhuman speed, predicting Miriam's every motion. The witch didn't fight back, but neither did she ever take a hit.

Miriam's chest burned with anger and her lungs burned with exhaustion yet she pressed on, backing the witch to the far side of the room, up against the door that led to the one place Miriam hadn't been in this underground facility. Briefly, Miriam considered there might be beasts in there. Ones that would rip her to shreds. She swung at the witch anyway.

This time, her fist hit squarely against the witch's delicate jaw. It almost felt as if the woman welcomed the blow this time. Blood trickled from her mouth. Miriam followed with another, only to have her arm seized.

The witch flashed a bloody smile as Miriam turned to meet Tanner's gaze. In that moment, she saw so much conflicting emotion inside him, and she knew that if she resisted—if she made another move toward the witch— Tanner, the closest family she had, would end her.

Miriam didn't fight as he dragged her away back into the main room. Brynn sat on the floor near the door of the cell, awake now and wiping blood from her face. Miriam had been so distracted by the witch, she hadn't even heard Brynn open the cell door.

Tanner threw Miriam back into the darkness of the cave.

"Tanner," Miriam pleaded. "It's me. Miriam. Don't do this. Fight it. You can fight it."

But he couldn't. She knew he couldn't. Men had committed cold-blooded murder under the influence of this parasite. Tanner would do the same if necessary. She told herself it wasn't his fault, but a small part of her hated him in that moment.

"Brynn," the witch said from beyond the door. "Prepare him for the procedure."

"No!" Miriam screamed, scrambling for the doorway. "Tanner!"

Brynn stood, slammed the door shut, and flipped the deadbolt. This time, the *clunk* reverberated deep within the stone, locking the door tighter than Miriam would be able to force open. She beat against the door despite the pain in her hands. Tears rushed down her cheeks. Eventually she gave up and slid to the ground, fighting against the hopelessness that threatened to invade.

If Tanner became a beast, there would be no bringing him back. He'd be lost forever.

And Miriam could do nothing to stop it.

Chapter 34 – Jillian

Jillian looked in horror at Tanner thrashing against the leather straps holding him against the gurney, a gag tied around his mouth to keep him from making too much noise. How Brynn had gotten him here in the first place confounded Jillian, but it was hardly the most concerning thing she'd encountered since returning to the cave. Somehow, Brynn had even tapped his vein to insert the IV. Perhaps the power of the parasite alone provided enough control.

"We can't do this," she protested.

The coyote lady didn't answer immediately, instead staring hard at Jillian. Never before had Jillian dared question her orders, certainly not directly. Brynn tended to act as the go-between and Jillian preferred it that way. She found the being in front of her unsettling, almost inhuman. That same feeling she would get when looking upon some almost-human version of a robot or artificially created art. The real-life incarnation of the uncanny valley.

"We can," the witch said. "And you will."

Jillian turned toward the bench which hosted a small refrigerator holding the seeker serum that she'd prepared, its amber hue glowing from within the confines of an ordinary vial. She'd agreed to the first beast out of scientific curiosity. By all accounts, Deke was a horrible human being. A domestic abuser. Possibly a murderer. She'd had greater reservations with the latest two beasts, but still went through with it because they were literal criminals, escaped from prison, and eager to receive the powers of the beast for their mistress.

But Tanner.

Tanner did not deserve what Jillian could only think of as spiritual death. His body would live on, but anything that made him *him* would disappear, consumed by both the serum and the will of the witch — a will that this young man most certainly did not share.

"Dr. Vance," the witch said. "I don't need to remind you what you've already done. The sacrifices that you've already made. In my new world, you will be safe, protected. Defy me now, and your career will be over."

Jillian knew the threat implied prison. She'd broken her own oaths, not to mention numerous laws. She wanted a way out, but self-preservation kept her in.

"Let me sedate him first."

"Like with the first?"

She'd sedated Deke, but the other two had been willing enough that putting them to sleep had been unnecessary. They were compliant as humans, even more so once they transformed.

"Exactly. He's unwilling, so it'll just be easier if I can sedate him," Jillian said. "You know how quickly they get strong. He could tear those straps and kill us before you could assert control."

Jillian focused on keeping her face impassive. Sedation would take a few minutes, and she wanted all the time she could buy. She didn't know what she would do with that time, but every second bought more uncertainty. More time for a miracle. A miracle that she didn't likely deserve. But this boy deserved one, and maybe the universe would grant it.

She shuffled through vials on the upper shelves until she found what she needed, then a syringe. She injected the liquid into Tanner's IV and watched the slowdown of his thrashing, the fluttering of his eyes. At least he wouldn't feel the effects of becoming a monster. He'd simply go to sleep as Tanner and wake up something else.

Once Tanner was fully asleep, the coyote woman pressed on. "There. Now do it."

Jillian sighed and turned toward the mini-fridge. She needed her miracle now.

The door slid open in response. Brynn stood on the other side, her face bruised and bloodied from a fight with Miriam that Jillian had missed.

"What is it?" the witch asked.

"We've got incoming," Brynn said.

"How many?"

"Hard to say. At least two. Cameras don't cover everything, though."

"The redhead?"

"Macy. Yep."

"More than you can handle alone?"

Brynn let out a small laugh and pointed at her face. "More than I can handle right now."

"Ok," the witch said, turning to Jillian. "Finish this. I'm going to need him."

"Of course," Jillian said. "He'll be ready in, um, thirty minutes or so."

That timeframe would have been accurate—if Jillian intended to follow through.

The witch pulled the hood of her coyote cloak up over her head, the snout of the long-dead beast resting on her forehead. Her eyes seemed to glow under that hood, her smile taking on the lupine features of her attire. Uncanny valley.

Brynn led the way. The witch followed. She had another chamber, higher in the cave, for commanding the beasts. Being so far underground seemed to give her less control, though Jillian thought she might be able to fix that flaw in later iterations of the serum.

No. No more.

She pushed aside her own curiosity. She swallowed her ambition. On one hand, she faced a life in prison. On the other, a life of self-hatred. She couldn't do that to herself any longer. She'd choose prison. Perhaps she'd find penance in a trial. Perhaps she'd be able to forgive herself.

Tanner wouldn't be awake enough to be of any help in the upcoming battle. Looking again at her mini-fridge, Jillian envisioned a dangerous path that might bring the power to end the witch once and for all.

It couldn't be Jillian, though. No one else had the ability to reverse the effects of this stuff. Of course, no one had ever done it, and turning back the physical effects of the seeker serum seemed downright impossible, but if she could get their minds back...maybe then. And her plan did not require turning anyone else into a beast. She would never do that again. But if she could only...

Path decided, test subject chosen, Jillian stormed out of the medical bay, walked across the computer room, and opened the deadbolt to Miriam's cell.

Chapter 35 – Macy

The plan, inasmuch as they had one, hinged on Rodriguez and his men approaching the clearing from the opposite side of Watermelon Ranch. Macy didn't really know if this had any tangible benefit, but everyone agreed it would surely increase their odds in case one of the groups literally met beastly opposition. With two beasts, Macy wondered if maybe they should split into even more groups, but with so few personnel, that risked leaving any one contingent far too undermanned to be useful.

She stood now at Steve's trailer with Kim and Gabe. Her team. It hardly seemed enough, no matter their skillset. They would wait here until they got the call from Rodriguez that his men were en route, at which point Macy and crew would hang back five or ten minutes before beginning their own journey to the clearing. The law would get there first. They'd bring their own weapons, of which at least a few would have the necessary stopping power to knock out a beast. That really left Macy, Kim, and Gabe as cleanup. Gabe thought it cowardly. Macy thought it wise.

"Once we get out there, we won't be able to communicate," Macy said. "The Clearing has no cell service."

Gabe nodded and took off again, pacing across the cattleguard and back, rifle on his shoulder. The nervous energy wafted off him, making it hard for Macy to keep her nerve.

"You've already said that," Gabe said. "Like at least ten times."

"Sorry," Macy said, more in habit than genuine remorse.

Kim leaned against Tanner's truck, a beacon of calm in stark opposition to Gabe. Macy could see through the cool exterior, though. Kim wasn't calm. The storm brewing in her eyes heralded a buildup of potential energy. Rather than expend it like Gabe, Kim saved it for the hike. And the fight.

Macy found it curious that Miriam would be attracted to two such different people as Kim and Gabe. But under the way each handled the situation, Macy found the common bond: a surety of self that Miriam only had when hunting, and rarely when it came to relationships.

Thoughts of Miriam became thoughts of Tanner. She knew no one with a stronger sense of self, not even the two people around her. He was only one man, but Macy knew he would fight with everything he had. If not for himself, then for her. Add Miriam to that fight, and Macy could not imagine a world where they would succumb to the evil of whoever held them. She counted on Tanner and Miriam getting themselves out as much as she did the law enforcement, or her own band of eager freedom fighters.

Was it blind hope? Maybe. But Macy thrived on it, nonetheless.

"We're gonna get 'em back," Kim said, breaking Macy's reverie.

"I know," Macy said, more quietly than she intended.

Gabe finally stopped pacing, giving Macy hope that he'd finally calmed down. Instead, he pulled the rifle from his shoulder and started fiddling with it. It worked — they'd already tested it. Gabe aimed well, his mark true. He would make the shot when it counted.

Macy's heart skipped when her phone started buzzing in her back pocket. She pulled it out before the second ring.

"Hello," she said, already expecting the voice on the other end.

"Ms. Donner. We're heading out now."

"Ok," Macy said. "We'll see you there soon."

"Sounds good," Rodriguez replied. "See you then. Be careful."

"You, too."

He hung up without a goodbye. Kim and Gabe both looked at her, already knowing what she would say.

"That was Rodriguez," she said. "They're headed out now."

"Let's go, then," Gabe said.

Macy looked at her watch. "Not yet."

He sighed in frustration. She shared it, but she would keep to the plan until she had no choice otherwise. She would minimize casualties and injury. She would not be reckless like her father.

"It's gonna be ok, Gabe," Kim said, clearly having sensed his distress.

He stopped, the anxiety finally boiling over. "Is it? It is going to be okay? My best friend and my... Miriam... are in trouble! They could be dead. And we're standing here doing nothing, trusting someone else to save them."

Kim remained calm. "Those *someone elses* are trained law enforcement."

"Yeah, well they're not trained beast hunters."

"No one is," Macy replied.

"Except Miriam," Kim corrected.

"You don't understand," Gabe said. "Miriam is... the best thing in this world. She's different. The world needs her."

Kim finally left her perch leaning against the truck. "You don't think I know that?"

"How would you? You've known her for, what? Five minutes?"

Macy watched as the tension between the two finally exploded. They'd been civil, but neither had been blind. Kim and Gabe fought for a common purpose, but, at the end of the day, had no choice but to be antagonists. They couldn't both have what they wanted.

Kim didn't back down, marching close enough to Gabe they could have kissed. Macy briefly considered the ironic humor that would come from that, but knew it wouldn't happen.

With Kim in his face, Gabe continued to goad her. "What? You think you're in love with her or something?"

Kim stopped and backed away, her silent response definitively answering Gabe's question.

Gabe's jaw dropped. Macy felt shock, herself. She could tell that Kim had feelings, of course. They'd begun all the way back at Misty Lake, but Macy never expected the feelings to be this strong. Not now. Not so early. Not when they weren't sure if Miriam felt the same way. Fear did weird things. For Macy, the fear of losing Tanner gave her resolve and focus. But for Kim, it seemed to have brought clarity.

Gabe didn't have a response for Kim's silent admission. He just turned from her and stalked toward the forest.

"Let's go," Gabe called.

Macy looked at her watch. Close enough. She took off after Gabe, Kim bringing up the rear, all of them stunned into awkward silence. Gabe stopped at the tree line.

"I don't know the way," he admitted, his pride wounded.

Kim passed him up and took the lead. They walked, quietly. Bickering would only make them easier targets in case something did hunt them. They'd escaped the beast's glare so long that Macy almost let herself be lulled into a false sense of safety, imagining that Rodriguez had already taken care of the threat and that she and her crew would waltz into the Clearing to see two dead beasts, Tanner and Miriam smiling and everyone else in handcuffs.

But nothing ever went that well. Macy and Miriam meeting all those years ago had evaporated everything of a normal life. And she desperately wanted to change that, hence the intent to retire from the cryptid hunting business entirely — once she got her fiancé back.

When they'd trudged a good way toward the clearing, Kim stopped.

"You should set up here," she told Gabe. "With the scope, you should be able to see the clearing."

Gabe crept a few feet off-trail and lowered himself to the ground, prone, letting the gun rest on the stand that folded out from the bottom. He closed one eye and looked through the large scope on top.

"Yeah," he said. "I see the rocks, but I don't see anything else."

"What about the men?"

Gabe pivoted the gun around, using it as a makeshift set of binoculars.

"I don't see 'em."

"Maybe they're on the other side?" Kim said. "That's the direction they'd be coming from."

Macy nodded. "Okay. We stick to the plan. Gabe. Stay here. If we need to, we'll draw the beasts into your view."

"You got it," Gabe said.

Macy looked to Kim. "Ready?"

"Yeah. Let's do this." Kim turned back toward the clearing, then stopped, and looked back at Gabe. "You got this, Gabe. I know you do."

Gabe looked confused and touched all the same.

"Thanks." he said. "Be careful. Both of you."

Macy and Kim took off alone down the path. It only took another couple of minutes before they came upon the clearing. With no trees to speak of among the rocks, the sun beat down and reflected off the stone, giving the whole place an ethereal glow. Macy couldn't hear a bird or a bug. There was no wind. And, perhaps most notably, no sign of a human presence. Just uncomfortable silence.

Kim vaulted to the top of the nearest rock and peered across the clearing before looking down at Macy and shaking her head. Macy waved Kim back down, and they crept as silently as possible, snaking between rocks until they reached the other side where Rodriguez and his men should have been. They found nothing there, not even a footprint or a disturbed leaf. Tracking did not make the list of Macy's skills, but even she could tell they'd never made it. And that did not bode well for their rescue attempt.

Macy whispered, "We have to go. We can't do this alone."

Kim nodded, no small amount of resistance in the dark black of her eyes. Macy reached out and squeezed

Kim's shoulder to show she didn't want to retreat either. But it made the most sense. Together, they turned back toward the path they'd come down just as the silence broke. Branches snapped. Macy thought she could feel the ground reverberating under their feet.

As Macy and Kim came around one of the large boulders, two beasts stood, shoulder to shoulder, staring at them, low rumbles rising from their chests. Macy recognized them both.

They'd ruined her wedding.

And now, she feared, they threatened to end her life.

Where the hell was Rodriguez?

Chapter 36 – Miriam

When the door opened, Miriam jumped toward it. She didn't know who or what she'd tackle, but the odds no longer mattered, and she'd happily take her chances with blind ferocity. The shadow fell compliantly to the floor as Miriam drew back a fist and nearly let it fly.

Jillian stared up at her, a little bit frightened, her hands raised at her face.

"I want to help you!" she yelled.

Miriam almost punched the woman anyway, but something in the tenor of Jillian's voice stopped her. Miriam stayed her punch and narrowed her eyes. She didn't unpin Jillian from the floor. She just waited for Jillian to explain herself.

"Your friends are in trouble," she said. "I can help you."

"My friends?"

"Yes," Jillian replied. "They're on the surface. She's sending both beasts against them. They'll be killed."

Miriam considered that Jillian was lying to avoid a beatdown. That she hadn't mentioned the more important matter didn't go unnoticed.

"What did you do to Tanner?"

"Nothing," Jillian said. "I swear. He's sedated, but I didn't turn him into a spear. I promise. You can check for yourself."

Miriam glanced toward the door to the medical bay, unsure whether letting Jillian up would prove dangerous. Ultimately, she decided to take the risk. She could overpower Jillian easily enough. When Miriam stood, Jillian sat up and backed herself against the computer desk, not even bothering to stand herself. Miriam took it as a sign that Jillian negotiated in good faith.

"Stay there," Miriam said.

"I will."

Miriam made her way to the medical lab, waited for the door to slide open, then rushed to Tanner's bedside. She studied the vitals on a nearby screen. They all looked normal. Of course, she didn't know what they might look like if he'd been turned into a beast, either, but surely they'd be elevated or something.

In this moment, she realized she couldn't verify Jillian's claim. Not without waiting to see what might become of Tanner. If Jillian could be believed, Miriam did not have the luxury of time.

"What friends?"

"I don't know their names," Jillian said. "The redhead, and her friends."

Macy.

Miriam started toward the door that led to the surface.

"Wait!"

Miriam turned back.

"I can give you the serum. Turn you into a seeker. Even the odds, maybe."

Miriam laughed.

"Are you joking? I'm not turning myself into a monster. I'll kill these ones like I killed the other two."

"With what weapon?"

"I'm sure Macy brought weapons. She's not stupid."

"We took the weapons."

"We who?"

"I don't know. Another one of her henchman. I haven't met him."

Miriam doubted that Macy would attempt a rescue without weapons and trained people. If anything, Macy tended towards risk aversion, though Miriam allowed for the fact that she may not have fully understood the depths of Macy's drive to retrieve Tanner. Love tended to be lost on Miriam most of the time. Or at least obscured enough that she didn't recognize it.

"How many came with Macy?" Miriam asked.

Jillian pointed toward the bank of computer monitors. "May I?"

Miriam nodded and Jillian stood up, quickly logging into the computer to reveal dozens of video feeds from all over Rose Valley. Miriam processed each one, recognizing notable places such as Mikey's, the police department, the newspaper, and a number of traffic cams at nearly every major intersection in town.

She wondered if the witch had installed these cameras or simply hijacked them. Either way, what Miriam had thought to be a nascent attempt at taking over the town was much further along than she imagined. Far enough along that Jillian's words felt true now. Of course the witch would have other minions. Maybe even in high places.

Miriam didn't have much time to ponder the motivation of it all. Surely revenge couldn't explain going to these lengths — for putting this many people in danger. What good would come from taking over such a small town? Unless the witch wasn't the head of her coven. Perhaps Rose Valley was just one of many cities that had already fallen to this cult. She pushed the conspiratorial thoughts away, choosing to focus on concrete information instead of speculation.

As Miriam worked her way through each small block of video, Jillian pointed to one in particular and drew Miriam's attention toward it. She saw Macy and Kim. No one else. It had to be some sort of ruse. Macy wouldn't be so reckless. She would have at least brought law enforcement. Dub, Cam, Jake. Unless they hadn't survived the wedding. If that many notable people had died, saving Tanner might have become Macy's only mission, regardless of risk.

"That can't be all of them," Miriam said. "Macy would have brought more."

"We don't have full coverage of the surrounding woods," Jillian said. "But, I don't see anyone else coming."

The screen next to the one they watched suddenly came to life with two hulking figures entering the frame. It only took Miriam a second to recognize them as the two new beasts. She hadn't seen them before, but they looked eerily familiar. Though the vantage point of the camera appeared to be high up in a tree, Miriam could still make out one of the beasts' missing arm, and one looked considerably taller.

She looked back and forth between the two screens. Kim and Macy, neither carrying a sizable enough gun, versus two monstrosities that could easily rip either woman in half with bare hands. Not a fair fight.

"She won't hesitate to kill them," Jillian said. "But if you take the serum, then you can fight her for control."

Miriam considered the option. Jake seemed no worse for wear, other than the occasional nightmare from a beast showing up on the grid. This new serum, however, clearly had new properties.

"What about the kraken parasite?"

Jillian turned in her chair and looked up at Miriam. "I've altered it. It'll give you greater control than earlier versions of the serum."

J.P. BARNETT

"But how do I know it's not going to kill me?"

Jillian sighed. "I guess I can't promise that it won't, but it's certainly the safer of the two. It's early. We haven't run exhaustive tests. This half of the parasitic entanglement evolved to survive in aquatic life, so it took some ingenuity to get it to work with human brains."

Miriam detected a hint of pride in Jillian's explanation. Disgusting.

"Can you cure me of it? After, I mean?"

"Maybe," Jillian said, her eyes losing focus as she descended into thought. "I've got some theories and some prototypes I haven't tried yet. I think I can cure the beasts, too. Though I don't imagine they'll ever be physically restored."

Miriam kept her eyes on the monitor and watched as Macy and Kim crossed out of one square and into the next, ducking around a rock and coming face to face with the two beasts.

Miriam weighed her options. She could sprint to the top and add one to the equation, but she still didn't like the odds of three regular humans against two super-powered ones. Yet she'd seen what could happen to the beasts when they got confused. They became aimless, which might buy Miriam the time she needed to get Macy and Kim to safety. Jillian offered her a way to do just that.

"How long?" Miriam asked. "Until it takes effect."

"Fifteen, twenty minutes, maybe."

Too long, but Miriam made her decision. The cost to herself mattered less than what she might stand to lose if she didn't take the chance. Macy and Tanner deserved a future, regardless of what Miriam's might be.

"Ok," she said. "Let's do it."

Chapter 37 – Dub

It ate at Dub, not being able to participate in Macy's raid on Big Rock Clearing. He told himself he did it for the strength of the group. He'd never been particularly athletic to begin with, and now his arm rested in a sling. He couldn't make it through the day without ample doses of pain medication. He felt useless. Maria tried to console him, and his kid could still bring a smile to his face, but he yearned to provide some sort of assistance beyond the resources of the Rose Valley PD.

His cowboy boots clopped against the shiny hospital floors as he worked his way toward the one person he wanted to talk to. When he arrived at the room, he rapped gently on the door. Kat opened it merely seconds after he knocked, her eyes red, puffy, tired. Dub hadn't seen her leave the hospital since Cam's accident.

Accident.

What a stupid word. Cam getting smashed by a human-created monster could hardly be considered an accident.

"How's he doing?" Dub said, his tone hushed.

"Better," Kat said. "He's in and out. The drugs make it hard for him to focus."

Dub nodded in sympathy and rested a hand on Kat's shoulder. "He's gonna be okay, Kat. I don't know anyone stronger."

She sniffled and managed a thin smile before gesturing behind her. "Did you wanna...?

"If you don't mind, yeah. I could just really use some of that strength right now, even if it just comes from his silence."

"I need food, anyway," she said. "I don't remember the last time I ate."

Dub stood aside and watched for a second as Kat shuffled down the hallway, then slid inside Cam's hospital room and shut the door. He sat at the stool next to the bed and looked into the face of his friend and mentor.

Though asleep and bandaged, leg up in the air, Cam looked as rested as Dub could remember. He tried to think back to the last time he could remember Cam taking a vacation and came up empty. The man didn't know how to quit. Even after he'd moved from Sheriff to mayor, he frequently consulted on cases. When a crime scene popped up, Cam would be there—sometimes before Dub could arrive. More than anyone Dub knew, Cam would want to be part of this. Like Dub, Cam loved Rose Valley and would do anything to protect it.

"Well, old friend," Dub said. "Looks like history repeats itself again."

Cam didn't answer, of course, but Dub took a pause anyway, as if Cam might suddenly wake from his drug-induced sleep to offer some nugget of wisdom.

"I hope I'm doing the right thing," he said. "Hanging back like this. It feels wrong, but also, it makes sense. Rodriguez is good." Dub laughed in the silence. "Hell, he's probably coming for both our jobs eventually. What do we have if we can't trust the future of Rose Valley, right?"

Dub felt a buzz in his pocket and instinctively reached for his phone. He patted Cam's arm with a smile. "Mind if I take this?"

The number came out of Dallas, but Dub didn't have it in his book. He tapped the answer button.

"This is Sheriff Higgins, Rose Valley PD."

"Hi, Sheriff," the voice said. "This is Officer Halka from Alcohol, Tobacco, and Firearms."

"Hi, Officer," Dub replied. "What can I do for you?"

"We just received a shipment from your department. Looks like a pretty big load of weaponry here. The sorta stuff we'd expect for a safari. There's no note on where this stuff came from, and we just wanted to follow up and ask a few questions."

Dub's mind started racing to put together pieces that he knew had just been flung in front of him. His first instinct told him it must be some mistake, a mix-up in the paperwork, but his pride warned him to play it closer to the vest.

"Sure, sure," Dub said. "We're always happy to help. Can I ask, real quick—who sent this particular shipment?"

"Let me check," the voice said, pausing briefly. "Looks like Officer Rodriguez? Does that sound right."

Dub's heart sank as his mind started connecting the dots. "And these weapons. Hunting rifles, ammo, and the like? For bringing down bigger game?"

"Yes, sir," the voice said. "Rodriguez didn't give us any context for where this stuff came from, and we usually like to keep records on things like that. I assume some sort of raid on your end."

The missing weapons from Watermelon Ranch. Rodriguez knew about those weapons. He knew they belonged to Skylar, and he knew the reason they'd been delivered to the ranch. Why would he have sent them to the ATF?

"Listen," Dub said. "I've got some stuff going on here. Let me give you a call back. This number good?"

"Sure," the voice said. "I'll be here all day."

"Great." Dub said, hanging up the phone without a customary send-off.

He didn't want to believe the direction this information led. He sighed and looked down at Cam.

"I think we might have been wrong about Rodriguez."

***

Dub pushed his cruiser to nearly a hundred, horn blaring, lights flashing. Thankfully, he'd mastered driving with one arm long before his most recent injury. The few cars on the road dipped out of the way as he flew through town, desperate to make it in time to prevent the worst.

He blamed himself. He should have seen the signs of betrayal. If only he'd noticed the malice instead of assigning it all to the ego of a young officer with designs on a promotion.

After his discussion with the ATF, he'd contacted the FBI and the Texas Rangers. Neither knew anything about the raid on Big Rock Clearing, or, in fact, about the attack on Rose Valley at all. Rodriguez had lied about their involvement, and that meant Macy's plan would be short a lot of valuable experience—and gunpower. Repeated calls to every number he had for Macy's group went to voicemail. Big Rock Clearing notoriously had no cell reception.

The entrance to Watermelon Ranch came on fast, but Dub only barely pumped the brakes, fishtailing the cruiser onto the gravel path then surging forward again. He slammed to a stop next to the other cars that had gathered under Macy's banners, one of which was another cruiser belonging to Rodriguez. The mole. The traitor. Dub could only pray no one had been hurt yet.

He vaguely knew the path to Big Rock Clearing. An entire life spent in Rose Valley gave him a mental map that rivaled any that a cell phone could provide. He didn't need GPS. He needed speed. As he sprinted across the yard toward the trees, he could already feel the burning in his chest. Some cops ran regularly. Not the ones in Rose Valley. Dub couldn't remember the last time he'd expended more physical effort than a stroll through the park. He told himself he'd institute a mandatory workout program back at the station once all this ended.

Long before he arrived, Dub heard the hallmarks of a war being waged. The screams and shouts brought him little comfort. He knew the sounds of a losing battle when he heard them.

"Sheriff?"

The voice caught him by surprise. Dub turned to see Gabe Castillo sitting up against a tree, cradling his head.

"What happened, son?"

"Your boy," Gabe said. "Rodriguez. He pistol-whipped me. Took the rifle."

From Gabe's vantage point, Dub peered through the trees and could barely make out the skirmish. With the scope on the now-stolen rifle, it would have been easy pickings to bring down the beasts as they walked into view. A good plan. Ruined by Dub's own blindness.

"Come on," Dub said, helping Gabe to his feet. "We gotta get in there."

"You sure you're up for that, hoss?" Gabe asked. "You're lookin' a little ragged. Didn't the doctor say you needed rest?"

"Ain't no time for rest. Not now."

"True," Gabe said, scratching his beard. "What's the plan?"

"Well, Rodriguez thinks you're out of the fight and that I'm in a hospital bed, so we try to stay out of sight. Find him. Take the rifle back. Kill some beasts. Wha'dya say?"

"Sounds good to me. I just hope we're not too late."

Dub hoped for the same, realistically expecting that they'd lost a few already. The sounds of war waged on, though, so not all had been lost.

"Here," Dub said, unholstering his firearm and handing it to Gabe. "You'll be a better shot than me."

"You sure, *jefe*?"

Dub held up his good hand and balled it into a fist. "I've still got this."

"If you say so, old man."

"I ain't that old."

Gabe clapped Dub on his good shoulder.

"Aahite, aahite. Let's go save the day, then."

Dub nodded and the two men crept through the woods in search of a traitor.

Chapter 38 – Macy

Kim broke away. Macy followed suit in the opposite direction, darting between two large boulders. The narrow crevices gave her an advantage where she should have had none, as one of the beasts struggled to squeeze through. The forced slowdown gave Macy time to dart ahead and try to get her bearings.

The pistol tucked in the back of her waistband seemed small and useless, so she didn't even reach for it. Instead, she needed to get this thing to follow her to the other side of the clearing, straight into Gabe's kill box. Kim would undoubtedly do the same, and if everything went to plan—which, of course, Macy did not at all expect—then Gabe would pick off the two beasts, and the worst of the threats would be dealt with.

A growl behind her sounded closer than she expected, and she glanced back to see a huge hand reaching for her. Just one, though. This beast only had one arm. That one arm, however, almost proved her undoing as she felt the tips of his mercifully clawless fingers graze her arm.

She lunged toward a particularly narrow crevice, turning sideways to squeeze through, the pressure of the two stones against her chest and back. For a second, she thought she might be stuck there, but she sucked in her breath and pulled herself free, popping out on the other side as the beast reached its arm in after her. It would have to find another way around.

Macy paused, having lost her way in the maze of boulders. She decided that right would take her to where they entered, then broke that way at full speed. She briefly saw Kim dart out and then back in, the two-armed beast close behind. She drew her gun to distract Kim's beast, but before she could fire, it also disappeared among the rocks. She fired anyway, her shot ricocheting into the forest. She would have missed, even had the beast not disappeared. She shook her head in a physical attempt to knock away the doubt in her. She'd only barely escaped Hogg Run. Why did she think she would fare better here?

A growl from above shocked her back into action as her one-armed beast stared down at her. The thing wasn't so stupid as to ignore the fact that it could go over instead of through. Macy fired a round toward it. It didn't flinch as the bullet hit it square in the right pectoral muscle.

For a brief second, she thought she recognized the man behind the anger, but her brain couldn't name that familiarity and she didn't have time to study it. She ran toward the front of the clearing at full speed, even as the beast jumped down, having missed tackling her by mere feet.

Knowing she couldn't outrun him, she squeezed back between two boulders, but this time the beast scrambled up. Everything went white as he hit her from the other side, her momentum keeping her just far enough ahead that she didn't feel the brunt of his full weight. It did, however, send her barreling into one of the boulders, her hands flying up a second too late to prevent her head smashing into stone. For the briefest of seconds, Macy lost touch with the world, her hands relaxing enough for her gun to fall to the forest floor.

No matter. It was useless anyway.

Somehow, she recovered quickly enough to roll out of the way. Like an enraged bull, the thing ran full force into the stone himself, dazing him enough for Macy to lurch away yet again. She could see the trailhead — her redemption.

"Gabe!" she yelled. "Here it comes!"

She dashed forward into the open space, the beast close behind. She ducked down to the ground, sure that a bullet would fly over her head. None came.

The beast grabbed her with its one arm and threw her back toward the boulders, but she came up short, skidding across the floor. The strength of one arm could not compare to two, even for this monster. Macy coughed, trying to regain the wind stolen from her chest. She ignored the blood that dripped from her mouth into the dirt. The beast advanced, his chest heaving as he looked down at her in disgust.

Disgust. Not from a mindless mutant. But from a human. A human that she'd fought before... in Gray's Point. She couldn't recall his name, but he'd been one of the dirty cops in the witch's cult. Last she'd heard, he'd been in prison.

With no time to contemplate what his presence meant, Macy scuffled backward, quickly hitting stone and ending the distance she could travel. Then, out of nowhere, a blur hit the beast from the side, causing him to stutter-step, but not lose his balance.

"Run, *chica*!" Gabe yelled. The end of his command came out strangled as the beast lifted him by the throat. Gabe kicked and sputtered.

Desperate to help him, Macy shot to her feet and took advantage of the fact that the beast didn't have another hand to grab her with by running hard into his side. Unlike Gabe's advance, Macy's weight didn't faze the thing at all, and she fell back to the ground. It didn't let go of Gabe as it looked at her with a snarl. She thought quickly and attempted a karate chop into the back of his knee. He buckled enough for Gabe's feet to find purchase just as the beast let him go and reached for Macy instead. By then, she'd ducked forward, prepared another blow, and jammed an elbow as hard as she could into the beast's groin. The beast stumbled backward and dropped to its knees.

"Nice," Gabe said, offering Macy a hand. "Let's go!"

Macy took Gabe's hand as he effortlessly lifted her to full height. They ran back into the boulders together, taking a wider path than Macy would have had to take alone.

They slowed on the other side, both turning to see if the beast was giving chase. For the moment, he appeared dazed enough to have lost their trail.

"What happened?" Macy hissed.

"Rodriguez," Gabe said. "He's not on our side."

Macy gasped as the realization truly hit her. "That means..."

"Ain't no one comin' for us, *chica*. Also, you're bleeding."

Macy reached up to her forehead and studied the dark red ooze that transferred to her fingers. It hardly seemed to matter in the moment.

"We have to retreat, then," Macy said, her mind immediately turning to Kim. "We have to find Kim."

"Sheriff's on it."

"Wait. Dub is here?"

"Yeah. Came to warn us about Rodriguez."

For all the good that did. Just then: a snarl from beyond the boulders.

"Split up?" Gabe suggested. "He can't chase us both. Take this."

Gabe produced a police revolver from the waistband of his pants and handed it to Macy. She took it, reluctantly tucking it into her own jeans. She never got used to the feeling, or the fear that she'd discharge it into her butt.

Macy shook her head. "No heroic sacrifices. We stick together. Come on."

She took off, expecting Gabe to follow. But, of course, he didn't. When had Gabe ever done the smart thing? And he'd given her his only weapon.

Without any time to backtrack, Macy squeezed forward, trying to carve an unpredictable path through the stones. After a few such zigs and zags, she realized the one-armed beast hadn't followed her.

Gabe better survive, cuz I'm gonna kill him.

Unsure of her next move, she certainly knew she couldn't retreat alone. She stopped, stilled her breathing, and listened for a clue as to what direction might lead her to Kim or Gabe or Dub. She got her answer off to her left as Macy heard a grunt that could have only come from Kim.

A few twists and turns later, Macy broke into a sizable space between a set of boulders where she saw Kim down on the ground. She spat blood into the dirt, tried to stand up, then wobbled before falling back to the ground. The beast itself—this one with two arms— held Dub against a rock.

Macy arrived in time to see a huge, balled hand land squarely on Dub's nose. The *crack* nauseated her. The beast dropped him, and his body crumpled to the ground. Macy didn't know if he'd survived the blow, but she opted to try to save the person still awake, darting to Kim and pulling her up by her armpits.

Macy felt the full weight of her. She didn't seem able to stand on her own.

"Kim!" Macy yelled. "Come on. Stay with me. We gotta go."

Kim nodded vacantly. Macy dragged her toward the smallest crevice she could see. It wouldn't work if Kim didn't come to her senses.

The beast turned just as Macy squeezed in, her escape forcing her to let Kim go. Kim leaned against the rocks. Macy looked into her eyes.

"Run," Kim squeaked out.

The beast slammed into Kim's body. Macy watched in horror as the stone scraped against Kim's skin, blood coming from seemingly everywhere. The impact surely broke some bones.

The shock of the pain seemed to give Kim some adrenaline, though. She twisted sideways and scooched her frail frame in next to Macy. The beast reached its hand into the crack, but couldn't get more than elbow-deep, keeping Kim just out of reach.

"Kim," Macy said, breathlessly. Kim looked at her, defeated. "Don't give up. We're gonna make it."

Surrounded by as much blood as stone now, Macy found it hard to believe her own promises. The beast snarled and growled, trying to get at them, but failing. As strong as these things were, they couldn't move boulders this big. The top sat at least six feet above them, keeping them safe from that direction as well.

They could wait here, she decided. The beasts couldn't get to them in such a small space. Eventually they'd give up. Or someone would come. Maybe Gabe.

The beast disappeared. To where, Macy could not say. She looked at Kim again, whose eyes closed halfway.

"Kim!" Macy yelled. Kim slowly opened her eyes. "Don't you go to sleep on me. We're going to get out of here. We're going to get Miriam and Tanner. Then you and me... we're going to live our happily ever afters. You hear me?"

Kim attempted a smile, her mouth bloodied.

"That's right," Macy said. "Think about why we're here. We can do this."

They just had to wait.

As Kim's head started to loll, Macy desperately searched for something to keep her friend awake.

"You know," Macy said, trying to sound calmer than she felt. "Miriam's a tough nut to crack. But she likes you. She really does. I know it's hard to tell."

For a moment, Macy saw coherency in Kim's eyes, which gave hope.

"I think you two would make a great couple, ya know," Macy said. "You both love the outdoors. Maybe you could go live in a tent somewhere. Become mountain-women."

Kim sputtered a laugh, blood spattering onto the rock between them.

They just had to survive.

"I don't think I ever told you thank you," Macy said. "For everything you did out at Misty Lake. And, most of all, for saving the otters. No one could have convinced Miriam to hide the truth like that. No one but you."

Kim seemed more awake. She smiled, this time less forced and more natural.

"Macy," she said, her voice hoarse.

"Yeah?"

"I'm..."

"You're what?"

Kim took a second to look down at her bloodied body. "I'm... this... hurts."

Macy laughed in spite of herself.

"Yeah."

"Miriam... better... appreciate this."

They just had to stay put. Help would come.

"She will," Macy said.

Then, a gunshot. The echo rang deep. It could only be from something heavy. Something big. Something that could kill the beasts. Had Gabe recovered the rifle?

Another shot. Macy heard the bullet ricochet off the rock above them. Then another, this one closer. Not Gabe. The truth of the matter came into focus. Someone was firing at them, and as small targets as they'd make wedged into such a small crevice, eventually a bullet would hit—or ricochet—into them.

"Kim?" Macy asked. "Do you think you can move?"

"I don't kn... why?"

The fact that she didn't already know told Macy all she needed about Kim's connection with reality.

But they had to move.

No more waiting.

Only surviving.

Chapter 39 – Miriam

The cave seemed like a maze as Miriam ascended. She looked carefully for the subtle markers Jillian had described, turning left, right, slowly snaking up.

She paused at a path leading to the witch's chamber, from which she controlled the two beasts. Jillian had warned that trying to confront the witch would be fruitless. She sat behind a massive steel door, and Brynn guarded her always. Miriam won the first fight with her doppelganger, but she couldn't be certain of success on a second. So she continued, waiting, hoping, praying that she'd start to feel the serum kick in.

And then, it did.

The force of emotion almost brought her to her knees. She felt shades of so many things. Anger, confusion, passion, and, perhaps most disturbingly, joy. Miriam stayed on her feet, forcing another step and then another, each one causing the sensations of other people invading her mind to grow. But if the witch could do this, so could Miriam.

Sunlight shone ahead as Miriam neared the mouth of the cave. This time she deftly avoided the traps, though they looked as if they'd already been disabled by someone. Instead, she stopped just outside the cave and tried to make sense of her emotions. Never one to dwell on her emotions, Miriam didn't know how to sort it all out. She couldn't name them or separate them. Jillian said to focus on one voice. One mind. Trying to control both would take practice, and Miriam didn't have time for that.

She heard the sounds of commotion around her but fought the urge to fight with her own body. Instead, she focused on trying to take control of another. With some effort, she started to see patterns. One of the minds seemed confused and scared, the other angry and lustful. She chose to focus on the confused one, hoping its mental state would make it more pliable to a new master. Jake had always described the experience differently, but this serum contained the kraken parasite. With her focus, Miriam started seeing flashes of imagery, which she quickly realized came from the vision of her beast.

None of it would give her enough knowledge to know what command to attempt. She used what she saw to navigate around the rocks until she came out on the other side, where Gabe flew through the air — thrown by the one-armed beast.

The hate raging from the beast before her couldn't be hers, but another flash of imagery led her to look up where she saw the other beast: two arms, chest heaving, standing on the precipice of a rock above.

She recognized him instantly, though wasn't sure if she knew him from his mind or his visage. Maybe both. This beast had once been Grimes, one of the witch's henchmen in Gray's Point. He'd been in prison, but her mind quickly recalled news that had seemed inconsequential from days earlier, playing in the background as she'd rushed through her apartment. Something about a prison break. It explained why these particular beasts so quickly complied with the witch's orders.

As the one-armed beast — Davies, if Miriam remembered correctly — stalked towards Gabe's battered body, Miriam put all her focus into commanding Grimes.

Gabe scrambled to his feet, woozy, and wobbly. He put up his fists as if they'd provide him any protection at all. As Davies got closer, Miriam began fearing she would fail. Grimes still stood on his perch at the top of the rock, but now he looked at her.

"Come on, Grimes," she whispered. "You know you don't want to do this. You never liked her anyway."

She saw something shift in his glare, then he leapt over her head — straight into the path of Davies.

Davies threw a punch with his one arm, likely aimed for Gabe, but Grimes caught it mid-air, using his other hand to pummel Davies in the ribs. Miriam didn't even know if she had control anymore as the two began grappling, throwing punches at each other, knocking one another to ground, growling and snarling. Gabe staggered over to her.

"What the hell, Mimi?"

With emotions barraging her, she could barely register Gabe's voice, much less carry on a conversation with him. When she didn't answer, or make a snide remark about his annoying nickname for her, his eyes widened.

"Holy crap," he said. "Tell me you didn't...."

Miriam managed to eke out: "Find the others."

"On it," he said, disappearing behind a boulder. Somewhere in the distance, Miriam registered a gunshot. Hopefully from a friend, but she saw no stray bullets hit either beast as they continued their epic struggle.

Davies may have only had one arm, but it packed enough heat to send Grimes to the ground with just one brutal blow to the head. Miriam drowned out the sounds of the gunshots and the worry for her friends, and refocused on her beast. She'd chosen him and she feared changing now would be too overwhelming, so instead she tried to will Grimes back to his feet. He rolled just as Davies attempted a stomp to the head.

Miriam pushed thoughts as fast as she could think them, unsure of what Grimes could truly understand, but when he grabbed Davies' ankle and pulled him to the ground, she knew that Grimes understood enough, perhaps even greater detail than she imagined. At Gray's Point, she'd proved to be a more adept pugilist than Davies, so if she could use her skills with Grimes' strength...

She began choreographing the fight in her head, imagining the whole thing as one big video game.

Grimes her avatar. Davies the endgame boss.

With both beasts on the ground now, Grimes rolled and straddled Davies, pinning his one arm and pummeling his face over and over with huge haymakers that smashed into bone so hard it reverberated through the woods. Even from her vantage point, Miriam could see the blood gushing from Davies' nose. She longed to do more than just see the fight. She wanted to feel it. To be able to anticipate how Davies might react or try to break free.

And break free he did, his one strong arm pounding the side of Grimes' head and knocking him to the ground. Davies pushed to his feet. Miriam willed Grimes to do the same. It quickly became a boxing match, each trying to dodge punches and landing ones of their own. Some landed. Most didn't. The transformation made them fast. Almost too fast for Miriam's mind to keep up.

But she held her own until something hard hit her from the side. She flew sideways, temporarily blinded, struggling to separate herself from Grimes long enough to register her attacker.

She managed it quickly enough to block Brynn's head-kick, as Grimes started fighting Davies all on his own.

Chapter 40 – Macy

The terrain made it hard for Macy to understand all factors at play. She managed to get Kim out of the narrow crevice without getting shot, and now they staggered toward the tree line, where Macy hoped to find escape or help. She found neither, but lowered Kim to the ground behind the largest tree she could see. With Kim no longer a threat, hopefully the bad guys would focus on Macy instead.

"Stay here," Macy said. "Be quiet. Stay alive."

Kim nodded.

She didn't speak, but looked alert enough to stay awake. Macy did her best not to make a face as she glanced over the blood and skin hanging from Kim's arms. They all looked like surface wounds, at least, like a really bad rug burn all over her body. Macy couldn't imagine how much it must have hurt, but she thought Kim would survive, even if she did come away with a few scars.

The shooter hadn't located them yet, so Macy gave Kim the best look of support she could and shifted away, following her ears toward the sounds of growling. She never thought she'd be one to run into the throes of danger, but somewhere out here, she had to find Gabe, at least. They would retreat together and return better prepared. She'd led the people she cared about most into a deathtrap. She couldn't imagine Dub having lived through what she'd seen, and she couldn't deal with losing Gabe, too.

She came around the corner to see....

"Mir!"

Miriam rolled away from a bruised and battered Brynn Kerrison. Macy couldn't make sense of the whole scene, but her attention shifted to two beasts in a death match. One of them threw the other against a tree. It shook so hard, Macy thought surely it would topple.

As the beasts raged on, Miriam sprung to her feet, threw a jab at Brynn, then dodged one thrown at her. Macy didn't even know where to help, but she had a gun so she pulled it out from the waistband at the back of her jeans and pointed it at Brynn.

"Stop!" she yelled.

Miriam shot her a side-eye, but Brynn didn't seem to notice, so Macy fired the gun into the air. When Brynn turned to look at Macy, Miriam took the opportunity to push Brynn to the ground and sit on her. Brynn might have outclassed Miriam on height, but not weight. Macy rushed over and kneeled on the back of Brynn's legs to make it even harder for the girl to escape.

"Are you ok?" Macy asked.

"Yes," Miriam said. "And no. It's a long—"

Miriam stopped short and screamed as she grabbed her head.

"What's wrong?" Macy asked.

Miriam didn't answer but shifted her gaze over to the war of beasts, where the smaller, two-armed one took one, two, three blows to the head from the other, knocking it to the ground. It didn't immediately return to its feet, and seemed to be almost unconscious. Macy looked between the fallen beast and her best friend, trying to understand the connection but coming up short.

"I...."

Below them Brynn squirmed, but the weight of both girls kept her at bay without too much trouble.

"She took it," Brynn said.

Miriam's eyes squinted in pain as she shook her head, as if to exorcise something within.

"Took what?" Macy asked.

Brynn didn't have to answer before the realization sank in. Somehow Miriam could control the beasts now. She was like Jake.

Wait. If she could control the beasts...

Macy shoved the thought aside, refusing to believe Miriam had been behind this all along. It didn't make sense, but there was no time to figure it out. First, safety, then answers.

She reached out to Miriam and touched her on the shoulder.

"Are you ok?"

"It hurts," she said in a raspy, broken voice. "It's like I can feel his pain, but only in my head. I can't... I can't explain it."

The forest fell temporarily silent. Macy felt an overwhelming sense of doom, spinning just in time to see the one-armed beast stomping toward them.

"Mir," Macy said. "You gotta do something."

"I'm trying."

Macy aimed her pistol at the beast and fired shot after shot. At such close range, each bullet hit with an audible *thud* that sprayed blood. Some spattered onto her face, causing her to shriek in disgust. The gun clicked. Empty. She slung it aside.

"We gotta go!" she yelled, standing and grabbing Miriam's hand and pulling her off Brynn.

With some effort and a little help from Miriam, Macy managed to get them both to their feet and dashing toward cover. As they ran between two boulders, Miriam turned.

"Wait."

Macy stopped to look behind them. The two-armed beast had risen again and rushed toward the one with one arm. The fight resumed, distracting the threat of the beast, but then came Brynn.

It suddenly made sense what Brynn meant to do. If she stopped Miriam, then the two-armed beast would be back on the side of evil. Macy couldn't let that happen. She crossed in front of Miriam, growled to psyche herself up, and ran straight into Brynn, who took the blow of the much smaller Macy without falling, only barely losing her balance. She pushed Macy's shoulders, causing Macy to stumble back several steps.

Macy knew she couldn't win a fight against this girl, and, frankly, she didn't even fully understand why she needed to fight her in the first place, but she understood the goal. Defense. She just had to keep Brynn away from Miriam. So, she didn't advance, she retreated, putting herself at the mouth of the opening between the boulders. The only way to Miriam now would be through Macy.

Brynn grinned as she approached. "I've wanted to do this ever since you and your boyfriend crashed the party back at Gray's Point."

Macy softened her knees, held up her hands, and used her forearm to block an incoming punch. Another came faster than she could stop, though, and she took the full brunt of Brynn's second to the jaw. It rattled her head. Her teeth chomped her tongue and she tasted blood. But she stood and took it, pushing forward and forcing Brynn back a few steps. Brynn gave up punching and instead tried to tackle Macy, but Macy twisted and spun, always putting herself back into the line of attack just before Brynn could slip past.

Recognizing her smaller size, Macy kept low as she went at Brynn and wrapped her arms around her waist. She buried her head in Brynn's stomach and squeezed as tightly as she could. Brynn could do nothing but pummel Macy's back, easy enough to take. They stumbled around like this, Brynn trying to advance and Macy trying to hold the line. But Macy could tell she lost ground. She wouldn't win in the end. She squeezed Brynn's waist harder, hoping to wind her.

Come on, Mir. Finish this.

Head buried in Brynn's torso, Macy couldn't see the beasts fighting behind them, but she could hear them growling and snarling, with the occasional blow hard enough to reverberate through the clearing.

Macy started counting the steps forward and backward. For every step away from Miriam, Brynn seemed to be gaining two or more. Before long, Macy felt the rock at her heels and knew she'd run out of room.

"Hey!"

The voice came from above. Brynn looked up. Macy let go just in time to see Gabe fall directly on Brynn, crumpling her to the ground.

Gabe pinned her arms. Macy walked over and looked into Brynn's angry hazel eyes. So many questions, so few answers. What had led this girl down this path?

Macy knelt, pulled back a fist, and hit Brynn so hard in the face that blood spurted from her nose.

"He's not my boyfriend," Macy snarled. "He's my fiancé, bitch."

Brynn's eyelids fluttered briefly, then her jaw went slack as she went unconscious.

Macy smiled and helped Gabe to his feet, as both turned toward the two beasts fighting it out in the clearing.

"What do we do?" Gabe asked.

"I don't know," Macy replied, looking back toward Miriam. She clearly wouldn't be helping as long as she controlled the beast. "But we gotta do something."

"Freeze!"

Macy and Gabe turned to see Rodriguez coming around the corner, rifle on his shoulder.

"Can't believe you let him have the gun," Macy said.

"Well," Gabe said with a smirk. "Let's get it back."

She shared a glance with him. Tanner's best man. An unlikely friend that they would have for life. As much as Gabe loved Miriam, he might have loved Tanner more.

Rodriguez yelled again. "Hands up! Don't move!"

Gabe looked at Macy with a grin. He was most certainly about to do something stupid. But maybe stupid is exactly what they needed.

He leapt forward. Rodriguez fired.

Jesus, Gabe. Not that stupid.

The shot missed somehow, as Gabe's forward trajectory switched sideways. The rifle, as large as it was, didn't reload quickly. Rodriguez fumbled with the mechanism but Gabe got there first, grabbed the barrel, shoved it to the side and swung a hard right. Rodriguez took the full brunt of it, his face contorted in pain. The gun stayed firmly in his grip, though, Gabe's strength keeping it pointing away.

As soon as Rodriguez turned his head back, Gabe threw another punch, less effective than the first, either from Gabe's fatigue or Rodriguez' expectation of the blow. Rodriguez recovered more quickly, juking backward and trying to wrestle the gun from Gabe's grip. The move worked, as Gabe's hand slipped from the barrel. Rodriguez quickly completed the reload, pulled the gun to his shoulder and held the barrel inches from Gabe's forehead. No amount of bravely stupid maneuvering could dodge that.

Rodriguez didn't fire, though, instead looking at Macy. "I will shoot him if you try anything."

Knowing that he'd been beaten, Gabe put his hands up. Macy did the same. Movement from behind Rodriguez caught her eye. Silent, almost imperceptible. She fixed her face to stone so as not to give away what came. Macy didn't think Gabe would be able to see past Rodriguez, which would put him in danger, so she tensed her muscles and readied to move.

The silent shadow was none other than Dub. Bruised. Bloodied. One eye swollen shut. And his good hand holding a rock that Macy wouldn't have been able to lift with both her hands.

Macy dove toward the nearest boulder just as Dub brought the stone down. Rodriguez shifted his aim toward Macy—a costly mistake. The gun fired. Macy felt some preternatural sense that the bullet very nearly hit her before she ducked out of view.

She peeked back around the corner to see Rodriguez crumple to the ground. Dub tried to smile, didn't quite get his lips to cooperate, then collapsed. Gabe rushed to him. Macy started to do the same, stopped by the sound of scuffling above her. She looked up and gasped. Above her stood a shadowed woman, elegant, inexplicably young, shrouded in the pelt of a coyote.

Suddenly everything came together. In all their adventures, all their hunts, only one evil had escaped their grasp. They'd put it behind them, foolishly confident she would never return. But she'd come for them, and brought so much destruction.

And she looked so incredibly young.

Macy didn't believe in mystical mumbo jumbo, but in that moment, she could not deny her own eyes. Someone had completed the ritual.

Deke hadn't killed Brynn's mother.

Macy looked to Brynn's unconscious body. If she'd killed her own mother, and the witch's crazy claim that doing so would restore the witch's youth was true, then that changed everything. They were no longer dealing with advanced science or forgotten monsters.

She surveyed the battlefield. The beast fight raged on. Rodriguez and Brynn had been taken out of the fight. Dub may have been dead. Miriam could only focus on the beast.

"Gabe," Macy said, motioning up with her head. His eyes went wide when he registered the witch. Whether he made all the connections, she didn't know, but as he stood, she could tell his confidence had taken a hit. No one's life had been more acutely affected by this evil woman than his. He'd grown up in Gray's Point, never free from her invisible control until Miriam had saved him. The witch had caused the death of Gabe's mother — the previous sacrifice to her eternal youth.

Once he shook off the shock, his face showed anger as he scaled the nearest boulder, jumped from one to another and flew toward the witch. He didn't connect, though, as she vanished into thin air. Moments later, the witch appeared on another boulder. Gabe looked down at Macy in shock and confusion.

For the first time, after having seen so many awe-inspiring things, Macy believed in magic.

She sure as hell didn't know how to combat that. If anyone could figure it out, though, it would be Miriam, so Macy's first act of business was on freeing Miriam from her trance. And to do that, she'd have to do the one thing she promised herself she'd never do again after Hogg Run.

Macy rushed over to where Rodriguez had fallen, knelt, and picked up the rifle. She'd never held a gun so heavy, so she lowered herself to the ground, lying down on her chest the way Miriam and Tanner had before when trying to land a particularly tricky shot. The barrel took away her ability to aim, its weight tipping it toward the ground. How would she...

Then she saw the small tripod, neatly folded up against the bottom of the barrel. She reached out and flipped it down. She looked through the scope at the two beasts in front of her, knowing she ought to aim at the larger one.

At first, she couldn't get a bead. They moved so fast, each punch shifting the other back so far that she lost sight entirely and had to move the gun. But then, the two-armed beast stopped trading blows and instead wrapped the one-armed beast into a bear hug. Miriam's beast spun away, presenting Macy with the back of her target.

Thanks, Mir.

Macy slowed her breathing, tried to remember everything Tanner had ever taught her about shooting, and pulled the trigger.

Chapter 41 – Miriam

The first shot lodged low in Davies' spine. Miriam focused her energy on instructing Grimes to hold on. She could sense the difficulty of the request, as Grimes pushed back against her psyche, somehow imparting the feeling of pain without any physical sensation. She insisted. He obeyed.

Miriam could hear Macy fumbling with the rifle, attempting to reload without really knowing how. She wanted to help, but couldn't spare the energy necessary to move from her position. She saw everything. Processed everything. But could only focus on Grimes.

Hope came when she saw Gabe sliding down the boulder above Macy, soon landing beside her and falling on his stomach. Much to Miriam's surprise, Macy swatted him away, allowing him only to help her reload. She fired her second shot. It hit true right into the back of Davies' head. Miriam knew the efficacy of the hit before seeing any physical sign, as all Grimes' pain and panic and stress suddenly stopped in her. She loosened her focus. Grimes released his bear hug. Davies slumped to the ground with an audible *thump*.

One beast down.

Macy gave up the gun this time, and Gabe quickly reloaded, no doubt intending to finish Grimes as well. Miriam could have held the beast in place, even, making it a sure thing.

Instead, she let her focus go enough to shout, "No, wait!"

Gabe heeded her command, but she couldn't spare any time to explain. If she did, she might lose control and never get it back. She could already feel Grimes resisting her, pulled in another direction — pulled in the direction of the witch.

Miriam swiveled her head until she found the old — now young — crone, perched on a boulder, her vacuous eyes trained directly on Miriam. It came down to willpower. Which one could send Grimes in to finish the job. If Miriam lost here, it would surely spell doom for everyone she loved. Grimes stood above Davies' body, his chest heaving, blood seeping from various wounds.

He looked at Miriam, then the witch, then back again. Miriam searched, focused, tried to find something in his mind that she could hold onto. Something that would mean more than any thread the witch might try to pull.

She felt anger. Confusion. Longing. Despair. So much despair. Miriam felt tears trickle down her cheek. Tears not from her, but from Grimes.

Then something new hit her. At first, she didn't know how to place it, but it mingled with memories of her own — feelings of losing Cornelius. The raw nerves in the aftermath of his death left her with only revenge on her mind. Grimes felt this here. Now. Without words or any confirmation that Miriam could have repeated, she knew that Grimes had not volunteered to become a beast. The witch forced him into servitude, and he hated her for it.

Miriam empathized. One of the hardest things in the world for her to do. And with that empathy she found the hook she needed. Grimes turned toward the witch and took off in a loping run. The witch seemed shocked at first, but she stood her ground, not pulling one of her vanishing acts. As Grimes drew closer, she held up her hands, the coyote cloak creating an impressively large, imposing silhouette. This did not stop Miriam or Grimes.

He leaped into the air, easily clearing the height of the boulder and reaching for the witch long before he arrived at her location. The witch's silhouette shifted. Grimes hit her with full force, then flew backward across the clearing, skidding across the ground before hitting up against a tree that shook from the weight of his body. Miriam momentarily lost control of him as everything she knew about the world suddenly came into question.

At the top of the boulder, where once a witch had stood, there now snarled a coyote the size of a grizzly.

Chapter 42 – Jillian

As a child, Jillian thought her father was the wisest man in the world. Only later did she learn that his wisdom mostly came from folk sayings and tired clichés. Right now, though, she clung to one of his favorites: *Necessity is the mother of invention.*

She'd been so close to so many breakthroughs, and suddenly, as the fight raged on above her, she understood how to overcome every hurdle she'd encountered. She viewed the serum on a level she'd never seen before, as if it existed in her mind as a 3D model she could pick apart at will. She'd been working nonstop since that realization, only occasionally checking the monitors to see the progress of the fight. She only hoped she could help in time.

Now, she stroked Tanner's hair as he groggily opened his eyes.

"How do you feel?" she asked.

He startled, sitting up quickly, then lunging out of bed, only to stumble and almost fall, catching himself by grasping to the side of the gurney.

"Easy, now," she said. "It's going to take a few minutes for you to get your bearings."

"What did you do to me!?" he shouted.

"Nothing," she said, holding up her hands. "I promise. I just...."

She reached for a syringe on the nearby table and showed him the clear liquid within. He looked at it without recognition. Naturally. She had just invented this particular cure, after all.

"It's a cure," she said. "A real one. The parasite is gone. You won't be compelled to protect her anymore."

He squinted his eyes at her, clearly not sure whether he should believe her. She wouldn't have believed her, either.

"Your friends need help."

She walked into the control room, expecting him to follow. He did, surprisingly solid on his feet. They watched as one of the beasts slumped to the ground and the other took off in a sprint toward the witch.

"Looks like they've got it under control."

"No, they don't," Jillian said.

"What the hell?"

They both watched as the witch transformed into a monster. A giant coyote out of myth and legend, though no specific one that Jillian could recall. She'd never seen the woman do this, in particular, but she'd come to suspect that she was more than a mere scorned villain. Now she had the proof. On camera. The world would never be the same.

"What am I supposed to do against that?" he asked.

"I don't know," Jillian admitted. "But I have something to even the odds."

She rushed back to the lab and came out with another syringe, this one with an amber liquid.

"This is what I've been theorizing. What I've been working on."

"What's it do?"

"It'll free the beast from her control. Give him his mind back."

"You mean that guy?"

He pointed at the screen, where the only remaining beast lay crumpled in a pile of muscle, possibly not even alive.

"He's not dead."

"How do you know?"

In truth, she didn't. But the spears were resilient. Nearly impossible to kill. Blunt force trauma wouldn't likely bring them down. Not unless the strength of this new coyote monster exceeded all logic and physics.

"He's alive. You know how hard they are to take down."

"How do we know he's not just going to turn against us?" Tanner asked.

"We don't," she said. "But while you were waking up, I watched the thing act on its own when Miriam lost control."

"Wait, what?" Tanner interrupted. "Miriam's in control of that thing?"

"Yes. She took the seeker serum. Long story."

"Of course, she did."

"Listen, I've got no promises for you, but I screwed up and I want to make it right," Jillian said. Another of her father's truisms popped into her head. "Desperate times call for desperate measures."

"I suppose it's better than turning me into a beast."

"All right," Jillian said. "Let's go."

As the door opened, leading up into the cave system, ear-splitting klaxons started blaring through the compound. Jillian covered her ears. She looked around frantically, trying to find the cause of the alarm, only for her eyes to land on the computer monitors, now all red with white bold letters that read: *Emergency destruction engaged*.

"What does that mean?" Tanner yelled, his voice barely audible.

"I don't know," Jillian said. "But I think we need to get out of here. Now!"

Jillian sprinted into the cave, Tanner close behind. It was time to find out whether necessity truly was the mother of invention.

Chapter 43 – Miriam

It had to be trickery. In Gray's Point, the witch used hallucinogens to force the squad into seeing horrendously impossible things. This giant coyote certainly qualified as a horrendously impossible thing. Yet, the sole remaining beast lay unconscious a good twenty yards away from the witch-coyote. That couldn't be explained by hallucinations.

Miriam tried to reach out to Grimes but found nothing. He was either unconscious or dead. She rushed over to Macy, who now stood over Gabe. He swiveled his body and the rifle around to the giant coyote. He fired. The coyote dodged by seemingly disappearing from one boulder and appearing on the next. Miriam couldn't believe her eyes, but didn't have time to work out the truth of what was happening.

"What do we do?" Macy asked. "We can't leave without Tanner."

Miriam balled up her fists. Her instincts told her to fight. To find a way to win. She didn't like backing down, but they had one rifle against a coyote that could, well, teleport. She hated even thinking the word, knowing in her core that such a feat should have been impossible.

"What's that?" Macy asked.

It took Macy drawing attention to it for Miriam to register a new sound. Klaxons coming from somewhere nearby. Help on the way? No. As she zeroed in on the sound, she realized it came from the caves below. She didn't know what it meant.

"Gabe," Miriam yelled. "We gotta run. We can't fight this. We have to get Tanner and go!"

"Get him," Gabe said. "I'll keep her distracted."

He squeezed off another ineffective shot as the coyote shimmered in place, as if somehow allowing the bullet to pass through.

Miriam knelt in front of Gabe and squeezed his shoulder. "Be careful."

"No promises."

He fired another shot.

Standing and turning to Macy, Miriam said, "Come on."

The two rushed toward the cave entrance, the sound of the klaxons growing in intensity as they neared it. As they reached the mouth, Jillian came bounding out, followed by a very awake Tanner. Miriam immediately went on the defensive, expecting him to turn against them, but he didn't. Instead he scooped Macy into his arms and buried his head into her shoulder.

"He's cured of the parasite," Jillian said. "I think."

Miriam didn't really believe it, but she also didn't have time to question it.

"What's with the alarms?" Miriam asked.

"Some sort of self-destruct system, I think," Jillian said. "To protect the lab probably."

"What triggered it?"

"Me leaving, but I don't know for sure. I don't even know what's going to happen when the countdown ends."

Of course, the witch would have a backup for ensuring that her dastardly plans didn't get compromised by someone trying to leave the cult. Though, how the witch could have predicted Jillian's betrayal remained a mystery.

Whatever self-destruct meant, Miriam suspected that it wouldn't be good. "We gotta get outta here."

Tanner lowered Macy back to the ground. "Yeah, but first, we have a plan."

"We?" Miriam asked. "You guys are besties now?"

Jillian held up a syringe. "We can free Grimes from her control. Then you won't have to command him anymore."

"Yeah, lady," Macy said. "I don't think that's going to help much. He's either dead or sleeping off the headache of a century right now."

Miriam turned her head instinctively as something beckoned to her. A sound, she thought at first, but in her head in lieu of the real world. Grimes wasn't dead.

"He's waking up," Miriam said.

"Then we better hurry."

Miriam turned to Tanner and Macy. "We gotta get everyone outta here. Get Dub, and Kim. Even Rodriguez and Brynn."

"You thinking explosion?" Tanner asked.

"Wouldn't put it past her."

"All right, we're on it," Tanner said.

"I'll get Kim away," Macy offered.

"I can get the Sheriff or Rodriguez, but not both."

"Gabe's over there," Miriam said. "He can help."

It wasn't like his shooting gallery practice was yielding results.

"What about Brynn?" Macy asked.

"I guess that's on me," Miriam replied. She turned toward Jillian. "Your plan better work. And we all gotta hope Grimes is gonna be in a fighting mood."

She suspected he would be. She'd never felt so much hatred toward a person as Grimes felt for the witch.

"Let's go," Miriam said.

Macy broke off into the woods to retrieve Kim. Tanner and Jillian followed to the clearing. Once there, she watched as the coyote teleported down from the boulders and stood only a few feet from Gabe's position.

"I'm out!" he yelled.

The witch had run him out of bullets, waiting to strike until he had nothing to fight back with.

He stood up, the rifle hanging loosely in his hands. The coyote lunged. He dodged backward just in time.

"Gabe!" Miriam yelled. "It's time to go. Grab Rodriguez."

Gabe looked back and smiled when he saw Tanner standing alongside Miriam.

"You got it, Mimi," he said, turning back toward the coyote just as it snapped again. He flipped the gun in his hand in one deft move and slapped the coyote across the jaw with the butt. The witch-wolf yelped and thrashed in place, giving time for Gabe to sprint away. Tanner met him at the pile of unconscious cops.

"Hey, bro," Gabe said. "Glad you made it out."

With a grunt, Tanner heaved Dub over his shoulder while Gabe slung the rifle over his shoulder, then scooped up the smaller Rodriguez into his arms like a giant baby. Miriam wouldn't have been able to lift either man. Miriam found Jillian just as the doctor injected her magic serum into Grimes' muscled bicep. He sat up and shook his head furiously. Jillian crept away back to Miriam.

The two women watched as the hulking beast pushed to his feet. Miriam felt nothing. Her intense and intimate connection with him was completely gone.

"I think it worked," Miriam said.

Tanner and Gabe scuttled past, the coyote hot on their heels. Grimes surveyed the situation. Miriam stood at the ready, worried he'd attack the first thing he saw. But he didn't. When they most needed a stroke of luck, Jillian had delivered.

Miriam quickly stepped out of the way as Grimes barreled headfirst into the belly of the coyote, sending her sideways and knocking her from a trajectory that would have surely caught the two retreating men. The coyote lunged back, snapping at Grimes but missing by inches. He used the opportunity to punch her straight in the nose, causing a yelp and a retreat. Oddly, the witch now seemed vulnerable in the same way a coyote would be.

Miriam pushed aside her curiosity and rushed over to Brynn's unconscious body, easily lifting the lanky woman into her arms.

"Ok," Miriam said. "Let's get out of here."

Jillian nodded, leading the way towards the tree line. The klaxons blared. The coyote and the beast squared off, dodging, fighting, rolling. She stopped at the edge of the trees and looked back.

"We can't leave him behind," Miriam said. "Not now. Not after you saved him."

She felt a surge of regret for mercilessly killing the first two beasts. She'd killed them because they had no hope of recovery, but now that there was hope, she couldn't let Grimes sacrifice himself like that. She looked ahead and viewed her motley crew shuffling away. Macy had joined, Kim leaning on her and limping alongside. Jillian wouldn't be able to carry Brynn.

"Go," Miriam said. "Get the gun from Gabe and bring it back."

Jillian nodded and rushed ahead. Miriam knelt and sat Brynn on the ground.

"Well, Brynn," she said. "Either I win, or we both die. We're in it together, now. Just like in Gray's Point."

Brynn didn't answer. Miriam laughed quietly. She never expected Macy to be able to throw such a strong punch.

Jillian returned with the gun, huffing along and barely keeping it from dragging along the ground. Miriam took it and leaned it against her shoulder. The weight caused her body to groan in painful agony. She'd lost track of the bruises, scrapes, and cuts. But this was what she did. How she was made. The pain felt natural. Proof that no matter the course, the outcome would be the same as it had been all the times before. When it came to bringing down monsters, supernatural or otherwise, Miriam did not know how to fail.

"There are no bullets," Jillian said.

"I know."

"What about her?" Jillian motioned to Brynn.

"You can't carry her," Miriam said. "I'll bring her when this is over."

"But what if you—"

"Go. Get out of here."

Jillian regarded Miriam with fear. Maybe a little curiosity. Clearly, the doctor expected Miriam to die, but Miriam planned otherwise.

"Good luck, Ms. Brooks."

"Thanks, Doc."

Jillian scuttled away. Miriam couldn't see the others anymore, which gave her hope. If this whole place blew up—which seemed the worst-case scenario—then at least she'd saved as many people as she could.

She borrowed a play from Gabe's book and flipped the gun in her hands, holding it by the barrel. The heft of it seemed inconsequential with the adrenaline flowing through Miriam's body. Or maybe the serum gave her strength. She didn't know, but she felt invincible.

She watched as the witch-coyote continuously snapped at Grimes, only to have him evade and attempt a counter. Both seemed adept at dodging, with neither landing many blows on the other. A true match of goliaths.

And so, Miriam intended to shift the odds in her champion's favor. She took off in a sprint towards the fray, sliding to her knees at the last possible second, pulling back the gun like a baseball bat and slamming it into the knee of the coyote's back haunch. The creature yelped like a dog.

The blow caused the witch to lose her balance briefly, skidding down on her hind quarters and almost crushing Miriam in the process. Miriam managed to slide out from the other side just in time, though, jumping back to her feet and turning just in time to see the beast land a massive blow to the coyote's jaw. Grimes didn't think it through, knocking the witch toward Miriam instead of away. She scrambled towards an opening between boulders and squeezed through right as the coyote slammed into the stone. Miriam used the gun and slammed it into the witch's canine ribs before she got back to her feet and lunged back towards the beast.

This time, Grimes didn't move fast enough. The coyote's jaws latched onto his forearm, eliciting a low growl the likes of which Miriam hadn't heard from a beast before. True physical pain. He pulled hard, but the witch held on, dragged away from Miriam and giving her the space to get back out into the open. Miriam battered the coyote's hindquarters, blow after blow with her gun-bat until she finally managed to get the witch's attention.

The coyote spun and snapped, managing to bite the gun instead of Miriam, a full half of its length disappearing between the witch's jaws. Miriam held tight to the barrel but felt it slipping through her fingers as the witch began wrenching it away. Miriam's fingers caught on the metal sighting notch at the end, slicing through skin and making her grip all the more precarious as she struggled to hold it.

But then she received an assist from Grimes, who grabbed the witch's tail and started pulling her backward. Miriam jerked in the opposite direction and the gun finally slipped free of the coyote's jaws, the potential energy of its trap knocking Miriam to the ground. Next time, Miriam thought, she'd make sure bayonets were installed on every rifle she used.

Annoyed with her tail being pulled, the witch turned again, setting her sites back on Grimes. She pounced. Grimes shuffled backward but hit a tree. He disappeared beneath the witch's muscled fur as she growled and snarled and bit. Miriam couldn't make out how Grimes fared, so got up, wiped the blood from her hands onto her pants, and brought the gun up above her head, slamming it down hard on the coyote's tailbone. When that seemed to have little effect, Miriam opted for a more vulnerable spot, using the butt of the gun against the witch's ribs. She yelped, then backed up as Grimes stood, holding open her jaws.

He wouldn't be able to hold the position for long. Lamenting the fact that she had no real weapon, Miriam tried to think creatively, considering her options only briefly before using the coyote's fur as handholds to climb onto the back of the canine. Though Grimes tried to hold her in place, the witch bucked and wriggled, making Miriam's ascent difficult, but not impossible. Eventually she managed it, straddling the coyote's back just behind its shoulder-bones.

Miriam slammed the gun down onto the witch-coyote's skull with an echoing *crack*. Then she did it again, and again, until finally Grimes could hold on no longer. The coyote's jaws snapped shut directly on one of his hands. Blood spurted, and when he pulled his arm back faster than she expected, Miriam realized he no longer had a hand. This fight wasn't going the way Miriam imagined.

Holding her perch solely with the strength of her thighs, she slammed the gun into the witch's skull two more times before finally being bucked free. She rolled onto the ground, but couldn't keep hold of her weapon. She came to a stop. The coyote moved toward her, but seemed to be smaller, its skin undulating, its fur seemingly disappearing. Miriam watched as the front legs morphed into frail human arms. The snout started to recede. Before the coyote could threaten Miriam again, it became just the witch. A woman in a coyote pelt, none the worse for the wear. All the injuries of the coyote seemed to disappear in the transition.

Fascinating.

Miriam could fight a woman. As the witch drew close, Miriam kicked at the witch's knees, landing a glancing blow that caused the witch to retreat and gave Miriam the time to get back to her feet. Then they stood face to face. Miriam glanced behind the witch to see

Grimes now on the ground, clutching his arm as blood poured from a handless wrist.

Miriam put up her fists and waited for the witch to make a move, praying that whatever ungodly energy allowed her to turn into a coyote was well and truly spent. When the witch brought up her own fists, Miriam thought maybe her prayers had been answered.

She attempted a jab, teasing at the witch, not really expecting it to land. But land it did, pounding the witch's blocking forearm. The woman hadn't shimmered, or shifted, or vanished. Miriam smiled a bloody smile, lunged forward, and tackled the witch, easily overpowering her to the ground. She straddled her and sent punch after punch at the witch's face. At first, the crone tried to block, but the assault left her too weak and Miriam felt like she could go on for days. Eventually her fists connected not with forearm, but with the delicate bones in the witch's face.

The witch's nose bloodied, then her mouth. Her eyes swelled. So taken with anger and adrenaline, Miriam lost count of how many punches she landed. Only when she felt certain the witch wouldn't pose a threat did she stop, leaving the witch wheezing for air, limp on the ground, only barely conscious. Miriam stood up. Suddenly she felt exhausted. Her arms heavy. Her breath laborious. She looked down at her torn and tattered clothes, covered in blood and dirt.

She moved toward Grimes, who looked up at her with wide, wet eyes.

"It's done," Miriam said. "Let's get out of here, before it's too late. Can you carry her?"

"Y-y-yes," Grimes said. The beast talked. Jillian had reclaimed his humanity, if not his body. Miriam wondered what kind of life he would lead now.

She offered him a hand, which he took with his one remaining. She jerked up hard, his weight almost pulling her down before he got his feet under him to aid in his ascent. She smiled at him, clapping him on his good shoulder.

"Good work."

Such an unlikely ally.

Miriam moved toward Brynn, surprised she hadn't yet gained consciousness. She bent over and pulled the girl up into her arms. She waited for Grimes to do the same for the witch. He pulled her up by her wrist and slung her over his shoulder like a sack of potatoes, needing only one arm to lift her small frame.

"Let's get out of here," Miriam said, turning toward the tree line.

Then the world exploded around them.

Chapter 44 – Macy

Macy gasped. Kim cried out. Jillian looked on with wide eyes. Gabe and Tanner immediately took off running toward the cloud of fire and debris rising above the treetops.

"Stay with them," Macy asked of Kim, who nodded, grimacing against the pain but otherwise cogent again. Macy didn't think Kim capable of running anyway.

Macy rushed off after the boys, her heart pounding not from the exertion, but the fear. If they'd lost Miriam. After all this.

With Tanner and Gabe by her side, she picked through the trees, not making it far before seeing the ramifications of the explosion. Branches burned, falling all around them. Stone from the boulders peppered the landscape.

"No one could have survived this," Macy said, tears forming in the corners of her eyes.

"Don't say that," Gabe replied, as he stepped around a rock that somehow was also on fire.

Tanner reached his hand out and Macy took it, intertwining her fingers into his. She had him at least. She would always have him. He squeezed her hand, pulling her along. She followed as if in a nightmare that she couldn't escape, each further step into the forest looking more like a warzone.

As they drew as close as they dared to Big Rock Clearing, they saw only smoke and fire.

"I'm going in," Gabe said.

Tanner held an arm across his chest in protest. "You can't, bro. You won't survive that smoke."

Gabe growled, but ultimately listened. He respected Tanner's experience too much to disobey, no matter how emotionally invested.

"Maybe she hid somewhere," Macy said, trying to voice hope into existence. "Or ran the other direction."

"Maybe," Tanner said. Macy didn't detect confidence in his voice, and when he pulled her into a hug, she took it as admission that he didn't think Miriam could have survived either.

They stood in silence, Macy wrapped against Tanner's chest while Gabe stared into the smoke as if he would serendipitously gain X-ray vision.

"Guys," Gabe said after a few minutes. "What's that?"

Macy peeled herself away from Tanner and peered into the distance, where she saw a silhouette forming. Her heart leaped at the chance that it might be Miriam, but the shadow grew too large, too fast. It could only be the remaining beast.

Tanner shoved Macy behind him as he squared his shoulder with Gabe's to create a wall of protection. Sweet, but Macy didn't think they'd be able to fend off a beast with nothing but their fists. She stood on her tiptoes to peek between their shoulders and watched the shadow grow closer and closer, until it finally broke through the smoke. It stumbled forward, then fell to its knees, dropping something off its massive shoulders.

Not something.

Some*one*.

"It's Mir!" Macy yelled, probably too loudly.

She rolled out from behind her man-wall and sprinted over, kneeling to the ground and cupping Miriam's head in her hands, feeling for a pulse. She found one. Surprisingly strong. Blood covered Miriam from head to toe, and she'd suffered no small amount of burns, but she was alive. Macy's tears came more freely now.

"She's alive!" she yelled at the boys, who had closed ranks around her.

"T-t-tell her... th-th-thank you," the beast uttered.

Macy turned her attention to him, his body also covered in blood, but so many more burns. One of his arms ended in a bloody mess, his hand missing. She could only imagine how much blood loss he must have endured. Tanner knelt beside him and took his good hand, somehow seeing through the terror of talking to one of these creatures and seeing the recovered humanity underneath.

"We're gonna get you some help," he said.

"N-n-no." His lips turned up into something resembling a smile, the scars and burns making it impossible for him to properly contort his face. He closed his eyes and collapsed onto the forest floor. Tanner couldn't hold his weight, but followed on his knees, never letting go of the beast's hand.

After a few seconds of silence, Tanner reached up to check for a pulse, but Macy could already tell he would find none. What a weird trick of fate that Miriam would end up being saved by a beast.

"Let's get Mir to a hospital," Macy said.

"What about the witch?" Gabe asked. "And Brynn?"

He looked longingly into the carnage left of Big Rock Clearing.

"We'll send out the authorities," Macy said. "For now, we need to take care of the people we can."

"Yeah," Gabe said. "But if that witch ain't dead...."

Tanner moved to Miriam, knelt, and picked her up in his arms.

"Miriam wouldn't have left her alive," Macy said, as sure of that fact as her love for Tanner.

Together, the three trudged out of Big Rock Clearing, Miriam in Tanner's arms.

Chapter 45 – Miriam

Three years later.

Stepping out of her rented Jeep onto the Rose Valley town square, Miriam smiled when she saw her nephew barreling toward her. She dropped to her knees to receive him, but a few steps out, he stopped, looked her up and down, frowned, then burst into tears. From a few feet away, Macy laughed before scooping the kid into her arms.

"Did Aunt Mir scare you?" Macy said in that annoying baby voice that only parents seemed to be able to muster. "Is poor little Cornelius upset?"

Tanner appeared out of nowhere with a pacifier. Little Cornelius eagerly took it, which quieted the mewling.

"Is it something I said?" Miriam asked.

"No," Macy replied, now bouncing the child on her hip. "He just doesn't get to see you much, what with all your galavantin' around the world and all."

Miriam couldn't argue the point. For the last three years, she'd hardly been in any one place for more than a few days.

The aftermath of Big Rock Clearing had left no doubt that the witch was finally and truly dead. Her remains had been charred and difficult to identify, but Miriam trusted the forensics. No more beasts. No more witches. And, sadly, no more Brynn. Having not saved her seemed the biggest travesty of the encounter, though losing Grimes also hurt. The mystery of the giant coyote remained just that.

All signs pointed to the witch being merely a woman, but despite being insanely busy, Miriam often spent her free time re-evaluating the evidence, sure that some secret of the witch's biology hadn't fully been unlocked. Any time a new genetic test came online, Miriam quickly ran it against the witch's DNA, sure it would find something out of the ordinary. So far, no luck. The rest of the world seemed keen to dismiss the tales of the woman's ability to shapeshift, but Miriam didn't let it deter her. It was the same with everything she ever hunted.

A few months after saving Rose Valley for a second time, Miriam had received a phone call from a guy in Hollywood. Apparently, he'd been watching her career with great interest and wanted to offer her a job. More than that, really. Her own show. She immediately declined, of course. Miriam could imagine few things less appealing than being famous.

But, the guy had been insufferably persistent, taking her disinterest as a bargaining technique. In the end, after a ton of extra offerings had piled up, Miriam relented. She didn't mind the money, but what she enjoyed most was the control. She chose the hunts. She got to keep the crew to just her and one camera operator. She didn't have to pay a dime for any equipment or travel. Who could turn that down? It was a blank check to live the life she'd always wanted. So what if she also had to film it?

She met Macy's comment with an understanding nod, then took in the sights around her. The entire population of Rose Valley looked to be filling the town square. A large white screen covered nearly half the courthouse in the center of the square, with chairs set up in neat rows for people to watch the premiere of the show Miriam had been filming for nearly a year. The hunt documented in the first episode was already a distant memory.

From next to her, a hand found hers. Warmth filled her, as her fingers intertwined with those of her camerawoman. Her friend. Her confidant. Her girlfriend. Maybe her wife one day, though the thought still scared Miriam, despite Kim's frequent discussion of the topic. For now, the fact that Miriam willingly engaged in public displays of affection seemed enough of a step. She even allowed Kim to lean over and give her a quick kiss on the lips.

"You ready for this?" Kim asked.

Miriam shook her head. "I don't think anyone could ever be ready for this."

"You're famous now."

"I guess."

The studio had offered her a screening of the first episode before it aired, but Miriam refused. She wanted to watch it here, with her people. Her family. She might not have been born and raised in Rose Valley, but she still thought of it as home. She and Kim kept a house in town, right across the street from Macy and Tanner who, honestly, spent more time in theirs since they also served as house-sitters. When Miriam and Kim crashed into town between filming episodes, they hardly left the house from sheer exhaustion.

Across the way, Miriam's eyes locked with Gabe's. He smiled and raised a can of beer. She nodded, noticing his crisp khaki uniform. After she'd become the pre-eminent cryptozoologist on the planet, work dried up quickly for Skylar. Now he spent all his time in the museum, with Tanner helping him tend to the place. Gabe had found a new career as a police officer, a profession that fit him well.

Miriam searched the crowd and found her dad, talking animatedly with some of the townsfolk. She dragged Kim over, clutching tighter to her hand. Miriam's relationship with Skylar had become stable enough, but he'd never fully embraced Kim, which made Miriam all the more interested in flaunting the relationship in front of him. Petty, she supposed, but some things never changed, even with fame and money.

She gave him a quick hug, exchanged pleasantries, then was immediately interrupted by Mayor Cam.

"Miriam." He said it so matter-of-factly that anyone else would have thought the man hated her. He didn't. At least, she didn't think so. "We have a couple of seats for you and Kim over here. Show's about to start."

They found their perfectly-placed seats in the center of the crowd. The first episode—if the studio had decided to air them in order—would document the hunt for Mothman in Point Pleasant, West Virginia. Of course, they'd found nothing. They usually didn't. The producers seemed a little worried about that, but to Miriam, the important thing was to properly show the world what she did. It was up to the editors to make that entertaining, not her.

She did know which hunt they'd saved for the season finale, and couldn't wait for that one to air. She half-expected the news to pick it up before they got that far. On the island of Tasmania, she and Kim managed to document a living, breathing Thylacine for the first time since 1936, when the dog-like marsupial had been believed to have gone extinct. They'd found not just one but two specimens, which implied a breeding population and the possibility of bringing the species back from the brink.

Despite all she'd done, finding the Tasmanian Tiger still alive was one of the accomplishments she was most proud of. It was the reason she did what she did. The reason her entire profession deserved a place at the scientific table. It helped that finding it also provided the confidence the network needed to renew her show for a second season, even before the first had aired.

Shortly after they sat, the giant speakers set up on either side of the courthouse came to life. The intro that Miriam had recorded just a few weeks prior started and she immediately felt her neck and cheeks flush with embarrassment. The audio engineers had been absolutely livid with her over how long it took her to get it right. The whole thing just seemed so forced and overly dramatic and silly, but Miriam went along with it by reminding herself that keeping them happy meant her show stayed on the air, and her feet stayed on the ground, hunting cryptids where they belonged.

Scenes of jungles and oceans flashed by, interspersed with Miriam creeping through the woods, dirty and disheveled, often wet with rain.

Miriam fought the urge to disappear, held down by Kim's hand in hers.

"It's gonna be great," Kim whispered.

Miriam's narration began: "As a child, my father raised me for one thing: the *hunt*. In me, he instilled the knowledge of two generations of cryptozoologists. Then, I forged my skills in the hot coals of Rose Valley—"

The crowd cheered so loudly here that Miriam only knew the next few lines by reading the closed captions.

"Cape Madre, and Gray's Point. I brought down beasts and krakens and witches. Now, I'm on the trail of more of these elusive creatures. The cryptids of legend and lore. My name is Miriam Brooks, and I am the—"

The screen changed to black as jagged red letters scratched their way onto the screen, as if cut into fabric by a large feline.

Miriam's voice finished the narration with: "Lorestalker."

She buried her face into Kim's shoulder as the crowd went absolutely bonkers with cheers. Kim laughed.

"That's so cheesy," Miriam whined.

"I don't know," Kim said. "I think you're a badass."

Miriam smiled to herself, looked back up at the screen and nodded. Kim had the right of it, even if Miriam had a hard time accepting it.

Miriam could never really think of herself as a badass. She struggled to believe she could even be considered *enough*. But, for the first time in her life, she could see a future where her life didn't have to be defined by the thoughts of others.

She could envision a life where she could thrive not just as a cryptid hunter, but as a friend, a daughter, a sister, an aunt, a partner, and, maybe, even a celebrity. Badass or not, maybe she would even learn to thrive as herself.

Acknowledgements

So, a series ends. Maybe. Though this book is designed to be the last in the Lorestalker series, I'd be a fool to make a vow never to return. These characters live in my soul, and one day they may demand another adventure. For now, however, I hope that Miriam and company live on in our imaginations while I go forth into new territory—I'm thinking demons.

My thanks, as always, goes out to the team at Evolved Publishing, Mike Robinson, Richard Tran, Gryphon Corpus, and Dave Lane (aka Lane Diamond). They've been there for every step, making my ideas shine brighter than I thought possible.

To Mistie, Amanda, Rachael, and Sammie, I cannot express enough gratitude for all that you've done to polish this book to its current form. People probably have no idea how valuable beta readers are, and each of you brings your unique experience to this story. Thank you.

I'd also like to acknowledge all the people who have influenced me over the years, even if not directly on these pages—my mother, my grandmother and grandfather, my sister, my two awesome nieces, and so many wonderful friends and family.

To my wife, Akaemi... I don't know what insanity made her agree to let me pursue writing so many years ago, but I'm grateful every day that she did, and for so many other things. She's my event planner, my champion, my alpha reader, my inspiration, and my best friend. Lorestalker wouldn't exist without her (quite literally — she came up with the name).

And, of course, I must thank the fans. I'm not a household name, but as I make my way out to events and meet people who like my books, I'm shocked and grateful every time.

Lastly, I need to thank Miriam, a fictional character who changed my life. When I first put her to page, I felt drawn to her. She felt the most me of any character I'd written. When Mike and others started pointing out that she seemed to be possibly on the spectrum, I scoffed. How could this character that I identify with so fully have ASD? After a lot of soul searching, therapy, and a visit to a psychologist, turns out there was a very good reason, made clear when I received my diagnosis — at the age of 41 — for Autism Spectrum Disorder. It changed my life. Everything about me suddenly came into focus and made sense. So, thank you, Miriam, for helping me find myself.

About the Author

J.P. Barnett grew up in a tiny Texas town where the list of possible vocations failed to include published author. In second grade, he worked harder than any other student to deliver a story about a tiger cub who singlehandedly saved the U.S. Military, earning him a shiny gold star and a lifelong appreciation of telling a good story.

Fast forwarding through decades of schooling and a career as a software engineer, J.P. Barnett stepped away from it all to get back to his first real passion. Years of sitting at a keyboard gifted him with some benefit, though, including blazing fast typing hands and a full tank of creativity.

As a child, J.P. consumed any book he could get his hands on. The likes of Stephen King, Michael Crichton, and Dean Koontz paved the bookshelves of his childhood, providing a plethora of fantastical and terrifying tales that he read way too early in life. Though the effect these books had on his psyche could be called into question, these masters of storytelling managed to warp his mind in just the perfect way to spin a fun yarn or two.

J.P. currently resides in Seattle with his wife and hellion of a cat, both of whom look at him dubiously with some frequency.

For more, please visit J.P. Barnett online at:
Website: www.JPBarnett.com
Twitter: @JPBarnett
Facebook: JPBarnett.Author
Instagram: JPBarnett.Author

What's Next?

J.P. Barnett always has at least one book in the works, so please stay tuned to developments and plans by subscribing to his newsletter at the link below.

~~~

www.JPBarnett.com/Newsletter

More from Evolved Publishing

We offer great books across multiple genres, featuring high-quality editing (which we believe is second-to-none) and fantastic covers.

As a hybrid small press, your support as loyal readers is so important to us, and we have strived, with tireless dedication and sheer determination, to deliver on the promise of our motto:
QUALITY IS PRIORITY #1!

Please check out all of our great books, which you can find at this link:
www.EvolvedPub.com/Catalog/

Thank you!

Printed in the USA
CPSIA information can be obtained
at www.ICGtesting.com
LVHW090117270124
770065LV00042B/907